CHIMAN

DESMOND LOWDEN

BBC BOOKS

For Annie

Published by BBC Books,
a division of BBC Enterprises Limited,
Woodlands, 80 Wood Lane, London W12 0TT

First Published 1990
© Desmond Lowden 1990
ISBN 0 563 20877 5

Set in 10/11pt Sabon Roman by Goodfellow & Egan Ltd, Cambridge
Printed and bound in Great Britain by Richard Clay Ltd, Bungay, Suffolk
Cover printed by Richard Clay Ltd, Norwich

Desmond Lowden began his working life as a film technician, then embarked on a writing career both as a novelist and a screenwriter. He is married with children and lives in Bognor Regis.

His novels include *Bandasnatch*, *The Boon Docks*, *Bellman and True*, *Budapesti 3*, *Sunspot* and *Cry Havoc*. For *Shadow Run*, a novel published by André Deutsch, he was awarded the Crimewriters' Association's Silver Dagger for 1989.

His television screenplays include *No Baby at All* for ATV, *The News Benders* for the BBC and the thriller, *Jake's End*, a 90-minute film directed by Jim O'Brien. He wrote the screenplay for *Bellman and True*, a 4-part serial and feature film for Euston films, starring Bernard Hill, produced by Michael Wearing and directed by Richard Loncraine. *Chain* is a 4-part film serial for the BBC.

CHAIN

The forecast had promised another fine June day, sunny and cloudless. But the first light of dawn was cold, bringing a thin white mist in from the sea. It reached the wide area of building land, and then the site itself, a great skeleton of girders surrounded by scaffolding.

Away to the left was a second site. Work had only just begun here, on the footings. And all that could be seen was a row of tall black pile-drivers. They were like cranes in the mist. Fat compressed-air tubes went up to their hammers. Though at four in the morning, they were silent.

Then there was a sound, the drone of a diesel engine.

A small flat-bed truck was reversing up a ramp. It stopped. Its tailgate fell down. And a long snake-like object began to uncoil from inside.

A chain.

It was fat-linked and heavy. It piled up on the wet boards of the ramp. And then boots came towards it, muddy site-worker's boots. They began to work the chain towards the edge.

It swung down, shaking out little clouds of rust. And far below it there was more rusty metal in the shadows. Reinforcing mesh, lining a deep shaft. One of the main structural footings.

The chain became still. The muddy boots turned as the site-worker looked back towards the truck. There was a second man there, up on the flat-bed. And he had his end of the chain around the drum of a winch.

He began to pay out. The chain began to graunch, link by link, across the ramp.

Then there was a different sound. Shackled to one of the links was something soft. It left a pattern of trails across the wet boards. There were shoes, smart Italian shoes. Ankles in monogrammed socks. Then neatly-pressed trousers. The man's body slid over the edge. It went gently, offering no resistance. *Rigor* had gone. He had been dead for some time as he swung out over the shaft.

LENNOX

1

It was late June, and the evening sun came low into the line of offices. Blinds were drawn. Wafers of yellow light found desks and cabinets and stack after stack of files. And there was that heat about the building, that stale heat people were glad to turn their backs on at the end of the day.

But in one of the offices a man was working on. He wore the neat grey suit of a civil servant. His pale sandy coloured hair was beginning to thin. He was thirty-nine, and maybe a little worried about being forty. But there was a breadth to him, a wideness of shoulder, a roundness of face. Something dependable, gentle even.

He glanced at his watch, got up and opened the blinds. Sunlight caught the curve of his large round glasses. The pale blue of his eyes leapt out, he seemed younger. And, as he dropped a couple of files into his briefcase, the long working day was there only in the tiredness around his mouth.

He went out along the corridor, and came to the security window at its end. A man in a dark blue uniform looked out at him.

'Early night, Mr Cassidy? Not often I see you out of here before seven.'

'No, that's right, Harold. But we've got people coming in to supper.'

'That's nice then. Have a good time.'

'Thanks, I will. Good-night.'

'Night, Mr Cassidy.'

Cass went down the stairs and out of the building. His car was parked in its bay, a small Peugeot 304. He dumped

7

his briefcase on to the front seat, switched on the ignition, and slotted a tape-cassette into the player.

It was Bach, the Magnificat in D. He listened to the opening fanfare, the trumpets rising up, golden, near-perfect.

And the city, as he drove through it in the summer evening, seemed golden and near-perfect too.

There were the wide avenues, the open spaces of a seaport. There were the canyons of the shopping centre, the neons of cinemas in the shadows. Then, as he turned right, the long Georgian terraces leading down to the park. And in the park itself a cricket match was being played.

He stopped in a queue of traffic and looked at the slow progress of the game, the white of the players, and the bright summer colours of the watchers on the grass. There was a calm about the scene, a calm hanging over this whole southern city of 60 000 people.

It gave him no pleasure to realise he had files on 12 000 of them.

The Bach was coming to an end by the time he reached an estate out in the suburbs. The houses were detached and of a reasonable size, built in the days of chimneys and wide plate-glass windows. And the plots were sizeable too, with long back gardens and well-established trees.

He passed the line of his hedge and turned into the driveway. Then had to jam on his brakes because a Volvo was blocking his path. A massive car, be-chromed, be-turboed, and brand-be-spanking-new. Cass smiled and shook his head. So Phil Benson had gone ahead and bought it, he thought.

Unlocking his front door, he went through a small hallway to a large L-shaped room. To his left sunlight streamed across a wide living-area. There were bookshelves, floor to ceiling, between every window, and magazines lying around. There were two large sofas and an armchair, none of them matching, all bought at different times. Not exactly *House & Garden*, he thought, and maybe a bit bashed, but comfortable.

To his right, however, in the shadows, there was order.

8

A long lightwood table had been laid for supper. The wedding silver had been taken out of its canteen, and the good crystal glasses. And beyond from the kitchen were voices, voices that warmed him. They came from the north-east, from Geordie-land. From his schooldays, and the first five years of his working life.

A man called Phil Benson was standing just inside the doorway. He seemed to take up most of it, gangling big-boned, with straight silvery hair. And he was beginning to put on weight, Cass saw, the face beginning to sag slightly, the stomach bulging over the tan trousers. But there was a smoothness about him. It was there in his wide easy mouth, his grin. The smoothness of money.

'Didn't hit that car of mine, did you?' he asked.

'No,' Cass said, 'not hard.'

'That's all right then.'

'But, I don't understand,' Cass went on. 'I mean, why buy now? The new reg comes out in August, what, six weeks' time?'

'Couldn't wait,' Phil said.

'Bit flash, that.'

'Oh, it is. It is.'

Cass grinned back. Then he went on into the kitchen where two women were standing.

The first, his wife Sonia, was bending over, turning potatoes in a roasting tin. The light from inside the oven caught her finely-boned face, the wings of her dark hair. While the sun from the open garden door showed her body, slight, athletic, through the folds of her Monsoon dress.

Beyond her, next to the door, stood Phil's wife Marianne, tightly dressed, and glowing. She always glowed. It came from the afternoons she spent in her garden, from her holidays, her shopping trips that brought in dresses of luminous lilac and yellow. Her wrist jangled now as she reached out for Cass, and she left a smear of lipstick on his cheek.

'The incredible Sonia,' she said. 'How does she manage to do a day's work and then produce all this?'

9

And all this, Cass saw, was the crown roast now sliding back into the oven, and the salmon-trout on a dish on the side.

Sonia shrugged. 'I like doing it,' she said. 'I like people sitting around my table.'

Her fingers were long and slim as she closed the oven door. There was a grace about her, about the way she cooked, the care she took. While behind her Marianne's ringed fingers walked boldly towards the salmon-trout and its jug of mayonnaise. They dipped in. She tasted. 'You don't mind, lover, do you?'

'No, of course not.'

Cass watched his wife's face, the pale translucent skin, the fierce intelligence that could rise up like a sword. But she remained calm, and he went over and kissed her.

'Not late, am I?' he asked. 'You said seven?'

'I did.' She nodded. 'But your friend Phil's getting a bit impatient.'

'Oh? Why's that?'

'Talking about going out to a pub.'

'But, isn't there something I could be doing here?'

Sonia pointed to herself. 'This one's got everything under control.' She pointed to Phil. 'And that one wants to show you his new car.'

2

It was impressive, the new Volvo. It wrapped itself around Cass with all the solidity of an aircraft. And facing him on the wide dashboard, aircraft-style, was a row of warning-lights.

'What's the light on the left for?' he asked Phil.

'Brake circuit failure.'

'And the next one?'

'Fault in the electrics.'

'And the next?'

'School-fees due,' Phil said.

Cass laughed. 'You're not into that now, are you?'

'Just started.'

Phil drove on slowing, signalling. They turned into one of the streets that led to old dockland, narrow and mean-looking. And a seedy-looking pub came up on the left.

Phil looked at it as they went past. Then stopped.

'What's the matter?' Cass asked.

'That pub, the Three Tuns, it sells Newcastle Brown.'

'Does it?'

'*Newcastle Brown*,' Phil repeated. Then turned round in his seat and reversed.

The kick-marked door of the pub made Cass uneasy. And the inside was no better, dim, and smelling of old stale lager. It was early too. There was just one other customer in the place, a young man in a green hooped sweater, sitting at a corner table.

Phil opened his wallet, ordered two bottles of Newcastle Brown from the barman, and watched as they were uncapped. He took a deep bite out of his pint, and then watched Cass drinking in small fussy rings.

'Doesn't mean anything to you now, does it?' he asked.

'What doesn't?'

'The ale, the north, any of it.'

'Yes, it does,' Cass said.

Phil shook his head. 'No, not any more. I mean, how often d'you go back there?'

'Christmas, Easter, to see my mother.'

Phil took another pull at his pint. And Cass turned to look at the young man in the corner, the hooped sweater, the razor haircut, the way he was staring fixedly back.

Phil put down his glass. 'I can see it all, my lad. You'll be just like the rest of them soon, drinking wait-wain-and-soda.'

'No,' Cass said.

But Phil nodded. 'You've merged. Merged into the soft south.'

Neither of them had seen the young man come over to the bar. Neither of them saw him pick up one of the

11

Newcastle Brown bottles. They just heard the crash as he hurled it across the room.

Phil spun round.

'Not you, skin, it's him.' The young man pointed at Cass.

'What?' Phil didn't understand.

And it happened fast. The young man feinted left, swung right, and caught Cass with the rings he wore on his right hand.

'For Christ's *sake*.' Phil tried to pull him off.

But the barman vaulted the bar. He closed in with a baseball bat.

There was a moment, just a moment, when it looked like a fight. Then the young man turned away. The bar-door banged. And he was gone.

Phil was angry. 'You took your time, didn't you?' he shouted at the barman.

But the man was looking at Cass. 'And you,' he said. 'You should know better than to come in here.'

They were back at home. Cass had his handkerchief to his face, trying to stop the bleeding. Sonia examined the wound. Then she swung round on Phil.

'How could you take him into a place like that?' she asked.

'What?'

'How could you be so bloody *thick*?'

And for the second time that evening Phil didn't understand.

'I mean, you used to work with him in the same office,' Sonia went on. 'And, all right, you may have been more junior then.'

'Then? That was six years ago.'

'Times have changed,' Sonia said.

'They certainly have.'

Sonia put her arm round Cass. 'Look, just work it out,' she said. 'He's now one of the Senior Crown Prosecutors in this city . . . And he just met a man he put away.'

3

There was a large piece of sticking-plaster on Cass' face. The bleeding had stopped. But his jaw throbbed, on and on.

The others were anxious. They tried to make him sit down.

'No, I'm all right,' he said. 'For God's sake, it was my own fault. I should know about the kind of work I do.'

They nodded. But beyond them now was a smaller figure, sitting cross-legged on the floor.

Alison, his seven-year-old daughter, had come back from Brownies. She was pale. The drab uniform was unkind to her, and her arms and legs seemed thin. But more than that, she was very still, her high-domed forehead like porcelain as she stared at him.

And it wasn't just the sticking-plaster, Cass knew. There was something else that showed. Something that shouldn't have been on a father's face.

He sat her on his lap, stroked her ash-blonde hair, asked her about the badges sewn on her tunic-sleeve.

'That's Homecraft,' she said. 'And that's Tracking. And today I started on Needlework.'

'And what did you do after?' Cass asked. 'After that?'

'Well, we sang, and we did the Brownie Trot.'

'The famous Brownie Trot.' He smiled. 'You've never shown me how to do that, have you?'

'No.' Her pale eyes were serious. 'No, I *think* it's secret, just for Brownies.'

He kissed her, held on to her. But her body was still tense in his arms.

When it was time for supper, Sonia let her sit at the table. Let her try the salmon, the crown roast, and a little splash of red wine before going to bed.

And later, it was the wine that did it, that stilled the throbbing in Cass's jaw, and brought the evening back on track. Phil drank too much as usual. He was sweating slightly, and his voice was loud as he held up his glass.

'Lovely, lovely Vacqueras,' he said. 'How about that colour?'

'Yes,' Cass said.

And Phil sighed, looking on round the table at the remains of the meat, the salad. 'Let's face it,' he said. 'Give or take the odd smack in the mouth, the best thing you and I ever did was come south.'

'You're right.'

But Marianne leaned forward between creamy shoulders. 'No,' she said to her husband, 'the best thing *you* ever did was come down here *and* get into private practice.'

'Well, yes. There's that,' Phil said.

'I mean, you said it yourself,' she went on. 'Working for the CPS was only a stepping-stone for you. You wanted a job down here. And they were recruiting prosecutors.' She turned to Cass. 'But the thing is, lover, they're *still* recruiting prosecutors, aren't they?'

'I s'pose so,' Cass said. 'I s'pose we're at about seventy-five per cent strength.'

Marianne smiled. 'Overworked,' she said.

And Cass knew what was coming next. It came every time.

'*And* underpaid.' Marianne's smile was wider.

Sonia got up. Her movements were fast as she began gathering up plates.

Phil saw it. He frowned at his wife. Then leaned towards Cass, put an arm round him. 'Oh, come on,' he said. 'Young Cassidy and I had some fine times together as prosecutors, didn't we?'

'We did,' Cass said.

I mean, d'you remember Sanderson? Old Judge Sanderson?' Phil made a fruity colonel voice. 'And when . . . ah . . . intimacy took place, was it . . . ah . . . unencumbered? Or . . . ah . . . through the fly-buttons?'

'Through the fly-buttons, m'lud,' Cass answered.

And Sonia stopped clearing away. She grinned. 'He didn't ask that, did he? In court?'

'Oh, yes,' Phil said.

'But, why?'

'Important point of law in Judge Sanderson's eyes,' Phil said. 'Wanted to find out if the act was . . . ah . . . unencumbered . . . or more hasty.'

'What's that got to do with it?' Sonia asked.

'Well, basically, if both partners extracted enjoyment. Or if there was coercion.'

Marianne leaned forward again. 'And was there coercion?'

'Difficult to tell,' Phil said. 'May have been to start with. But, as far as I can remember, intimacy took place seventeen times over the weekend.'

'Seventeen times.' Marianne sighed.

Then they all turned. Alison was at the doorway in her nightdress.

'What's seventeen times, Mummy?'

'Nothing,' Sonia said.

'Seventeen times . . . multiplication table,' Cass said.

'What's that?' Alison asked.

'Seventeen times one is seventeen. Seventeen times two is thirty-four. Seventeen times three is . . . ' Cass looked round at the others for help.

It was after eleven. The Bensons had gone, and Cass was stacking the washing-up machine in the kitchen. Then, behind him, he heard Sonia drop a saucepan into the sink with a crash.

He turned, surprised, saw how she'd splashed her blue Monsoon dress, her favourite dress. Saw how she was dabbing at it angrily with a cloth.

'What's up?'

'Need you ask,' she said. 'That bloody woman Marianne needling me all the time.'

He went towards her, felt the sharpness of her shoulders, tried to smoothe them out with his fingers. 'Oh, come on,' he said. 'Marianne's Marianne. You can handle her.'

'Once I could, yes.' She nodded. 'But in the past year or so, I don't know . . . since they've got rich.'

His hands closed together, worked on the muscles of her neck. 'Look,' he said, 'usually you're angry about impor-

15

tant things. Your work, those kids of yours at the day centre, probation officers, town hall . . . But these are friends of ours.'

'We've got other friends,' she said. 'Sometimes I feel we're at a turning-point with those two.'

He was more than surprised, he was shocked. 'For Heaven's sake, we've known them for years. I mean, Phil . . .'

'Oh, Phil's fine,' she said. 'He's kind, he's funny, he's been funny ever since university.' She hesitated, 'But . . .'

'But, what?'

'Well, he's not a *real* lawyer any more, is he?'

'What d'you mean?'

'All he does is conveyancing. Commercial work. It's property, property, property all the time with him.'

'What's wrong with that?'

She looked at him. 'I don't know. Sometimes I feel like a northerner, a po-faced northerner. I need space around me. Not people conning their way towards every square foot of land.'

Cass nodded. 'We did both choose to come here,' he said. 'And we knew it was boom town, one of the most successful cities in the south.'

But later he wasn't so sure. It was when he'd finished in the kitchen, and was catching the late night news on TV.

It was loud.

There were shouting men, a mob of them, and a great many uniformed policemen.

And a name that was new to him . . . Lennox.

'Picket-line scuffles broke out today at Lennox Freezers plc,' the announcer said, 'the major kitchenware manufacturers of Polling Lane, Westwood. Yesterday union leaders rejected a final offer that included natural wastage, early retirement, and some redundancies. While a spokesman for the company claimed that . . .'

4

The next morning, Friday, Cass spent in court. And it was the recipe as usual.

The Chief Magistrate was a lady of around sixty, with thin tight lines on her face. The younger magistrate in the Jaeger dress was frowning, trying to look older. And the last of the three was a company director with a Caribbean tan.

Facing them in the dock was an eighteen-year-old boy. He had one ear-ring, a dirty T-shirt and jeans. Bullet-headed and bullet-faced.

The court-clerk got up and turned to him.

'Your name is Terence James Grayling?'

'Yes.'

'You were born on 19 September 1971?'

'Yes.'

'You live at Flat 16, Normanscourt, on the Oakleigh Estate?'

'Yes.'

'The charges against you are that, firstly, on 22 June, you were guilty while drunk of disorderly behaviour. And that, secondly, on the same date, you occasioned actual bodily harm on a British Rail official in pursuance of . . .'

Cass' jaw was aching again. He leaned close to Samantha, his assistant, and asked her for another Veganin. She opened her bag and rummaged through it in that mumsy way she had. Cass watched her, dark-haired, plumpish, confined by her black court-clothes. And not for the first time he wondered how long that wide Welsh smile of hers would last in Court.

Then she was pushing his notes towards him, nudging him to his feet.

He cleared his throat, and addressed the Chief Magistrate. 'Ma'am, I have very little to say in this matter. The defendant was observed, on the day in question, on the 17.22 train from Waterloo. He was seen to be carrying a six-pack of strong lager, and to have a bottle of white rum in his pocket . . . He drank four of the cans of lager during the journey, and took frequent sips from the rum. On a number of occasions he staggered uncontrollably into other passengers. And when asked to refrain, replied with a well-known phrase . . .'

The recipe as usual.

Something that was usual, too, happened when the magistrates went out to confer. Because the court became smaller, just a group of people. The tall grey-haired figure of the court-clerk, the usher in his black gown, and Banham the defence solicitor.

'Getting your whites out this Saturday, Arthur?' Banham asked.

'That's right.' The court-clerk nodded. 'First time this year.'

'Who're you playing for?'

'Registrar's Eleven,' the court-clerk said.

'With your son running for you, I'll bet,' the usher said.

'Absolutely not,' the court-clerk told him. 'I'll have you know I scored thirty-two in the match last year. Three fours off their fast bowler.'

And it was at this moment that Cass looked across at the dock, no more than fifteen feet away. And saw the bullet-headed Terence Grayling leaning forward, sizing up the man who could score three fours off a fast bowler, interested.

Interested or not, he got a £200 fine and probation.

'Your name is Tracy Ann Rawlinson?'

'Yes.'

'You were born on 4 March 1970?'

'Yes.'

'You live at Number 79 Haldane Way, on the Oakleigh Estate?'

'Yes.'

Cass looked from the court-clerk to the new defendant, the nineteen-year-old girl. With her T-shirt, her very short creased skirt, her badly-dyed pony-tail, she was fat, spotty, a mess.

The court-clerk cleared his throat.

'The charges against you are that, firstly, on 15 May this year, you went into Ryman's shop on the High Street, and there stole a Personal Organiser, valued at £52.'

Cass shook his head sadly. In his notes he ringed the words Personal Organiser.

'And that on the same date,' the court-clerk continued, 'you went into Zara's Boutique on East Street, and there stole a Victoria Principal stretch-fit boudoir suit.'

Cass sighed. His jaw ached.

The recipe.

As usual.

5

The sign facing the road said CHALCOTT DAY CENTRE. Behind it was a row of tall lopped trees. And then a wide area of grass.

There were seven young children on the grass, three black, four white. They wore long paper sacks. The topmost corners of the sacks had been cut away to let their heads poke through. And the same sack-corners served as paper hats.

They were painted bright green, these hats. And bright green cardboard spines had been stuck on to the paper of the sacks. Spines that belonged to some weird carnival animal. Because when the children formed a line, each clutching the sack-tail of the child in front . . . and when the foremost child had a great cardboard head stuck on top of its shoulders . . . they became . . .

A dragon.

It was Sonia who had arranged all this, designed it, found the materials, and set the children to work. And now she stood back and faced them.

'What do dragons do?' she called out.

'They roar! They *roar*!' the children shouted.

'How fast do dragons run?'

'*Very* fast!'

And, nudging and pushing each other, they ran the dragon away across the grass, turned in a wide wheeling movement, almost coming apart. And ran back.

'And what do dragons eat?' Sonia called out.

'Gorgon*zola*!'

They collapsed in a heap, laughing. And Sonia laughed too. But then became serious as she turned and saw the little girl sitting on her own. The girl who hadn't run with the others, hadn't shouted.

Jo-Ann.

Sonia went over to her. She helped her out of her paper sack and walked her over to the low brick building of the care centre, holding her hand.

During the next few minutes, in the play-room, Sonia attended to Jo-Ann. Finding her apron, finding her chair, finding her a large white sheet of paper, paints, and a brush. Then she left her alone. It usually worked. Jo-Ann liked painting.

Walking slowly around the rest of the group, Sonia came to a small black girl. She was hunched in fierce concentration over her paintbrush, stabbing at a wild maelstrom of colour.

'That's nice, Nessie. Very nice,' Sonia said. 'What is it?'

'Apple.'

Sonia moved on to another painting, a precise, minutely-detailed scene of people and cars and buildings. She pointed at a figure in it. 'Who's this here, Dorinda?'

'Crockett,' Dorinda said. 'And Tubbs. And a junkie. And our nan's car. And . . .'

'I see,' Sonia said.

She came back round the corner of the table, returning to Jo-Ann. The girl sat as small as she could, her face as white and buckled as a broken ping-pong ball. And the sheet of paper in front of her was untouched.

'Nothing coming today, Jo-Ann?'

The little girl didn't answer.

Sonia crouched down, put one arm around her, and picked up the paintbrush. She loaded it with paint. 'Here we are . . .

Look, we could sort of put in a hill here . . . And then a tree . . . And then, maybe, what d'you think? A farmer?'

She gave Jo-Ann the paintbrush, but the girl didn't move. Sonia leaned even closer and felt the seat of the chair she was sitting on. 'Have we had a little accident, Jo-Ann?' she asked softly.

Suddenly Dorinda laughed.

And just as suddenly Jo-Ann was across the table at her, jabbing with the sharp end of her paintbrush.

Sonia managed to haul her off in time.

The social worker sat in Sonia's office. It was her weekly call, and as usual her face was gaunt over her loose-leaf file. She looked at a page, the sad facts and figures there. 'Nessie? How's she coming along?' she asked.

'Well, she's been arriving on time,' Sonia said. 'She wears clean clothes. And she's even got comics now, and sweets.'

'And does her mother meet her?'

'No, her Auntie Doreen. She says her mother's got a part-time job at Sainsbury's.'

'Haven't heard about that. I'll check on it.' The social worker turned the page. 'And Jo-Ann? Any recurrence there?'

Sonia frowned. 'Yes, today,' she said. 'She went for Dorinda. It could have been nasty . . . I mean, I try. We all try. But we haven't got eyes in the back of our heads.'

'No.' The social worker looked at the file again. She sighed. 'It's been reported that she's been out in the streets a great deal, getting into fights, stealing.'

'Oh, God.'

The social worker leaned forward. 'Look, I've called round there, but it's just not working. Her mother insists on an appointment. And by the time I get round there, she's . . . well . . . hidden everything away.'

Sonia nodded.

'You don't think you could dream up some excuse and take Jo-Ann home?'

'Tonight?'

'Sorry, I forgot. It's Friday.'

'Doesn't matter,' Sonia said. 'I'll go.'

6

Cass drove Samantha back from the magistrates' court. He parked in his bay outside the CPS building. Then looked at the stack of brief-boxes on the back seat. 'D'you think you can manage half of that lot, Sam?' he asked.

She nodded. He piled her up, and they went into the building and up the stairs.

Harold the security man saw them coming. He moved quickly out from behind his desk, and relieved Sam of her load. 'You mistreat that young lady, Mr Cassidy,' he said.

'Don't think so,' Cass told him. 'She's of good Welsh stock.'

Harold came on with them to the office. He put the boxes down on Cass' desk. Sam went on to her desk and then turned, holding a piece of paper. 'There's a message here,' she said, 'from your wife.'

'What is it?' Cass asked. 'Trouble?'

'No, she just wants you back at four-thirty, to meet your daughter from school.'

'Does she say why?'

'She's taking one of the children home from her day centre.'

Cass turned to Harold, spread his hands. 'Four-thirty,' he said and shrugged.

'It's happened before, Sir. And you've managed it before.'

'On a Friday night?' Cass asked. 'With all the week's work to tie up?'

Sam came forward, her pale Welsh skin glowing against her dark hair. 'I can do it,' she said. 'I'm perfectly capable. I've sat through the court-cases with you all week.'

'You sure, Sam?'

'Mr Cassidy . . .'

Cass tried a short cut home. But it turned out to be a long cut. Because out on the industrial estate he found the road blocked by metal barriers, and a queue of traffic being directed away by a police sergeant.

Cass stopped, and wound down his window. The police-man came forward, waving him on. But then his face changed.

'Oh, Mr Cassidy. Sorry, I didn't recognise you.'

'What's the trouble, sergeant?'

'It's the picket-lines, Sir, at the Lennox factory.'

'The what?'

'Lennox Freezers, Sir. It's been on the local news.'

'Oh, yes.' Cass remembered.

'Moving up into the big league, Sir. I mean, there were only a few here yesterday. But look at it now.'

Cass did so, and saw the pickets, five-deep, red-faced and angry in the sun. He saw the placards, NO LAYOFFS, NO TO MANAGEMENT LIES. Then the line broke. There was a surge forwards, a roar, as vehicles tried to come out of the factory gates.

And the sergeant was right, he thought. It was the big league. There must have been five or six hundred men there. And maybe fifty uniformed police.

'If it goes on like this, Sir, I reckon you'll see a few of them in court.'

'Looks like it.' Cass nodded. And then turned off where he was directed, down a side-street.

It led to another side-street, which in turn led on to the crowded ring-road. And it was a quarter to five by the time he got home. To find Alison already there, in the kitchen, cutting a huge Marmite sandwich with a bread knife.

'Here, let me do that,' he said. 'You'll hurt yourself.'

'*I* can do it.'

She was upset, he saw. She didn't want to hear about mummy taking another little child home. She put the sandwich on a plate and said she was going upstairs.

Sadly Cass made himself a cup of tea, and went through to the long L-shaped living-room. He passed the table where Phil and Marianne Benson had sat last night, and came to the living-area. The afternoon sun found pink roses in the cover of the armchair. It streaked the wall of brightly-coloured books and music cassettes. Cass found a tape of *Rigoletto*. He put it on, and started on his weekend's files.

23

Some ten minutes later Alison came in.

'You all right?' he asked.

'Yes.'

'You sure? Nothing you want? Another Marmite sandwich?'

'No.'

She came over until she held the floor in front of him. 'My knickers are Aged Fourteen Years,' she said, 'and they fell down in Brownies.'

'Oh.' Cass put down his pen. 'Looks like the management has boobed.'

'Yes.'

'Well have you got any others?'

'Got them on.'

She came closer, then slid on to his lap. 'What's the music?' she asked.

'Opera,' Cass said. '*Rigoletto*.'

'Mmm.' She nodded. 'What are they singing about? I mean, what's happening?'

Cass listened. 'Well,' he said, 'there's this group of people.'

'Where?'

'In this tavern.' He saw her frown. 'This restaurant.'

On the tape, Rigoletto began to get emotional.

'He seems to be moaning a bit,' Alison said.

'He's just got the bill.'

Alison smiled.

Rigoletto got louder, more emotional.

'What's he saying now?'

Cass thought a moment, then translated. 'Outrageous,' he said. 'Twenty-eight quid for three hamburgers?'

Alison laughed, and wriggled in his lap.

7

Next to Sonia, on the front seat of her old Mini, sat Jo-Ann. Her face was taut, looking ahead. And through the windscreen, getting closer, was Jo-Ann's home.

Oakleigh Estate.

Blocks of flats, drab fifties' flats, street after street of them. And not a signpost out.

Sonia drew up in the damp shadow of a building. She got Jo-Ann out. They went into a stairwell of grey concrete. There was the snicker of beercans on the tiled floor, the smell of urine. And on the walls, graffiti . . .

DEBBIE WATERS BUMMED UP. PLUS SHE ENJOYED.

SUZANNE MEYER IS A BICTH.

Sonia shivered. She shivered more up on the third-floor corridor where it was warm and sweating. Doors were open, and there was the thump of every bass-guitar in hell.

Jo-Ann, a tiny figure, heels clicking, led her past Flats 36, 37, 38. She stopped outside 39. The lock was broken, and she went in.

There was the sound of soap, loud American soap. Jo-Ann pushed open another door, and stopped.

It was a bare room. Sonia could see just part of it, a stained red settee, and the television.

Jo-Ann's mother sat watching it. Or rather lay watching it, a shapeless woman, her hair flattened to her head. Her eyes were half-closed, and she had a foil strip of pills just by her hand.

Beyond, on the arm of the settee, sat her boyfriend. There was foam on his T-shirt, and a six-pack of Stella on the floor.

And the television, the loud American soap, was soap-flakes, was whirring white granules. No picture.

A man brushed past Sonia in the hall. She smelt his beer-breath, and was afraid only after he'd passed. He went on into the room with a small portable TV, and put it down by the other one.

'S'okay, I got Lynn's,' he said. He was slack-faced, dirty-jeaned, exactly like the boyfriend.

He plugged the TV in, then transferred the aerial from the faulty set to the new one. The soap appeared, bright-lipped and gleaming.

And from Jo-Ann's mother and her boyfriend there came

a movement, the first movement Sonia had seen since she'd been standing there . . . As they transferred their gaze from one TV set to the other.

Half an hour later Sonia sat facing Cass. He listened as she talked for some time. She was small and angry behind her thin hands. But what worried him most was that she spoke so quietly.

'I mean, at the end,' she said, 'all I could think of was what had I ever done for that woman? With all my training? What had any of us done, come to that? . . . Except give her cheap booze, cheap pills, and *Dallas*.'

Cass nodded. He could see the Oakleigh flat as Sonia had described it. He could see how little sense it made against her own home. The sunlight streaming in through the window. Alison pedalling her cycle out on the lawn. And *Rigoletto* playing on.

'For God's sake, that poor bloody woman,' Sonia went on. 'There was a time when she tried, *really* tried. After her older boy got taken into care, she used to go with Jo-Ann to the rec, both of them on the bus . . . Have you any idea how much it costs to go by bus nowadays?'

'No, not really.'

'Well, two returns came to two pounds forty. And even that's come to an end because . . . '

Cass held up his hand. 'My love, in any city of the world you're going to find an Oakleigh Estate, aren't you?'

Sonia leaned towards him. 'You didn't let me finish . . . I mean the bus-trips came to an end because the whole damn recreation-ground was torn up. It's two-bedroom flats now, quality development, starting at eighty-four grand.'

'Yes,' Cass said. It was true.

'And the trips to the swimming-pool ended because that went private. Membership five quid, day-tickets two quid, for *children*.' She spread her hands. 'But of course it's more than a swimming-pool now, it's a *complex* . . . Squash, indoor golf-range, sodding *dry-ski* slope.'

If only she'd raise her voice, Cass thought. But she didn't. She spoke with quiet desperation, emphasising words just by tapping her knee. And her eyes, those dark eyes, never left him.

He stood up. 'All right,' he said, 'granted there are certain flats out on Oakleigh where you'll find the no-hopers, and the well-Stelled.'

'Yes.'

'But there are other flats, well cared-for flats, where you'll find people earning three hundred and fifty a week, working overtime on building sites.'

'Yes,' she said again.

'Well, they've got ambitions, plans.'

'Plans for what?'

'I don't know, put down a mortgage on a council house maybe.'

'I'll tell you about council houses,' she said. 'For example, out in the village of Copthorne. Nice little village, you remember?'

'Yes.'

'Well, a council house there sold for a hundred and five grand this week. It was in the paper.'

Cass whistled.

'And even around Oakleigh . . .'

'Oakleigh isn't smart.'

'*Around* Oakleigh,' she said. 'I mean, go where I was this evening. Leave the Oakleigh Estate on that road to the park. One second it's balconies filled with washing and bicycles. The next it's yucca plants and BMWs.'

'Scratched BMWs, I'll bet.'

'Exactly.' She looked straight at him, and spaced out the words, '*Dallas* . . . has . . . left . . . the TV screen. It's there for real now, staring them in the face.'

'Yes.' Cass nodded slowly. He moved closer, put his arms round her. 'My love, you're not the only one who brings the Oakleigh Estate home with you. I deal with it every day as well . . . But in the evenings I switch off. I have to, or I'd go crazy.'

'Quite.' She looked up at him a moment, then pulled away. 'So you just sit down again and listen to your opera.'

27

8

The next morning Cass got up early and went to the supermarket. He bought garlic sausage and oak-smoked ham. He bought French bread, gruyère, strawberries and raspberries. Then he drove back home.

'We're going on a picnic,' he said to Sonia.

They drove to where they sometimes drove on a Saturday, Brendan Point overlooking the sea. Far out, there was the dark shadow of the Island, but the water this side of it was quicksilver. And there were yachts, and the luminous colours of sails.

Cass removed the back seat from the Peugeot and lay with his head on it. Sonia sat next to him, spreading out the picnic. And Alison ran like a loony up and down the hill, trailing a buzzing insect-kite.

There was wine. He'd brought a bottle of Anjou in the cold box, and maybe he drank too much of it. He remembered the sea-breeze getting up a little. Remembered the kite-string going straight up into the air, and Alison tying the end of it to his foot. He even remembered the garlic sausage and the cheese.

But then his eyes closed.

'Strawberries?' Sonia asked.

'Yes,' he said sleepily.

'And cream?'

'Yes.'

'Where d'you want the cream?'

'Yes.'

'On your head?'

'Yes.'

She poured. And suddenly he opened his eyes, lay quite still.

Alison giggled.

'Raspberries as well?' Sonia asked.

'Why not?' he said.

Carefully she put raspberries on his head, with the cream. 'And you'd like them all squashed up? Mushy?'

'Of course,' Cass said.

She leant over him, mashing the fruit and cream into his hair. Still he didn't move. Until Alison started laughing, louder and louder.

With a roar he got up and chased her, down the hill. But he'd forgotten about the kite attached to his foot. It jerked up and down, shrieking crazily. If he'd run any faster he would have broken it.

He gave up, reeled the kite in, and walked back up the slope to Sonia. She threw him the roll of paper towel and watched while he cleaned the mess from his head.

'Good for the roots,' she said.

'Got to be, yes.'

He made a ball of the dirty paper towel and squashed it down into the cold box. The wind dried his hair and he looked at the day, the shining day.

'Perfect, isn't it?' he asked.

'It is.'

'And there's more to come.' He sat down beside her. 'Do you realise that this time next week we'll be on holiday?'

'Of course I do,' she said. 'I've been thinking about it all the time.'

'Going to be marvellous. Driving down through France, looking for cheap hotels and expensive wine.'

'I'm not sure about the wine.'

'I am.'

She began to collect up the dirty picnic things. 'So what about this coming week?' she asked. 'Is it going to be busy?'

'Busy?' He sighed suddenly. 'After Friday night pub-opening? All day Saturday opening?'

He turned away from the yachts and the shining water, and looked at the city sprawling to the east. At the tower-blocks on the edge of it, grey, seemingly always in shadow.

Oakleigh Estate.

9

At twenty past nine that evening an old blue Transit left the
Oakleigh Estate. Fifteen young men were crammed into it.
They were dressed identically, and there was a strange
hysteria about them, a strange wild sweat.

Up front, a young man called Pike was driving. He was
nineteen, and in the passing headlights it was possible to
see him more clearly. The dark strides, the green sweater
with the coloured hoops, the expensive hair-style, razor-
cut. He reached behind him, took the vodka-bottle that
was offered. 'Thanks, skin.'

'Get it down you, Pikey. Neck it back.'

Pike drove for about half an hour out into the country.
The air was dry. It smelt of hedgerows and burnt grass.
Then there was a village. Pike turned left and parked on the
common. From where he could see the pub.

It was smart. There were those old-style bubble
windows. There were a million signs for credit cards. And
a blackboard outside that said TROUT & ALMONDS,
PEPPERED STEAKS, OUR FAMOUS HOUSE RED.

Just before ten they went in there. It was full of yahs and
their bastard voices and their Perrier. Pike went to the bar
and ordered fifteen pints of Stella. The barman recognised
him from earlier in the week. The landlord looked up,
nervous. He edged towards the phone.

Pike smiled at him. He smiled at the blue blazers and the
women in their bastard velvet headbands and their bastard
low-heeled shoes. The Stellas came. He handed them out to
the others and they dropped them on the floor.

A wave of Stella and broken glass went out. The
landlord picked up the phone. Pike jumped the bar and
grabbed it from him. Then he dialled three nines, and
handed the receiver to the frightened man.

He went back over the bar, and there was mess. There was
bastard Perrier all over those blazers and bastard low-heeled
shoes. Chairs were over. Tables were over. Fat men and thin
piss stockbrokers were getting up and running.

They ran for the kitchen, but they were slow. Pike and some others caught them up, and they were tooled. Bastard trout and almonds, he thought, bastard peppered steak. And our *famous* house red.

10

The CPS offices were quiet on Sunday morning. Only Harold the security man was there, jingling his keys on a chain. He looked at the clock. He went downstairs to the main entrance of the building, opened the double doors, and chocked them back. Then turned and saw the big furniture van out in the car-park. Well, he thought, at least they were on time.

There was a man with them called Barry Oldfield. He was down on Harold's list, and he seemed to be in charge. He ordered the unloading of the chairs and desks and worktops. And then Harold took him back inside the building.

They went through the entrance-hall and turned left just before the stairs. Facing them was a big oak door. To the best of Harold's knowledge it hadn't been opened in twenty years. Until last week, that was, when it had been scrubbed, when the whole suite of offices inside had been scrubbed. And painted out, and a new vinyl floor laid down.

These people needed it like that, apparently, for their computers.

Inside it was dim, despite the paint and the new floor. There was oak panelling up to shoulder height, oak partitions. And darker wood too, strangely old-fashioned. The big mahogany letter-rack, the chart-lockers, and the rows of drawers that had held card-index files. Harold looked round at the pictures on the walls, the old cargo-ships steaming against blue sky. And then at the display-model of a ship in a glass case. Three foot long, it was, and every hand-rail, every line of rigging in place. Beautiful handiwork, he thought.

But the man called Barry wasn't impressed. 'What is this?' he asked. 'A museum?'

'No,' Harold told him. 'Shipping office. They went bust in the sixties. Hasn't been used since then.'

He led Barry up the three steep steps to a smaller office. It was glassed on three sides like a tallyman's booth. And the fourth wall, they found, had a large framed map on it of the city and the docks. Or rather the docks as they had been, years ago.

Harold tried to be friendly. 'I s'pose your guv'nor'll sit in here,' he said. 'So he can watch over the rest of you.'

'McRae, you mean?' Barry's mouth curled. 'I tell you, McRae's just going to love this place.'

The man's accent was London. And he smelt of London too, fags, fry, that burnt kind of smell you get on the underground. He moved fast, and he was all sharp edges, the dark gelled hair, the square glasses that magnified his eyes, the pointed lapels of his suit.

Harold left him to it. He looked at his clipboard, and the morning went by as he ticked off entries on the lists. The office furniture was brought in from the van. The four big desk-top computers with all their bits and pieces came too. And then the Telecom men came to instal a tangle of coloured wires.

It was just before midday when McRae turned up. And Harold was surprised. He'd been expecting someone like Barry, thirty-fiveish, sharpish, tired behind his glasses.

But McRae was very different.

He wore one of those designer suits, the kind that looked baggy and crumpled, and was meant to. It pushed his hands forward in his pockets as he walked, bent his head down. And his head was strange. There were these big bushy eyebrows and staring eyes. There was this greasy chestnut hair that went straight back, and then fell in waves round his shoulders. And his slab-white face was thin, beaky, listening to voices of its own.

More, he was *young*.

Harold couldn't see him as the man in charge. He was more like some pop star looking for the keys of his Rolls.

He walked around the outer office, followed by Barry.

'I know it's not much, Bob,' Barry said. 'But it's the best they could do in the time.'

McRae said nothing. He just began pacing the room, looking down at the floor.

Barry pointed to the Telecom men. 'We'll have the cables in by tonight. Fax, the lot. And we'll be up and running by Tuesday.'

For a moment McRae looked as if he was going to say something. Then he backed off, and began pacing again, finishing up by the door. He left the room.

Harold couldn't make him out.

Nor could he make out why this new super-fraud team had come down from London.

11

Monday morning was never a good time for Cass. And this one was definitely bad. He began to realise just how bad when he saw a certain name on the court-list.

'Pike?' he asked. 'Lee Trevor Pike?'

'Yes,' Sam said, looking over his shoulder. 'Why? D'you know him?'

Cass nodded, thinking back to last week, the kid who'd come at him in the Three Tuns. And Pike, it now seemed, had been busy. He'd done over a country pub on the Saturday night.

He went through the file of police statements. Then looked up suddenly.

'They're trying to say he dialled three nines *himself*?'

'Yes,' Sam said.

In Cass' mind there was always a neatness about the magistrates' court. The lightwood panelling, the lightwood benches, a feeling of matters to be settled without fuss.

And Pike, standing in the dock, was neat too. The green-hooped sweater, the carefully-cut hair. In fact the only thing that spoiled it was the sticking-plaster over his knuckles.

Cass faced him, feeling the thin piece of sticking-plaster on his jaw. It seemed to him there was a direct line between the two, and that everyone in the courtroom could see it.

He began.

'May it please you, your Worships, we now come to a disturbing matter. Proof, if it were needed, of an extremely violent age.' He turned to the dock. 'Lee Trevor Pike . . . known member of a football gang called the Wrecking Crew . . . and a young man who, outside the football season, takes the violence of the terraces out into the peaceful countryside.'

He paused, checked his notes.

'In my view he is extremely lucky to be facing only four charges. Others will arise before this case reaches the Crown Court, as I'm sure it must. The mode of trial only is in question this morning.'

He looked up at the magistrates, lined, worried men.

'The facts, your Worships, are these . . . on Saturday *morning* last, Pike drove out alone to the small country village of Dunsford. He there entered the Lamb public house. Business was slow, and he was able to engage the barman in conversation . . . A part-time barman, your Worships, a young, inexperienced man. Because he let slip that the police response-time for the premises was thirty-five minutes.'

One of the magistrates frowned.

'Perhaps I should explain,' Cass said. 'The police station in Dunsford closes at 6·45 pm. After that time, calls are put through to the central station here, eighteen miles away . . . Therefore the time the police allow to respond to a 999 call from Dunsford is thirty-five minutes.'

The magistrates nodded, looked grim.

'Armed with this information,' Cass went on, 'some fifteen members of the . . . Wrecking Crew visited Duns-ford again on the Saturday *evening*. Pike drove them down the B486 in a blue Transit van. With them he entered the Lamb public house at around ten o'clock. And, in the space

34

of twenty-five minutes, with utter impunity, he took charge of the devastation.'

He glanced at his notes again. 'The pub is now closed. Damage is estimated at £4000. And, more importantly, seven customers were taken to casualty, suffering from . . .'

Suddenly Pike stood up in the dock. 'I was never on the B486. I was never in that pub. I do not own a blue Transit van.'

The Chief Magistrate turned to him. 'Be seated, Mr Pike. Your turn will come in a moment.'

Pike sat down, and softly muttered, 'Wankers.'

Court finished late, and Cass took Sam into the nearby Pizza Express. She ordered green salad, garlic bread, and a Perrier.

'You'll fade away,' Cass told her.

'That's not what my husband says.'

They ate, and then Cass opened a file out on the table. 'As you know, Sam,' he said, 'I'm going on holiday at the end of the week. So maybe we'd better get this Pike thing sorted out.'

'You mean, I could be prosecuting?'

'Well . . .' Cass shrugged.

She was excited. She'd never taken on anything of this size before.

Cass found the police statements, pulled them out of the file. 'All right, what d'you think of these?'

'Well,' she glanced at them, 'fourteen separate statements, varying descriptions. But they all see the youths as five-nine to five-ten, slim build, green hooped sweaters.'

'And how many kids are you going to see looking like that on a Saturday night?'

'What? . . .' She went back to the statements. 'Okay, the pub landlord . . . a good witness.'

'But he owns the place, doesn't he?'

'Yes, but I don't see . . .'

'He's got all his money tied up in it,' Cass said. 'He's not going to come through on the day.'

Sam frowned. She turned pages. 'Okay, the blue Transit,

reg number UVM 420T . . . Nothing on the National Computer. But Pike was seen driving it a fortnight ago, leaving the Mirabelle Club.'

'Mmmm . . .'

'And then,' she said triumphantly, 'there's Sergeant Dawson from the Hillside Station.'

'What about Sergeant Dawson?'

'He was called to a domestic last week. A Miss Tania Capel, who turned out to be Pike's girlfriend.' She read on, her voice rising. 'What's more, Sergeant Dawson called back there yesterday. Miss Capel had heavy bruising of the face and neck, said she wanted Pike locked up. And she came straight out with it, no prompting . . . Pike had skinned knuckles late on Saturday night. He boasted that he'd been down at the Dunsford pub. *And* he'd driven the others down there in his blue Transit. She knew its number was UVM something.

Cass let the silence hang. 'Did they find the logbook at his place.'

She looked down the page, frowned again. 'No.'

'And what does Pike say in his statement?'

'Well,' Sam found it. 'He claims . . .'

Cass held up his hand. 'I don't even have to hear it,' he said.

'What?'

'He doesn't own a blue Transit. Maybe he drove one once, but it was for a friend who was pissed.' He shrugged tiredly. 'Last Saturday night he was nowhere near Dunsford. Went sea-fishing, with witnesses . . . Skinned his knuckles on the side of the boat . . .'

He touched her arm. 'Look, we're going to have to do a lot better than that if we're going to get this into the Crown Court. For God's sake, we're dealing with a *football* gang.'

He reached out and closed the file. Then he stiffened. There was a prickle on the back of his neck as if somebody was watching him.

He turned. Somebody was. It was a young man, a strange young man with shoulder-length hair and a thin white face.

Cass saw the same face some three hours later. It came into his office. Along with a crumpled designer suit and expensive shoes.

'Mr Cassidy?'

'Yes?'

'The name's McRae.'

Which figured, Cass thought, because the voice was thin, Scots, carefully articulated.

'What can I do for you, Mr McRae?'

'Quite a lot actually.'

Cass frowned, pointed to a chair. Though McRae didn't sit down. Instead he began pacing the room.

'The thing is, I only arrived here yesterday,' he said. 'They've put me downstairs, in the old offices.'

'That's bad luck,' Cass said.

But McRae ignored him. 'Have you heard of Lennox Freezers?' he asked suddenly. 'Local factory. They've got a big labour-dispute on at the moment.'

Cass nodded. 'It's been on the local news.'

'Exactly,' McRae said. 'Well the reason I'm down here is to make certain investigations into Lennox Freezers. And you might say I'm going to be helped by this dispute. There are going to be people in court, prosecutions, and so on.'

'Is that right?' Cass asked.

'Yes.' McRae was quite serious. 'But what I thought I should mention, Mr Cassidy . . . I need *you* to prosecute for me.'

'No.' Cass shook his head. 'No, not me.'

'Why not?'

'Well, picket-line trouble? It's going to be a continuing saga, isn't it? Daily appearances? Drag on for weeks?'

'Yes.'

'Well, as it happens I'm going on holiday at the end of this week. Car-ferry booked. Everything.'

McRae looked straight at him. 'Then somebody in the car-ferry office will have to get their pen out won't they? Change the date?'

'*What?*' Cass was amazed. 'No, it's out of the question.'

'I wouldn't bank on that.'

And it was the look on the man's face. Cass got up, angry. 'First thing in the morning,' he said, 'I'm going to have a word with Royston, my Area Chief.'

'That would be an awfully good idea.'

12

It was just after six, and the news was showing on TV. Sonia got up and switched the sound down.

'But, he can't do it, can he?' she asked. 'Can't change our holiday just like that?'

'Course he can't,' Cass said.

'Why don't you ring Royston now?'

'He wouldn't like it,' Cass said. 'Don't worry. I'll catch him tomorrow.'

She shook her head.

'What's the matter?' He got up too. 'Don't you believe me?'

'Oh, yes. Yes, of course I do,' she said. 'It's just . . .'

'Just what?'

'Well, all this has come on top of a very bad day.'

He went over to her, sat her down in an armchair. 'What is it? Somebody at the day centre?'

'Yes,' she said, 'a little girl called Jo-Ann. D'you remember me telling you about her?'

Cass thought a moment. 'The mother and the boyfriend sitting there in that flat,' he said. 'And the two television sets.'

She nodded. 'And the six-pack of Stella. And the moggies.'

'Oh,' he said. 'Mogadon.'

'Turns out there was a chemist's shop broken into, out Ryefield way,' she told him. 'A hundred and fifty strips missing.'

'How d'you know that?'

'The police found them at the flat. They've taken statements. They're going to prosecute.'

'Oh, God.'

There was silence. Then she turned to him. 'Cass, I've lost,' she said. 'Lost a-bloody-gain.'

He put his arm round her. It always affected him when she swore, swore softly in that way she had.

'And that little girl,' she went on, 'she's going into care.'

'Not necessarily,' he said. 'There's still a good chance.'

But she shook her head. 'It all happened before, with Jo-Ann's brother. Two years ago.'

He was silent.

She twisted suddenly away from him. 'I mean, what d'you do after years and years of no bloody money? And then some bloody man comes along with a strip of pills? . . . You lie down, put a cushion under your head, and whack them down.'

'Yes,' Cass said.

Her voice became quieter, frightened. 'I saw Jo-Ann today. She didn't say anything. But inside she's screaming. She's up against a wall.'

Cass sat on the arm of the chair next to her. He pulled her close, stroked her hair.

Then he looked up.

He saw the TV, silent, its sound switched off. But the newsreel film was of men fighting with police, placards, NO TO MANAGEMENT . . .

Lennox.

He watched as a car, a metallic red Rover came out of the factory gates. Watched as men broke through the police cordon. The car went towards them, was lost behind a forest of waving hands. Hands which, Cass suddenly saw, held iron bars and lumps of concrete. They smashed at the windows, at the roof. They grabbed the car, rocked it, rocked it higher. Turned it over.

And maybe it was because the TV sound was switched off. But somehow the men's faces got to Cass. The anger, the mouths taut, wide open . . .

Screaming. Sonia's words came back to him. *Up against a wall.*

13

At ten past nine the next morning Cass went in to see Area Chief Prosecutor Royston. And at twenty past nine he came out again, his face grim.

He walked down to the ground floor of the CPS building and stopped outside a large oak door. He'd passed it every day for years, knew it led to an empty suite of offices once owned by a shipping firm. But things had changed. There were new steel locks, high-security locks. There was a press-button entry system, and a closed-circuit scanner looking down at him. He should have been warned.

But he wasn't. He was angry as he was led through to some inner office. And his anger grew as he saw the thin Scotsman draped across a desk in his designer suit. Saw his face in particular.

McRae was grinning.

'You got the news from Royston, I take it?'

Cass nodded. 'I'm on attachment to you.'

The man's grin widened.

'But why?' Cass' voice rose. 'For god's sake, why me?'

McRae shrugged. 'Because you're a boring old fart,' he said quietly. 'But, so they tell me, the least boring among the prosecutors here.'

Cass couldn't believe he was hearing it.

And McRae got up from the desk. 'They also tell me you get things right. The squeaky-clean laddie from Newcastle. No deals with naughty ladies or Town Hall.'

'*What?*'

The man came close. He eyed Cass up and down. 'Quite the local caped crusader,' he said. 'One sees the rippling muscles of Batman . . . Pow, Splat, Ker-Plok.'

Furious, Cass' head came up. 'Just who the hell d'you think you are?'

'I'm Boy Wonder, Batman. Didn't you know?'

He went away towards the door, then turned. 'But you can call me Robert McRae,' he said. 'Investigator. Serious Fraud.'

'Oh, big stuff,' Cass said. 'Like fraud wasn't serious before.'

'Correct.' McRae opened the door and leaned against it for a moment. 'You can forget your Guinness director, walking down to the beach with 5.2 million tucked in his sandals. You can forget your Johnson-Matthey.' He beckoned Cass outside. 'Fraud, Batman, can be defined as taking a million pounds from someone, or taking a pound from a million people . . . But this, this is taking a pound from *322 million people* . . . Jumbo Euro-Size Fraud.'

They went down some steps and into a big outer office. Anger hadn't allowed Cass to see it before. But now he saw the old oak panelling. And against it, strangely, bright white worktops, white metal shelving, and machines.

There were four of them, big desk-top computers with complicated extras. Operators were bending over them, and a secretary was hurrying between. McRae brushed his way past her. He picked up a huge bound file from a desk.

'Information from the Department of Trade and Industry,' he said, 'concerning 1992 . . . You've heard of 1992?'

'Course I have.' Cass was still angry.

McRae smiled at him. 'The date when the whole of Europe's going to be one great big happy family,' he said. 'Frontiers disappearing, trade barriers disappearing, not to mention currency regulations . . . In short, Batman, a time when any businessman will be able to do business in any other part of the Community. Buy premises, start trading, take the money and run.'

Cass sighed. He wondered how long he'd have to put up with this Batman business. Tiredly, he watched McRae riffling through the pages of the huge file.

'Rather a fat volume, wouldn't you say?' the man asked. 'And getting fatter. New directives coming out of Brussels every day . . . *Total* chaos . . . ' He snapped it shut. 'And your average British company director's not bothering to read. No tits in it.'

'Look, this is all absolutely riveting stuff . . .'

McRae held up a hand. 'But certain *European* gentlemen have started moving early, *well* in advance of 1992,' he said. 'They've taken advantage of this chaos I was talking about, and they've come across the Channel. Started looking through company lists here.'

'What?'

'European take-overs . . . Cross-border mergers.'

'Listen,' Cass said. 'I'm just a Crown Prosecutor. I deal with assault, burglary, rape . . .'

'I was coming to rape,' McRae said.

He led the way over to one of the desk-top computers, and tapped the man there on the shoulder.

'Run the horror-comic, will you, Barry?'

Words appeared on the VDU, Italian words, and a great many figures. Cass watched them without understanding. The man called Barry homed in on certain data. While McRae paced up and down behind him, shooting occasional glances at the screen.

'This comes from a couple of recent raids by our *carabinieri* chums,' he said. 'Little factory outside Turin. They manufacture pumps . . . And see those dates? Delivery dates? See how they keep falling behind?'

Barry tapped at the keys. There was more Italian data.

'Sunny Rimini,' McRae explained. 'Ever been there? All those Eyetalians picking their noses in the sea? . . . What we've got here is another little factory, turning out heat-exchangers. But they're waiting for pumps, aren't they? Waiting forever? They go out of business.'

The data speeded up. Cass' mind was in a whirl.

'Group office, Milan.' McRae was still pacing. 'Who, of course, have their cheque in the post. It's in the post *seven* months . . . And at the same time, container-lorries are being sent back from the Italian border. The drivers, you see, have the wrong documents. They have the wrong documents *every* blasted time.'

'What are you saying?' Cass asked. 'That other firms are going out of business too?'

McRae didn't answer.

The next block of data that came up on the screen was in French.

'Switzerland,' McRae said over Cass' shoulder. 'Had an

uncle who lived there once. Very steep country. Very. He had to slide down the mountain on a tin tray just to pick up his morning paper . . . Before that they used to yodel the news up to him.'

'For God's sake,' Cass said.

'What I mean is,' McRae moved closer, 'news doesn't travel very far in Switzerland. Doesn't even cross the street.'

And on the computer-screen Cass saw data that even he could understand.

CREDIT SUISSE GENEVA TRANSFER TO UNITED OVERSEAS BANK GENEVA U.S.$720 000.

The jokes were finished with. What came Cass' way now were precise, clearly articulated words. It was a quality he'd met before in certain Scotsmen. And despite himself, he was impressed.

'One more little factory I have to talk about,' McRae said, 'right here in this fair city.'

'Lennox Freezers.' Cass nodded. 'The picket-line business.'

'Exactly. And what, in your opinion, is all that about?'

'Well, according to the television, mass redundancies.'

'As far as the workers are concerned, yes.' McRae nodded. 'But, what do the management say?'

Cass shrugged.

'*Selected* redundancies and early retirements,' the man went on. 'A process of streamlining, in short. The firm is tooling up for a new line in white goods.'

'But, why should they be doing that?'

'Lost orders,' McRae said. 'They claim their old products, fridge-freezers, were way behind the market-leaders.'

Then he stopped, arms to his sides, waiting.

And Cass got there. 'Fridge-freezers? . . . Those pumps you were talking about and those heat-exchangers?'

McRae nodded slowly. 'Oh, yes,' he said. 'Parts from Italy, body and assembly from here, and decisions from *Christ* knows where.'

'What do you mean?'

'Remember those cross-border mergers?'

'Take-overs?'

'Exactly.'

'But surely . . .' Something still wasn't right. '. . . Surely you can't guarantee to take a factory over just by squeezing it dry. You just leave it wide open to predators.'

'Not if you've marked your card,' McRae said quietly. 'Not if you know a certain Mr R.A. Gotto, finance director of Lennox Freezers. And you slip him $720 000 through a Geneva bank.'

And Cass remembered the Swiss data. 'But . . . but haven't you got evidence of that?'

'Evidence of what?' McRae asked. 'That Mr Gotto's got a chum in Geneva? And he sold this chum his collection of Dinky toys?'

'Seven hundred and twenty grand?'

'All right, sold him a holiday house . . . whatever . . . The man's a *finance* director.'

Cass nodded.

'And besides, Gotto's on holiday at the moment . . . In Europe, so they tell me.'

It was after lunch. They were walking down past the library. The park was on their right, the wide grassland of the cricket field, with the square in its centre roped off.

'Time is what it's all about,' McRae said. 'My little laddies and I, we're always getting there too late . . . But now . . .'

Cass frowned.

'Work it out,' McRae told him. 'Lennox Freezers . . . Only a quarter of the work-force still with jobs. The rest outside the gates, throwing rocks at them.'

'Yes, but . . .'

'*Plus* the fact that the Union's orchestrating the whole thing. They *want* their people in court, talking.'

'And you want me there, making them talk?'

'I need half a dozen martyrs, the firewood piled up underneath them. I need them away from the magistrates

44

and pushed through to the Crown Court.' He turned towards Cass. 'Don't you see? Six weeks' delay. Time to get the Press interested. Get policemen digging under rose-bushes.'

'Yes,' Cass said.

'Can you guarantee that?'

'If the dispute starts getting out of hand.'

'Oh, I think it will,' McRae said.

14

It was dark in the Lennox factory yard. The police were starting the delivery-run later tonight, at around a quarter past ten. Trying to make the people outside think it wasn't going to happen. Trying to make them drift off to the pubs.

But they were still there outside the gates, beyond the police cordon and the barriers and the barbed wire. A bigger mob than last night, and they were setting up that beat, bashing dustbin lids with spanners, metal on metal.

And inside the gates, the Chief Inspector thought, it wasn't much better. The factory drivers were nervous. They went towards their lorries quietly, closed the cab-doors quietly, and waited before starting their engines.

There were four of them, four big artics. Unmarked. This was since the ambush of last night, the broken glass on the road. And the driver, coming in to work, who'd been chased into the multi-storey, and done over by six men.

Nothing proved, of course. Nothing ever was.

The Chief Inspector waited too, before signalling the police outriders to start up. He decided to put in one last call to Archie.

'What's it like out there?' he said into his PR.

Archie's voice came back, loud and angry against the roar of the mob outside. 'I don't know,' he shouted. 'Looks more like six or seven hundred than five.'

'*Seven* hundred?'

'They know you're coming. They're organised. They've got people on the roof opposite with glasses.'

'Oh, shit,' the Chief Inspector said quietly. 'So what do we do, Arch? Up it?'

'Have to.'

The Chief Inspector made one more call. It brought three riot-buses in from the end of the street to park outside the factory gates.

Ninety men.

De-bussing in full view.

15

The magistrates' court had lost its smallness, its intimacy. It was filled to overflowing. The public benches, the Press benches, the three rows of defence lawyers.

And the ten men in the dock, bandaged, sullen, their eyes like coal.

The court-clerk was working his way through them.

'You are Mr Denis Slattery?'

'Yes.'

'You were born on 17 March 1968?'

'Yes.'

'You live at . . .?'

Cass sat with Sam by the piled-up brief boxes. And in the whole of that crowded courtroom he felt just one person's eyes on him.

McRae's.

Because McRae didn't know yet about the phonecall of last night. The long phonecall Cass had taken at his home . . .

But the court-clerk was going on.

'You are Mr Robert Hickman?'

'Yes.'

'You were born on 3 January 1944?'

'Yes.'

'You live at Number 17 Downside Road, Westwood?'

'I do.'

'And do you plead guilty or not guilty?'

'Not guilty.'

Cass looked at Hickman, a man of forty-five, older than the others. He was thick-set, dark, careful. A union man, as Cass well knew.

The court-clerk was now addressing the Chief Magistrate.

'May they be seated, Sir?'

'They may.'

'Please be seated.'

The ten men sat stiffly, angrily. And the silence grew.

Cass got to his feet. He turned his back on McRae. 'May it please your Worships,' he began, 'it is not my intention to outline the industrial dispute at Lennox Freezers plc. That lies outside the jurisdiction of this court. All that can concern us now are the actions of the ten men appearing here. Actions which have led to violence outside the factory gates.'

He paused.

'Your Worships, I am advised that a major cause of this violence is the departure of lorries from the factory yard. Lorries which are delivering goods outwards, and are impeded from their lawful course by these men . . . Last night there were very ugly scenes. Far uglier than have been seen in this city for a long time.'

The magistrates nodded. They knew their role in this piece of theatre.

'I am also advised,' Cass consulted his notes, 'that on the first day of this dispute, twenty policemen were on duty. But that on Monday night last there were ninety. And that last night, Tuesday, there were in excess of one hundred and fifty . . . Obviously this cannot be allowed to escalate further.'

Cass kept his eyes on the magistrates, never once looked at McRae.

'It is for this reason,' he went on, 'that the police ask, and the Crown concurs, that these proceedings be dealt with swiftly, by a magistrate's court. By which I mean, the

47

Crown asks that the defendants be charged with a Summary Offence under Section Four of the Public Order Act. And that, as a condition of bail . . .'

McRae got to him in his office, before lunch. He was angry. And anger, Cass saw, brought back the comic-book jokes.

'*Summary* offences? *Magistrates*' court? Holy Christ, Batman, what d'you think you're doing?'

Cass shifted behind his desk. It was a moment before he spoke. 'Listen. I had a phonecall last night . . . from Royston, Area Chief Crown Prosecutor.'

'Royston? I thought he was on the side of justice and truth.'

'He was,' Cass said. 'Until *he* was phoned up by the Assistant Commissioner.'

'And the head of the Sewage Department maybe? The *whole* of Gotham City?'

Cass sighed.

'You were nobbled,' McRae said then.

'No. My duties, as laid down by the Code, were explained to me.'

'Is that right?'

Cass nodded. 'Number one,' he explained, 'is there sufficient evidence for the case to go on to the Crown Court?'

'Of course there is, man.'

'Number two, is it in the public interest?'

McRae hissed in his breath. 'It's political.'

'No,' Cass said again.

'What is it then?'

'Understandable, from a police point of view.'

'Jesus.'

'Listen,' Cass said, 'the police are on a hiding to nothing. Every day it gets bigger. Every day they're in the middle of a mob. And every time they raise a hand, they're on TV . . . *They* want it contained.'

McRae looked at him steadily. 'And you?'

'Well,' Cass hesitated, 'one thing I know. When there's

violence, when property's threatened, and it gets out of hand . . . then a lot of things start to happen, very quickly.'

'One thing you know, Batman.' McRae turned away in his chair.

And as he did so, the designer suit caught around him, became like any other suit. And he became like any other thin young man, Cass thought, up against the system.

'All right, can they get away with it? The police?'

'Oh, yes,' Cass said. 'They can charge what they like. Undercharge if necessary. Even when it's a case of, as on Monday night . . . ' He held up a piece of paper. ' . . . Six men on the picket-line smashing up a Rover car, turning it upside-down.'

'What?'

'Didn't you see it on TV?'

McRae turned back, flapped a hand tiredly.

'It still went down as a Section Four Offence,' Cass said. 'No further evidence required . . . At least, not *against* those men.'

He pushed the piece of paper towards McRae. And suddenly McRae knew he'd had it ready, he'd had it ready all the time.

'I've made a couple of notes in the margin,' Cass said.

16

The pub was all leatherette seats, TV quiz-games, symphony bloody orchestras playing pop. And McRae didn't like it. But it was the pub where the journalists had told him he'd find Robert Hickman. Union man.

He was there at a table, slack-limbed, staring down at his scotch. And he was fed to the teeth, McRae saw, with magistrates and the due process of law.

'Mr Hickman?'

'Yes?'

'Saw you in court this morning,' McRae said. 'Trouble is, I expected to *hear* you in court too.'

49

Hickman grunted. 'Who are you? The Press?'

McRae showed his warrant card. There was a flicker of surprise.

'Have you heard of us, Mr Hickman?'

'Heard you exist.'

'Oh, we do,' McRae said. 'And the thing is, you and I, we're trying to get into the same building.'

There was more than a flicker of surprise. McRae sat down. He got Cass' piece of paper out of his pocket.

'I'd like to talk to you about a car,' he said. 'A Rover, F370 MXD, metallic red.'

Hickman didn't answer.

'It was bashed about by some friends of yours last Monday night . . . Now, why was that?'

Hickman still didn't answer.

'Seems there was a reason.' McRae read from the paper. 'Evidence of a Mr Jack Oldfield, electrician . . . "The car drove right at us. Me and five other members of the picket-line. Right at us on purpose."'

'That's what Jack said, yes.'

'What do you say, Mr Hickman?'

'Well,' the man hesitated, 'I don't know about it being on purpose. I just couldn't hold the others back.'

'Why?'

And Hickman showed a trace of anger. 'This car, all right, it was being driven by Mr James Denton, Assistant Director, Finance. And right bastard.'

McRae waited.

'Look,' Hickman leaned forward suddenly, 'is this an interview? Official?'

'Well . . . '

'Because I'm not too fond of policemen right now. None of us are.'

'I'm not a policeman, Mr Hickman. But there is one present.'

'Where?'

'Next door, playing darts.' McRae pointed. 'And you'd like him. He's hand-picked, got blue all round his mouth.'

'What?'

50

McRae mimicked a man licking a ballpoint pen and writing.

And slowly Hickman grinned.

It was later. They were close together over the table, and they were drinking large ones.

'All right, we had news on this lot,' Hickman said quietly. 'January last year. Way before anything started.'

McRae waited.

'There was a letter sent to a shit-hot firm of lawyers in the City, Jarrold and Jarrold.'

'Letter?' McRae was startled. 'But, how did you get to hear about it?'

'This isn't the stone age. We don't all come to work on bikes,' Hickman said. 'We've got secretaries on our side. And higher-ups.'

'I see.'

'No, you don't. There was a signature on this thing . . . R.A. Gotto, Finance Director, Lennox Freezers.'

McRae frowned. 'Which would explain your dislike of his assistant, Mr Denton.'

'Yes.'

'And his metallic red Rover car.'

Hickman nodded.

'Tell me about this letter,' McRae said.

'Well, what it did, it asked for legal precedent . . . I mean, strictly *legal* ways of driving a successful factory into the ground.'

McRae whistled softly. 'And was there an answer?'

'Oh yes, it outlined a series of steps.' Hickman said. 'Scrap the old production-line, and go over to something new like tumble-dryers. Automate the plant. Offer a new contract to a reduced work-force with reduced hours.'

'Which they did?'

'Only the last part. The rest of it they didn't have to.' Hickman showed anger again. 'All they had to do was spend a few bob. Have plans drawn up, budgets. Place *provisional* orders for the new plant . . . You see what I'm talking about?'

51

And McRae did. 'Tell me,' he said. 'Did you actually manage to get your hands on these letters?'

'Jesus, if I had.' Hickman sighed. 'If I'd been able to deep-throat that lot to the Press.'

McRae sat back in his chair. He thought a moment. 'Okay, this is what you do,' he said. 'You think back to last Monday night, when that car drove at your friend Jack . . . And you find the man standing next to him, who was injured.'

'Injured? There wasn't anyone standing next to Jack who was injured.'

'Exactly.'

'I don't understand,' Hickman said.

'It's easy,' McRae told him. 'You find a guy who's been working on his garden recently, his rockery maybe . . . and dropped a rock on his foot.'

The man looked up.

'And then,' McRae said, '*I* talk to my policeman friend next door. Get him to sign a laundry-slip.'

And for a second time Hickman grinned.

17

The laundry-slip, as McRae called it, had its results. Because at two o'clock the next afternoon James Denton, Assistant Finance Director of Lennox Freezers, turned up at the CPS building.

He was brought to the interview-room. Which, McRae thought, was just like interview-rooms the world over. A wire-glass window, cream walls with a couple of Public Information posters, and that smell McRae knew of old. The smell of men trying not to show they were frightened.

Denton wasn't frightened. He was ten years past that, greying, with thin-rimmed glasses, and thin around the mouth. And there was his cream linen suit to back him up. Not to mention his 2K wristwatch, and his 48K a year before you got to the gravy.

He sat down at the table where Detective Sergeant Roderick was waiting. He said he was a very busy man. He said he appreciated that he'd been asked to call at the CPS building, and not at the police station where the Press were jumping around.

And all the while he was sizing Roderick up.

Which was fine, McRae thought from the back of the room. More than fine, it was perfect. Because Roderick came from the local CID pool. He was too young, too full of himself, too sharply-dressed. No more than a whisker away from the yobs he usually chased.

And Denton saw it, saw the flush there was about the boy, the sweat. And as time went by he took charge, got uppity.

'But this is *insane*,' he shouted suddenly. 'Those tear-aways on the picket-line attacked my car. They smashed the windows, kicked in the doors, totalled the roof . . . And you accuse *me* of dangerous driving?'

'Yes, Sir, but . . .'

'But bloody *what*?'

'Well, Sir, as I explained to you,' Roderick said, 'I have statements from these six men. And then there's the doctor's report on Mr Spencer's leg.'

'I didn't go *near* anyone's leg. I stopped well short . . . Look, I've been driving for twenty-two years.'

'I understand, Sir. But of course we need to hear your side of it. And examine your vehicle.'

Denton's lips became thinner. 'That's going to be difficult.'

'What d'you mean?'

'Well, I expect it's on its way to some car-auction by now.' The man shrugged. 'I took delivery of a new one this morning.'

It was time, McRae thought, to intervene. He went forward with his briefcase and sat down.

'A new Rover?' he asked.

Denton turned. And he wasn't warned, not yet.

'Yes,' he said, 'the fleet people have managed to find me one.'

McRae smiled. 'That's very impressive.'

'I don't see why. They handle all our business. It only required a signature.'

'From your Finance Director?' McRae kept the smile on the boil.

'What?' Denton frowned. 'No, he's abroad, on holiday.'

'But you do know the Finance Director?' McRae asked. 'Well, of course you do, you're his assistant.' He opened his briefcase and got out a file. 'Let's see, it's a Mr Gotto, isn't it? A Mr R.A. Gotto? . . . Director of Lennox Freezers? Director of Sherenson plc? Director of . . .?' And he was enjoying himself now. ' . . . Refrigerazione Marchetti, Turin? . . . Bank deposit holder at the United Overseas Bank, Geneva? Account Number S43826? . . . Where, on 12 March this year, he received a transfer for $720 000?'

Denton's mouth opened. 'Who are you?' he asked.

'Robert McRae. Serious Fraud.'

McRae started as he always started, from six feet away, leaning back in his chair, and with a lot of paper on the table.

He went through it all once, and then went back, narrowing down the questions.

'You were at every forward-strategy meeting bar that one?'

'I never even *heard* of that one,' Denton said.

'Never heard why millions of pounds worth of new automated plant was approved?'

'No.'

'Oh, come on, man, you're Gotto's deputy. And your office *typed* that letter to Jarrold and Jarrold, smart-ass lawyers in the City.'

'No.'

McRae smiled. It was fine by him. He had time.

By four-thirty in the afternoon he was sitting closer, and he'd brought in more paper. Italian company records, in the original and in translation.

'Motore Apalico, Rimini,' he said. 'Refrigeration

pumps . . . And, d'you see it? The meeting out there at the factory? Where you all agreed the slowdown?'

'What meeting?' Denton asked.

'July 10, last year.'

'I wasn't there.'

'Your name's down in the bloody *minutes*.' McRae pointed. 'For God's sake, we've cleaned out that factory, had it *investigated*.'

Denton shook his head.

Fine, okay, plenty of time.

But then there wasn't.

Because, during a break around five o'clock, Roderick came up to him in the corridor.

'Sir?'

'What is it?'

'His office has been on the phone, Sir. Mr Denton's office. They want to know why he's being held here and not down at the station.'

McRae looked at him. 'You gave them the line, did you? About the Press boys?'

'Yes, but . . .'

'But, what, laddie?'

'Well, the problem was, their call was transferred to me from your office. Serious Fraud.'

McRae swore, and went back into the interview-room.

He worked fast, as fast as he dared, but it was seven o'clock before he began to get anywhere.

With telexes, a great pile of them.

'This $720 000,' he said. 'Traced forward to your friend Mr Gotto. Traced back, as you can see, to Lamorisse Achats-Ventes . . . Which is a Mickey Mouse company acting for Viallonga . . . Which is Italian again, if you understand me, and *definitely* not in the ice cream trade . . .'

And it was a quarter to eight before he was close. By which time he was speaking softly, crouching, next to Denton's chair.

'It's always the big men who get out, who know their

55

way out,' he said. 'But the men coming up, like you, they fold . . . they're folding all around you . . . Milan . . . Turin . . . Rimini.'

He put his arm round Denton. 'Then there's *afterwards*. How your family'll see it. I mean, they always say it'll be all right. Wives say they'll wait. Kids say it doesn't matter. We see it all the time.' He paused. 'But after Ford prison, well . . . It's just a sort of a house and a sort of a job. And of course there are memories of that other house, the nice house. Summer, kids on the lawn, cricket with a soft ball . . . all poisoned. The way a house can be poisoned for a woman.'

Denton breathed in and out, slowly, experimentally. 'All very poetic,' he said. 'But I've told you again and again, I know absolutely nothing about . . .'

Then he folded up. The shine went out of his face, his watch, his cream linen suit. 'All right,' he said.

McRae got up. He signalled Roderick to take over, and he moved away to the corner of the room. Pain went through him. Because he could see it, *see* . . . that house, that lawn, the cricket with a soft ball . . .

Every time.

18

Friday was a big day in court for Cass. And he didn't get back to his office till four o'clock.

To find McRae lying back in one of the easy chairs.

The man had maybe twenty sheets of paper in his hand, stapled together. He held them out. 'Denton's statement,' he said.

Cass skimmed through the first two pages. 'Unsubstantiated,' he said, 'Mmmm, maybe that . . . Definitely not that . . . Hearsay . . . Hearsay.'

He looked up. 'A good QC would throw three quarters of this out.'

'That's what I thought,' McRae said.

Cass frowned. 'So what are you going to charge him with?'

'Oh, traffic offences. Reckless driving and the rest of it.'

'I don't understand.'

McRae didn't say anything.

There was something wrong. Cass looked at the statement again. 'One o'clock this morning?'

'What?'

'It was one in the morning when this was signed?'

'Yes.'

'So where's Denton now?'

'As I heard it, he went into work at the Lennox factory.'

Cass moved closer, watching the man's face. 'Denton left here at one this morning? And then went into work at nine?'

'That's right.' McRae shrugged. 'Seeing as how it's Friday, the last day before his boss Mr Gotto gets back from holiday.'

'What?'

'And seeing as how there's a certain letter, signed by Mr Gotto, still on disc.'

'Jesus,' Cass said softly.

'It was a choice between reckless driving, and one hell of a lot else,' McRae said. 'He understood that.'

Cass stepped back. Anger, the long day in court, welled up in him. 'Well, listen, I don't know anything about this. Anything at . . .'

Then he stopped. 'Wait a minute. Sergeant Roderick . . .'

'What about Sergeant Roderick?'

'Didn't he say the Lennox factory rang up yesterday? Found out that Denton was being interviewed by Serious Fraud?'

Cass was still angry as he cleared up for the weekend with Sam. 'On Monday morning,' he told her, 'there are going to be a hell of a lot of police reports. And I'll want them on my desk before nine.'

'*Jawohl*,' she said.

He looked at her. 'Sorry,' he said, lowering his voice.

'Doesn't matter.' She did so too. 'But why so many police reports?'

'The Lennox business.' He sighed. 'It's Friday night. Rent-a-mob night.'

'You mean, they'll be bussing people in?'

'No, it won't necessarily be the unions,' he told her. 'It'll be anyone who wants a punch-up . . . law-bashers . . . guv'nors' men.'

'Guv'nors' men?'

'Anyone with a score to settle,' he said.

And the thought stayed with him, grew on him, as he drove home later. Something was going to happen, he was sure of it. Nor was the tension broken when he found Sonia and Alison out in the garden, immersed in a game of swing-ball.

He didn't join them as he usually would have done. He went back into the living-room, poured a drink, and switched on Radio 3.

To find his sort of peace.

Michaelangeli was playing Schumann's Winterszeit. Cass sat down. He listened to the sound of the piano, fine-boned, melancholy, and small.

19

Outside the factory gates the sound was huge. The beat of metal on metal, the chanting, the roar.

It was going to be different tonight, the Chief Inspector thought. Archie had told him there were more than a thousand men out there.

And inside the yard it was different too. The factory-drivers had gone. TNT men had been brought in to take charge of the lorries. And they'd done all this before.

Because there was a routine they'd worked out.

The first man got into his cab. He slammed the door, *ker-chunk*, then fired the motor and started revving it.

The second man got in, *ker-chunk*, and fired up too.

Ker-chunk, the third man. *Ker-chunk*, the fourth. Until the revving was like the sound of some huge animal. It echoed back from the walls of the yard.

The men outside fell silent.

Then headlights came on, from lorries and police out-riders. The Chief Inspector was dazzled. He started to give the signal, but they were already going past him.

Fast.

At first it was clear what happened outside the factory, clear as day in the police floodlights. The lorries reaching third gear, twenty-five miles an hour, before coming to the gate. The uniformed men there swinging them open. The men with riot-shields and helmets beyond. The horses beyond them, the barriers, the barbed wire.

And then the mob, still silent.

But as the outriders came through there was a roar from split-mouthed men. Split-legged too as they took wire and barriers. Took horses, pouring around them and between their legs. Took on riot-police, the line of shields and visors breaking up like glass.

A loop of men, the first of them, spilled out across the road. A police outrider was hurled to the ground, his engine screaming. Other riders swung out and round, giving way.

The police were fast. A new formation of riot-shields came in, a new machine, glinting in the light.

But men got through. They ran at lorries in the shriek of brakes, leapt up on running-boards, battered at locked doors and windows.

The road was screams, was a mass of men falling, clawing at each other as they fell.

Confusion.

Except where, further along the road, a Transit van was parked.

Inside the van was the sweet white smell of vodka. There were four young men, all wearing the same green sweaters with coloured hoops. Three of them had vermin-killing catapults. And the fourth, Pike, was getting ball-bearings from a box.

He straightened, looked out of the van windows at the mob. At the confusion, the flaring riot-shields, the rearing horses. Then he saw the outriders reforming, and the first of the lorries getting away.

Pike opened up the rear doors of the van. He and the others squatted there, steadying their elbows on their knees. By the time the first lorry came past it was picking up speed again. The young men fired. A cab side-window went white. A hole appeared. Just about in line with a man's head, Pike thought. The lorry swerved, mounted the far kerb, its side-walls rattling like thunder. Pike laughed. But the vehicle straightened, brushed a fence, went on.

The other three lorries passed, and they hit two of them. Well, they would've done, Pike thought, with four of them firing. And the last was special. Its windscreen snowed. And then as it came on, its far cab-window snowed too. The driver at the wheel one-armed and screaming.

More outriders came. Pike shut the doors. He got out the vodka bottle and passed it round. Then he remembered why he was here. Not the target-practice, that was just the icing on the cake. The real action was to come.

He moved to the front of the van, slid back the passenger door and climbed up on the roof. On his right were factory railings. Beyond them the factory car-park. And the cars there were the yah kind of cars you would expect, executive crap.

Pike got a piece of paper from his pocket. It had a number written on it, F380 JMP. And underneath, dark blue Rover. Brand new.

20

In his cream-coloured suit, James Denton walked over to his car. His new car, he still couldn't remember the number exactly . . . F380 JM something.

He found it, unlocked the doors, and dropped his briefcase inside. And, he thought savagely, all it contained were his weekend files. Not the letter, the letter McRae wanted.

Denton didn't know what to make of that. All day long he'd had the same answer . . . the keys to the data-safe were in use.

He got into the car and drove slowly towards the factory-gates. To his surprise he was waved through. There was a solid row of riot-shields on either side. And the crowd, or what he saw of them, were being kept back.

He turned right, passed more police and the odd scuffling groups, and picked up speed. He passed a battered Transit van parked by the factory railings, and for a moment wondered why it was there.

Some five minutes later he saw the van again. It was in his mirror, not far behind him as he drove through the industrial estate. And Denton wondered about that too. He'd heard about an ambush, five men in a van with spanners, and he speeded up.

But the van came closer. It was on his tail as he left the estate. *On his tail*, its bumper smashing at his rear. And there were kids inside, laughing.

Denton cut left *fast*. He went under the ring-road and came to crowded streets. He needed them, needed the evening shoppers spilling out from the pavements. And a policeman.

But there wasn't any law about, and he took risks. He kept in second gear, and, sweating, weaved in and out of strolling shoppers, getting flashed by oncoming cars.

But the van stayed with him, six inches from his rear.

He jumped a traffic light. He hit the camber of the crossroads *hard*, and the van did the same, lipping up under his bumper, corkscrewing him.

He went on. On the far side was the business-area. Cold stone buildings, empty, locked up for the weekend. Not a person in sight. Denton drove faster. He cut corners, howled round them, but the van kept up. Then on his left, incredibly, red light. The last of the evening, the last of the sun, coming across a park.

Denton swung left, and immediately knew he was wrong. There was a dead end sign. There were high railings at the end. And not an alley, not a gateway out.

He parked up against the railings. For a moment he thought of running. But then the kids were coming for him, four of them, all in the same kind of sweater.

Denton locked the doors. He looked at the park, red under the setting sun. He tried not to look at the kid with the crowbar, or the kid with the pliers. But he heard the voice.

'Hello, skin.'

Out on the park they were playing cricket, the bowler coming up to the crease. He bowled just short of a length, on off-stump. And it would turn, he thought. It would come in.

But the batsman gave himself room. He hit against the spin, hit high, his head coming up.

Out in the covers a fielder ran back. Then he stopped. He saw a figure in white, another fielder, out near the boundary.

'Yours,' he shouted.

But the ball hit the ground. The other fielder made no move. Or rather made strange moves, weaving on his feet, moaning.

He wasn't a fielder, but a man in a white shirt and cream coloured trousers. And on his shirt, at nipple-level, were two red stains.

21

At ten on the Saturday morning Cass was waiting down by the old docks. It was cloudy. A cold wind was coming up the estuary, kicking over the piles of rubble behind the quays. There was dust and flat grey land, not a soul in sight.

Until McRae turned up in his car. He'd arranged the meeting down here. Said he needed the air.

And Cass needed the air too when he heard the news.

'Kids?' he asked. '*Kids* did this to Denton?'

'With these, yes.' McRae held out a pair of pliers. 'And they stuffed them in his trouser-pocket afterwards.'

'For Christ's sake,' Cass said. '*What* kids?'

'Who knows? Lots of people turned up last night, looking for action.' McRae shrugged. 'Maybe a couple of notes changed hands.'

'But, couldn't Denton identify . . .?'

McRae shook his head. 'He's not saying anything. Not any more.'

Cass shuddered. They walked in silence along one of the deepwater quays. It was deserted too. The cranes were idle, black against the sun.

'Look,' Cass said then, 'when we started on this thing, you said it was just a factory being run down. A take-over.'

'Seems to be more than that now, doesn't it?' McRae said. 'How about take-overs? Take-overs, plural?'

'What?'

Thin as a scarecrow in his suit, McRae spread his hands. 'Listen, we've reached an *impasse* with Mr Denton. So now we're turning our attention to his boss . . . Mr Gotto.'

'Gotto, yes.' Cass remembered. 'What d'you think? You think *he* arranged this . . . this episode of last night?'

'No, not really.'

And McRae's face was strange. There was just the flap-flap of waves against the dock, and the flap of his suit.

'What are you trying to say? I don't understand.'

'Batman, Gotto's away on holiday.' McRae came closer. 'Meant to be somewhere in the Med. Meant to be flying his own aircraft.'

'*Meant* to be?'

'All right, he's been gone three weeks, and he hasn't taken his plane. We've just found it at Lydd airport?'

'You think he's done a runner?' Cass' mind was racing. 'With that money he had? What was it? $720 000?'

'No, it's not as simple as that, $720 000's only a drop in the bucket. There's a lot more we've found that can't be accounted for. Not by ordinary banking means.'

'You mean, hot money?'

'Oh, I do, yes. And the man's somewhere in the middle of it all.'

McRae turned away, fumbling in his jacket pocket. Then he produced a photo, a polaroid, taken at some flying club. It showed a twin-engined Cessna, and by it, a smart-looking man in his forties. He wore a short-sleeved shirt and his hair was slicked down, neatly parted in the middle.

'Gotto,' McRae said. 'But, don't worry, Batman, the forces of justice and truth have been set in motion. We'll find him.'

CHAIN

In the dawn of that June morning, beyond the row of black pile-drivers, the body hung on the chain.

The man hung full length, shackled by his neck, and it was possible to see more of him. The smartly-pressed trousers, the short-sleeved shirt, the hair still neatly parted down the middle. Only his face was untidy, showed horror.

Then he was moving again as more of the chain paid out.

And a second body came into view.

The feet, shoeless, bare. Then jeans, a T-shirt. Then a girl's face, terrified, wound round by long blonde hair.

In life she had been young, high-cheekboned, beautiful.

But in death the joke was bad.

There were words on her T-shirt.

At the top, a name, FLASHMAN'S.

And underneath, WHERE THE BIG BOYS HANG OUT.

VICKY ELLIOTT

22

It was seven-thirty in the morning. Cass sat on the edge of his bed, buttoning up his shirt. Then he went to the wardrobe and chose a tie.

Through the open door he heard Sonia padding from the bathroom. Heard her stop on the landing, then her voice.

'Alison, come on,' she said. 'It's getting late.'

Sonia came through into the bedroom and untucked her towel. The back of her neck and shoulders were flushed from the shower. He could smell her lemon soap, her warmth. And there was always a calm about her in the mornings, he thought. She woke from a deep sleep, refreshed as a child, and for a while the tensions of the previous day were gone. He fancied her like mad in the morning, always had.

She turned and grinned at him. 'No,' she said, 'you haven't got time.'

'I know.' He nodded sadly.

'So, what's it going to be today? Are you in court?'

'Mostly.'

'And the usual kind of stuff, is it? Drunks? GBH?'

''fraid so.'

Still naked, she came towards him and nibbled his ear. 'My love, my dearest arsehole,' she said, 'three weeks ago we had our holiday cancelled.'

'Yes,' he said.

'On the orders of Mr McRae.'

'Yes.'

'But in the past ten days you haven't really *done* anything for McRae. Just your usual kind of stuff.'

'That's the way it goes,' he said. 'I'm only on attachment to Serious Fraud. I give advice as and when they're ready.'

The ear-nibbling went on. Then her mouth came close to his. 'And when might that be, pillock-brain?' she asked. 'I mean, are we going to get a holiday this year or aren't we?'

He kissed her. 'I'll talk to him,' he said, 'McRae.'

'When?'

'Today maybe.'

She pulled back. 'Maybe?'

'Well, that's the funny thing,' he said. 'Nobody seems to have seen him for a couple of days.'

23

There had been a light summer shower at around eight that morning. And when McRae got back to his hotel room, his suit was wet and sticking to him. He wiped his handkerchief across his face, and looked at the half-dozen or so phone messages he'd picked up at the desk. All from Barry. All wanting him to ring in.

McRae turned, checked that the phone was still off the hook. Then he looked at his room, the mess, the litter of folders that crossed the carpet, and the cassettes over by the video recorder. Two piles of them. Those he'd seen and those he hadn't.

Film show courtesy of Belgian Fraud.

And it was matinée time, he thought, once again. For a moment he stood there, pale and dripping. Then he inserted another cassette, knowing it was going to be like the others, hand-held stuff, grainy and blurred . . . bars, airport lounges, moving taxis.

But it wasn't. This time the camera was static and high up. It looked down on a sunlit business street, thirties buildings, grey streaked stone. A title said it was Geneva. Then there was the usual little box in the top left-hand corner of the screen. The date, 26.4.89. And the time, 14.48 and counting.

At 14.48 and 30 seconds a grey Mercedes came along the street. It slowed, parked at the kerb. Two men got out, both in business suits, carrying suitcases. And with them was a girl.

McRae couldn't see her face because she had her back turned. And she wore a headscarf that covered her hair. But she followed the men with long loping strides. A looker, he thought. Had to be.

The three of them crossed the pavement and went in through a frosted glass door. The camera tightened up and showed a name, *AGENCE ORIENTALE*. Which was a new one, McRae thought. But it was going to be like those other new travel agents that sprung up half a world away, in Karachi or Calcutta. Sprung up for a couple of months, then disappeared.

The camera moved to the left. It came to a window that was half-frosted and half-plain. It tried to zoom inside, tried opening up a stop or two in the bad light. But there was nothing. Just vague movement, vague shapes.

And what could you expect, McRae thought, from this kind of surveillance operation? A camera shooting from fully eighty yards away? . . . For God's sake, it had taken two years to get this far.

At 14.50 the picture cut. At 15.03 it reappeared again, tight on the frosted glass door. The two men came out. They were no longer carrying the suitcases. They weren't carrying so much as an envelope. But McRae knew what they had. The kind of thing they had.

Then, suddenly, he saw the girl again, turning to face camera. And she *was* a looker. Tall, calm, and a graceful way with her hands as she unknotted her headscarf in the sunlight. Long blonde hair, he saw. A wide smiling mouth. High cheekbones.

24

There were going to be those kind of mornings, Cassidy thought. Mornings when Alison got down to breakfast finally at ten past eight. When half-way out to the car, she suddenly announced she hadn't got her English book. When the traffic was bad, and he was late, late . . . late . . .

Sam was already in Court One by the time he got there. She had her hair coiled in a chignon. She looked very smart in a pale, lace-fronted blouse. But, when he came closer he saw she was panicking.

'They've changed the order,' she said quietly.

'Who has?'

'The usher. He's just told me.'

'Talk me through it,' Cass said.

'Well, number one, Jeffreys, he's jumped bail,' she said. 'Number two is just a holding date. They're going to start with number three.'

He looked at the court-list. 'Elliott?' he asked.

'Yes, and it's the one we thought was going to be tricky,' she said. 'The one we were going to look at again in between cases.'

'Where is it?' Cass asked.

She turned to the pile of brief-bags. 'Here *somewhere*.'

They found it only moments before the magistrates came in. There was the standing, the bowing and the sitting. Then the court-clerk turned to the defendant in the dock.

'Your name is Victoria Susan Elliott . . .?'

Cass didn't hear any more. He had his head down and was reading, reading fast. Right up until the moment when the pleas were entered.

'To the charge of theft of a vehicle,' the court-clerk said, 'guilty or not guilty?'

'Guilty.'

Cass looked up. And he was amazed. He'd expected the kind of girl who got into this kind of trouble. Barrel-armed, stony-eyed, the leader of the pack.

But this one was very different. There was a curving line

to her as she stood in the dock. She was calm and poised in a beige summer suit. Expensive. A mile away from the streets.

'To the charge of theft of £850, guilty or not guilty?'

'Guilty.'

And there was something appealing about her. An innocence. The dark, well-shaped hair, the lack of make-up, the smoothly-freckled face. Just nineteen years old.

'To the charge of criminal deception?'

'Guilty.'

No defiance, no pretence. Just that calmness of hers. And all the time, a slow lazy smile.

The court-clerk turned to the Chief Magistrate. 'May she be seated, Sir?'

'She may.'

'Please be seated, Miss Elliott.'

Cass got to his feet. He played for time, fiddling with his notes. Then he began.

'May it please your Worships, I would like to start by mentioning the statement by a Mr Jackson. He is collection manager for the Scimitar Finance Company. And he states that, on 20 February this year, his company entered upon an agreement with the defendant concerning an MG Metro car, registration number D437 AOR.'

In the dock Victoria Elliott nodded.

'The deposit paid was £500,' Cass continued. 'The out-standing credit was £2400. Which, together with charges for credit, interest, and documentation, totalled £3250.'

The magistrates were taking notes, and Cass waited.

'By May of this year £435 had been repaid,' he said then. 'The balance outstanding was £2800. And, by the terms of the agreement, Miss Elliott had no authority to sell the vehicle . . . This was pointed out to her when the contract was signed and in a subsequent letter that she admits she received.'

Again Victoria Elliott nodded, smiled. And for a moment Cass thought she was playing with them, all of them. But she wasn't. She was just lending herself to the trial, he saw. Didn't believe she was there.

He cleared his throat and went on. 'We now come to the statement of a Mr Hambling, a motor dealer of Carthage Road,' he said. 'On 17 June this year Miss Elliott phoned him to say she had a car for sale . . . They met by arrangement. They agreed on a price of £850. Miss Elliott asked to be paid in cash . . . And at the same time she signed papers to show that the vehicle was hers, with no outstanding claim on it.'

The Chief Magistrate leaned forward. 'This Mr Hambling, and the £850 owing to him,' he said. 'I understand that it's to be repaid . . . Will that be by Miss Elliott herself?'

Cass paused, and turned to the defence solicitor, Fred Dyer.

Dyer got up. 'No, by her father, Sir,' he said. 'Miss Elliott no longer has the money.'

'Oh?' said the Chief Magistrate.

'The fact of the matter is,' Dyer hesitated, 'she's spent it.'

'£850?' The Chief Magistrate asked. 'In one month?'

'She has . . . one or two commitments.' Dyer sat down quickly.

Cass glanced again at Victoria Elliot's smiling face. And he didn't want to, but he knew he had to go into a little aria. It was expected.

He gripped the lapels of his jacket and raised his voice. 'I'm sure Miss Elliott has commitments,' he said. 'I'm sure it will be claimed she's a teenager bewildered by modern sales-techniques. Bank-cards and credit cards arriving with every post.' He paused. 'But, Your Worships, Miss Elliott has admitted she read the fine print. And, far from being a bewildered teenager, she has in fact eight O levels and three A levels to her credit . . . And, until last year, was at the local polytechnic, studying economics.'

The magistrates frowned at this, frowned hard. Then one of them leaned forward.

'Excuse me,' he said. '£850 . . . It doesn't seem a great deal for a D-registered MG Metro.'

'No, Sir,' Cass said. 'In fact the vehicle was crashed. It was sold in a crashed condition.'

'I see.'

Fred Dyer got up quickly. He was nervous. 'There are antecedent matters, Your Worships. Matters it would not be in the interest of my client to go into.'

The Chief Magistrate frowned. 'You mean, another offence?'

'Offen*ces*, Sir,' Dyer said softly.

The magistrates conferred. Then they conferred with the court-clerk. The Chief Magistrate turned and beckoned Cass and Dyer to approach the bench. He leaned down, spoke softly. 'I am in a certain amount of difficulty here,' he said. 'There is not, as you'll understand, a great deal of leeway in sentencing. And I wouldn't want anything too drastic to happen.'

'No, Sir,' from Dyer.

The Chief Magistrate turned to him. 'So I was wondering . . . Would your client agree just to *touch* on these other matters?'

Dyer went away, he whispered to Victoria Elliott. She smiled and nodded.

Cass went back to his place. He saw that Dyer was uneasy, more than uneasy.

'Well, briefly, Sir,' the man began, 'there was a traffic offence. My client was in collision with another vehicle that had stopped at traffic lights.'

'Offen*ces*, Mr Dyer. You said offen*ces*,' the Chief Magistrate said. 'Was there an altercation?'

Dyer, lost, turned to Victoria Elliott for help.

'No, no altercation,' she said clearly. 'As a matter of fact it was a police car I hit. And the officer was quite nice about it, really. What he said was, "But, Madam, how d'you stop when *I'm* not here?"'

There was laughter.

Cass bent to a notepad. And with his pencil wrote, SHINE ON YOU CRAZY . . .

. . . DIAMOND.

It was evening. He was back at home, in his living-room, choosing an album from the record-rack.

An old album, the cover creased and torn, from his student days.

Wish You Were Here.

Pink Floyd.

And he played it as loud as he'd played it then. So loud, in fact, that Sonia came in from the kitchen.

'What's with the Floyd?' she shouted.

'What?'

She went to the stereo and turned the volume down. 'Must be ten years ago when you bought it.'

'More like fifteen.'

'Second childhood, is it?'

Cass shrugged and went away to an armchair. He sat down. 'Something I meant to ask you,' he said then.

'What's that?'

'Well, I had a young girl in court today. First offence. And the magistrates have asked for a social enquiry.'

Sonia turned. 'Isn't that unusual for a first offence?'

'It's an unusual case,' Cass said. 'But, look, they've assigned a probation officer . . . George Adams . . . What's he like?'

'I don't know.' Sonia frowned. 'A bit heavy. Goes by the book.'

'Oh.' Cass sighed.

And Sonia looked from the Pink Floyd album to his face. 'Is she a looker, this girl?' she asked.

'No,' he answered truthfully. 'No, not really.'

25

In his hotel room McRae had come to the end of the video-cassettes. He sat on his bed, smoking. He was going to have to get stills made, he thought, blow-ups, digitally enhanced. He was going to have to get back to the Belgian fraud people, maybe go over there in the end. And he sat there thinking, the filter-tip clenched between his teeth, a wolf-like look about him as he sucked in smoke.

Then there was knock on the door.

McRae didn't move.

'Bob . . . Bob?' It was a man's voice.

Still he didn't move.

'Come on, I know you're in there. They told me down at the desk.'

Slowly McRae got up and opened the door a crack. Barry's pale square face was there, the tinted glasses, and the dark gelled hair.

The man was worried.

'Look, do I have to come and get you out of bed like this? At seven in the *evening*?'

McRae shrugged.

'I mean, how long is it going to go on? When are you going to show up at the office?'

McRae opened the door wider, and Barry came in. He frowned at the mess, the scattered videos, the half-touched lunch tray. And he wrinkled his nose at the smell.

McRae smiled lightly. A good laddie, Barry, he thought, but a bit of a careful dresser, a bit of an aftershave man . . . Definitely your anal tendencies.

The man turned. 'Look, can we go and have a cup of coffee somewhere, Bob? And, for Christ's sake, do some talking?'

'Fine by me,' McRae said. 'We can go up to the roof garden.'

He picked up his jacket and led the way out to the lift. 'Roof is right. Garden is not,' he explained. 'You know the kind of thing, where you're sitting by the kitchen ventilators and staring at a stack of beer-crates.'

But he'd left out the wind, the wide wind of a seaport. It kicked at the umbrellas above the tables, and flattened the rows of geraniums in their pots. McRae ordered coffee. He looked out over the parapet at the long grey sheds of dockland, and the idle cranes. Always idle, he thought. The men out on the golf-course with their lump sums.

Then he got hold of himself. Barry was talking, talking seriously.

'Bob,' he said, 'are you sure we're handling this thing right?'

'No, not sure. Never sure.'

'Only you can't go walkabout like this. I've been getting calls. High-level calls.'

'Who from?'

'The Police Commissioner for one.'

'God the Father, you mean.'

'And Royston, the Area Chief Prosecutor.'

'God the Son as well. What's he want?'

Barry sighed.

'Well, I suppose it's understandable,' McRae said then. 'They're going to be worried men, Barry, aren't they? Their beautiful city's been on TV. The Lennox factory's gone down the tubes. Three thousand workers have got the sack. And a finance director called Gotto's gone missing.'

But Barry shook his head. 'That's old news, Bob. It all happened a fortnight ago. People are saying we've got it wrong.'

'People can say what they like.'

'But why not throw them a little something? Tell them this man Gotto was picking up dollar transfers through a Swiss bank?'

'*Was*,' McRae said. 'You know as well as I do, Barry, the transfers have stopped. The money's coming in via a different route now, according to our Belgian friends . . . Why the hell d'you think I've been watching home movies downstairs?'

'Okay, Bob. Okay.'

But McRae hadn't finished. 'And it's not just a few thousand dollars, it's a bloody great raft,' he said. 'It's feeding this take-over business we're looking at, and I'm not putting *that* out on the news.'

'No,' Barry said. 'But, it would help . . . I mean, help me if . . .'

'You're asking for my opinion?'

'That's right.'

McRae stood up. He looked once again at the distant cranes of dockland, the grey foreshore. Then he walked off.

Barry followed him to the corner of the parapet and looked out towards the south. The waterfront was closer here. And there was no longer greyness but colour.

New dockland.

There were bright village-style houses out on narrow quays. There were the swaying masts of a marina, the shifting patterns of sails. And closer, a large shopping mall of green glass and red girders . . . cafés, restaurants . . . a multi-screen cinema . . .

McRae looked down at it. 'All right, you said I've been going walkabout, and I have . . . Down there.'

'But, why, Bob?'

'Why?' McRae turned to him. 'You've seen it on the map . . . Channel Village. One of the biggest dockland developments on the south coast. Eighty-five acres. Millions up for grabs . . . Doesn't it mean anything to you?'

'Not really.'

'Well, maybe things'll look clearer when you've got me a rundown on all the companies involved.'

'*All* of them?' Barry was startled. 'For God's sake, how long d'you think that's going to take?'

And McRae grinned. 'How long before you want me back in the office?'

26

In the early evening a man walked up the path to a smallish detached house. He wore a dark creased suit and a rugby club tie, though by now he was ten years past playing. And he changed his briefcase from one large hand to the other before he rang the bell.

A woman came to the door. He saw the resemblance between her and her daughter immediately. 'Mrs Elliott?' he asked.

'Yes?'

'My name's Adams, George Adams, Probation Officer,' he said. 'I rang earlier.'

'Oh, yes.' She was nervous, very nervous. But, he thought, most of them were.

She led him down the hall to a newly-decorated sitting-room. It was a pale green, and the sofa he sat on was green too. He put his briefcase on his knees and opened it. But all the time he was looking round.

People were always calling him old-style, he thought, a bit of a rugger-bugger, but he saw the chill there was to the room. No books, no newspapers, nothing lying round. The furniture expensive, and the TV huge.

And he saw too how quietly Mrs Elliott moved. How she looked older than forty-two, her face seeming to come from Marks and Spencer's with her clothes. Even how, at a puff of wind, her lipstick and her tight curls could go. Everything fall away.

He spoke gently as he got the file from the briefcase, explaining that a social enquiry meant no more than a few background facts. He was only here to help her daughter Victoria.

'Vicky,' she said. 'Vicky'.

He nodded. And for a moment was silent, looking at the file.

'Now, as I understand it,' he began, 'during her first year at poly, she lived here at home with you.'

'Yes.' She was eager. 'And it was fine then. Everything worked out so well.'

'But, the second year,' he checked his notes, 'she moved out to this flat . . . 23 Cranleigh Gardens?'

'That's right.'

'And did you notice any change in her?'

'Well, she got thinner, much thinner. I kept telling her to eat more.'

'But, apart from that?'

'Nothing, really.'

He turned a page. 'And yet, at the end of this year, she was asked to leave the poly, because she didn't pass her exams.'

'None of us could understand why,' Mrs Elliott said quickly. 'I mean, she worked, worked all the time.'

'But, *after* she left,' Adams insisted, 'she stayed on at Cranleigh Gardens, with these other students . . . Doing what, exactly?'

Mrs Elliott's hands went to her hair, ran through the tight curls. 'Well, nothing much, really. Not for a couple of months. My husband went to see her.'

'At the flat?'

'Yes, he called round. He was in the habit of calling round. It was all quite amicable. They chatted . . . And gradually she got herself together. Got a job in a building society.'

Adams made a pretence of glancing at his notes. He knew the next question already. 'Mrs Elliott, your husband works for a building society, doesn't he?'

'Yes.' She shrugged. 'And he might have helped her a little. But he didn't insist. He'd never do that.'

'No.'

'Anyway she was good at the work. Got promotion.'

'And bought the car,' Adams said.

Mrs Elliott's hand went to her hair much faster, flattening the curls.

Adams smiled at her. He said how well the colours matched in the room, the light green, and the darker green of the suite.

Then, 'Mrs Elliott, is your husband in this evening?'

'No,' she said, 'he's out, I'm afraid.'

'Would there be any chance of seeing him tomorrow then?'

'He's . . . he's very busy at work.'

Adams looked at his file again. 'The reason I'm asking,' he said, 'is because I understand he's paying the first amount that Vicky owes. The £850 to this Mr Hambling who bought the car.'

'Yes,' she said, 'he's doing that.'

'But the rest of it?' Adams said. 'The sum that's owing to the hire purchase company? I mean, can he help out there at all?'

'How can he?' There was a wildness about her suddenly. 'It's such a vast amount. He doesn't know where to *start*.'

Well, Adams thought, he could have started by turning up in court this morning. For that matter, so could she.

He turned, and pressed the cushion on the sofa next to

78

him. 'Mrs Elliott, you said your husband called round at Vicky's flat, was in the habit of calling round there. But was she, I mean, in the habit of calling here?'

'Of course. All the time.'

'About how often would that be?'

'I don't know. Once a week, once every ten days,' she said. 'She'd drop round with her friends. We'd have coffee or something. Or, I don't know, a glass of beer.'

'Nice friends, are they?' Adams asked.

'Oh, yes,' she said. 'Quiet . . . But Vicky's a quiet girl.'

27

In the small white-tiled cubicle Vicky Elliott screamed. She screamed, she danced up onto the pedestal. Pulled the chain, cavorted like an ape. Then, unlocking the door, she walked past the row of basins and went back to the bar.

The bar was long. It pulsed to the flicker of coloured lights, thumped to the beat of heavy metal. And, two deep around it, were the usual customers, the spending customers, men aged from twenty-two to thirty, sweating, the jackets of their business-suits piled up on stools.

Vicky lifted the bar-flap. She walked to the far pumps where Jane was serving. Jane who had the spiky black-dyed hair, the lashes, the lips. Who was hard.

Or pretended to be.

'Six pounds-eighty, seven pounds-eighty,' Jane said to the man she was serving, and took a ten pound note. Then she turned to Vicky. 'Where've you been?'

'Out to have a scream.'

'Bad as that, was it?' Jane moved towards the till.

'Seemed like it at the time.'

'Who was it then?'

'Baldy,' Vicky said, and turned to the one man among the shouting customers who was quiet. Quiet and still. His eyes dull behind his Special Brew, his bald head shining.

'Oh, him,' Jane said.

'I mean, I can stand most of it.' Vicky raised her voice. 'Stand the jokes. Stand Wicked Wanking Willie . . .'

'I know.'

' . . . But it's those drawings, those *sodding* photo-copied drawings.' Vicky shivered, 'How anyone can bother to get hold of them, bother to put them through the office photocopier, and then come in here with a dozen in their pocket . . . *Jesus*.'

Jane opened the till. Then she looked up. 'What d'you reckon?' she asked. 'Reckon it's time he moved up the charts?'

'Definitely.' Vicky grinned.

She moved on to an alcove at the back of the bar. There was a notice-board facing her. And, blu-tacked to it, a vertical column of names. Names on cards. She thought a moment, then picked one out, stuck it higher up on the list.

'All right, darlings, she thought. Childish. Totally childish, but there you go . . .

She went back to the bar and served a few more of the shouting herd. Then she found herself opposite Baldy again. He raised an empty glass.

She fetched another bottle of Special Brew. He watched her pour it. 'So what's that you've got back there?' He pointed.

'Back where?'

'Over there, where you were just now?'

'Oh, that,' she said. 'Nothing.'

'Has to be something,' he said. 'Well, doesn't it.'

'Nothing important.'

But he grabbed her wrist.

'All right,' she said, smiling above her anger, 'it's a chart.'

'What kind of chart?'

'Sort of top twenty.'

'Pop tunes, you mean?'

'No,' Vicky said, widening her smile, and saying it lightly. 'Perverts . . . Perverts who drink here.'

'*What*?'

Vicky saw the sweat on his face, the shock. 'And you're

chart-buster of the week,' she said. 'Just moved up five places.'

Baldy was angry. A screech of laughter went up from the men around him, and he was angrier. 'I want to see the guv'nor about this,' he said.

'See who you like,' she told him.

'No, I mean it.' Baldy's grip tightened on her wrist. 'You get him. You bring Neill here.'

Neill, she found over by the kitchen swing-doors. He was with Simon, a third-year student who worked as a waiter.

And, Vicky found as she got nearer, there was drama going on. Another drama.

'Look, my son, don't worry about it,' Neill was saying. 'Just relax.'

'But, it's insane.' Simon was flushed.

'Sure it is,' Neill told him, 'But she's a customer. She's American. And Americans are like that.'

'She wants to know what's *in* everything,' Simon insisted. 'What's in the Beef *Bordelaise*, what's in the *ratatouille*.'

'Course she does, the cow.'

'But,' Simon couldn't believe it, 'she even wants to know what's in the chicken and ham *pie*.'

'So what did you tell her?' Neill asked.

'Octopus,' Simon said.

'You did right son.'

And Neill laughed. That big laugh that rolled up through his body. He was a large man, broad. And there was a roughness to him, the cracks of his face, the dark matted hair. But the surface was gloss. It was the flash of his Rolex, his cufflinks, and the blue shantung suit that he wore.

He turned and saw Vicky. 'Lovely.' He put an arm around her.

'I don't feel all that lovely,' Vicky said.

'You've got problems too?'

'At the bar, yes.'

She followed him over there. And she felt that force he had, that violence people often misjudged. But, like the silk

81

of his shirt, it was real. It raised the temperature ten degrees as he walked behind the bar. Always did.

'Hi, Neill.'

'Nice to see you, Neill.'

'Nice to be able to see you.'

The usual stuff.

Except from Baldy, who waited in silence.

Neill moved towards him. 'Hear you wanted me,' he said. 'What's up?'

'It's those girls,' Baldy said sourly. 'Those girls you've got behind the bar.'

'What about them?'

And Baldy drew himself up. 'Know what they've got back there? Top twenty chart. Top twenty perverts . . . Perverts they call us.'

Neill grinned, came out with his big laugh.

'I don't see what's funny.' Baldy's voice rose. 'We're your customers, aren't we? And Rog over there, he's the small-eyed pervert, apparently.' He pointed. 'And Chris, he's the pocket-billiards pervert.'

'Oh, come on,' Neill said. 'Lots of people know about it. Lots of people . . . Don't we, fellers?'

The fellers did.

'Everyone except me.' Baldy got to his feet. 'And it turns out I'm the bald-headed pervert.' He slammed his glass down on the counter. 'Well, d'you need my custom, or don't you?'

Neill waited, hands wide, shoulders wide. 'I need your bald head.'

'What?'

'My son,' Neill leaned towards him, 'the human body loses a quarter of its heat through the top of its head. More, if it's bald.' He reached out, tapped the man's shiny skull. 'Few more of you baldies around, and I don't need to turn on the heating.'

Baldy kicked back his bar-stool, turned, left.

There were jeers, catcalls. Neill laughed again. But then he was quieter as he took Vicky away to the back of the bar. He looked at her.

'Get to you, that one, did he?'

'A bit,' Vicky said.

He moved closer. She felt the silk of his jacket. Real, she thought. And he was real. He was the same to everyone, jet-setter or pisshead. And she'd never met that in a man before.

'Darling,' he said then, 'the way they sell drink is with big colour posters. Sell it to heroes.'

'Yes,' she said.

'But *we* sell it to people who want to get pissed, go broke, be king for a day.' He looked at her. 'Only one rule in this place . . . Sod the Customer.'

'Yes,' she said again.

He kissed her gently on the cheek, then straightened her T-shirt.

The shirt that was the same that Jane wore, that Simon wore, everybody who worked in the place . . .

FLASHMAN'S, it said.

WHERE THE BIG BOYS HANG OUT.

28

It was mid-morning when McRae turned up at the office. And, as he looked round, it pleased him. It had from the first day he'd seen it.

A sense of continuity, he thought. The wood panelling and the old high-arched casement windows from shipping company days. The glass case with the big white model of the liner inside. Even the blackboard where they'd marked up dockings and sailings.

And, against all that, the white racks of hardware that now filled the room. And the quietness of the work in hand. The new dockings and sailings, the electronic link-ups of modern fraud, the soft pebble-click of computer keyboards.

What didn't please him, however, when he went through to the inner office, was to find Barry at the map. The big old wall-map of the port, where the docks were a faded brown, the water a faded blue, and the deepwater channels white.

Because Barry was working on its glass front . . . with a felt-tip pen.

'What's this?' McRae asked. 'Defacing a priceless antique?'

And Barry turned, neat as always in double-breasted grey.

'No,' he said, 'just bringing it up to date.'

'Is that right?'

'Yes.' The man nodded. Then showed a curving span he'd drawn in across the wide estuary. 'This is the new bridge, for example. The road-bridge that goes across the river.'

'I know it.' McRae sighed.

'And this.' The man pointed to an area he'd shaded in. 'This is the new dockland development you showed me the other day.'

McRae looked. He saw how neat the shading was, and the label above it, Channel Village. Then, closer, he saw the little white flags that had been blu-tacked to the glass.

'Flags, is it now?' he asked. 'Little flags?'

'What's wrong with that?' Barry asked.

'This is not the CID,' McRae told him. 'This is not some anal little circle drawn on a map. Everybody inside the line being guilty. Everybody outside going free.'

Barry flushed. 'I was trying to help,' he said.

'I see.'

'I mean, you remember you asked me to check out the companies involved in the dockland scheme?'

'Yes.'

'Well, those flags show the sites that belong to a certain developer.'

'And who might that be, Barry?'

'It's a group called Packham Leisure. A venture capital company, specialising in the leisure industry.'

'And why, if I might ask, is it so interesting to us?'

Barry told him.

An hour later, when McRae was sitting thinking at his desk, Barry came in with a list of phonecalls. 'These are the most urgent ones, Bob,' he said.

McRae looked at them. 'So God the Father has rung up five times?'

'That's it.'

'And God the Son, four times?'

'Yes.'

McRae looked further down the list. 'And our old friend Cassidy, twice.' He rubbed his chin. 'I think I'll go for the Caped Crusader.'

He left the office and went upstairs. At the entrance to the CPS offices he waved at Harold the security man. Then he walked on along the corridor, turned right, and knocked on a door.

Cassidy was in. He had that girl Sam with him. And between them on the desk there must have been, by McRae's reckoning anyway, half a pine tree's worth of paper.

'Morning, Batman,' he said.

Cass looked up. And the girl was startled.

'Busy, are we?' McRae went on.

'What's it look like?'

'Only I was told you'd phoned. Wanted to see me.'

'That's right.' Cass nodded, 'I've got a problem.'

'What's that?'

'It's to do with my wife.'

'We've all got problems with our wives,' McRae said.

There was a flicker of annoyance in the bright blue eyes. 'Look,' Cass said, 'she wants to know when we're going on holiday. I mean, as she points out, my attachment to Serious Fraud is hardly essential right now.'

McRae was thoughtful. 'Tell you what,' he said. 'Maybe I should fill you in on a few details . . . Why don't we slide down the Bat-Pole and have an early lunch?'

Cass got up from his desk. He was more than angry. 'Could you do me a favour and drop this Batman business?' he asked. 'It's not very funny at the best of times.'

'Sorry,' McRae said. He looked at the man's glasses, his

neatly-knotted tie. 'It's just every time I see you . . . Those gleaming pectorals. Those little black boots.'

They went downstairs, past the surveillance cameras outside Serious Fraud, and out into the sunlight. McRae led the way over to his Audi, unlocked it, and they drove in silence through crowded streets. Then, in a queue of cars, they reached the old dock-gates of the port . . . Entrance to Docks 5–6 . . . Entrance to Docks 3–4 . . . And, at Entrance 1–2, a big circus-coloured signboard that said CHANNEL VILLAGE.

The sunlight was wider here, the land cleared, and they drove towards the masts and rooftops of the new marina. McRae slowed. He parked in the shadow of a huge pavilion, and they walked around it to the waterfront.

The circus colours were back again, the green glass roof of the shopping mall, the red of its girders, and the blue of its stairs and walkways. There were also restaurants, open continental-style on to the quay. One of them had the smell of charcoaled fish, the smell of coffee. And Cass stopped. 'When are we going to have lunch?' he asked.

'Later,' McRae told him. 'There's something I want you to see first.'

They walked on around the quays. It was low tide, and the pontoons were maybe twenty feet below them. There were gleaming hulls down there, packed close together, the creak of fenders, and the slap of rigging. But McRae turned away from the harbour. He took a footpath between new village-style houses. And, a minute or so later, they were out on open ground.

It was white under the sun. There was a haze of cement dust, and the tracks of big earth-moving vehicles. 'What's going on here,' McRae said, 'is Phase Two of the development. The completion date, February next year.'

'I know,' Cass told him. 'I live here, remember.'

'But, maybe there's something you don't know, Batman.'

'What's that?' Cass asked. They walked on.

'All right. Remember a man called Gotto? Finance Director of Lennox plc?'

'Yes?'

'We've learned a little more about him.'

'You mean, where he is?'

'No, he's still missing. Vanished off the face of the earth,' McRae said. 'But, d'you remember his awfully healthy bank-balance? The dollars? The hot money?'

'Of course.'

'All right, as it happens, money has cropped up again. But not just a trickle, like before . . . A flood . . . A damn great pipeline pumping into the country.'

'What?'

'It's to do with a company called Packham Leisure,' McRae said. 'And it turns out that Mr Gotto is on their board of directors.'

'What?' Cass asked again. 'What's Packham Leisure?'

They walked on, round a row of builders' huts. 'That is,' McRae said.

And Cass looked where he was pointing, at a large building site some way over the rough ground. '*That*?' he asked.

'What's the matter, Batman?'

'Well,' Cass said, 'I've read about it, haven't I? Going to be a big leisure complex? Swimming-pool? Gymnasium? Squash courts?'

'Yes, I told you, leisure. Packham Leisure.'

'But, come on. A thing of that size can't be founded on hot money.'

'Oh, no, you misunderstand me,' McRae said. 'Packham isn't a property company. It's involved with venture capital. It operates in the money market, and *finds* investors, legitimate investors . . . But, to do that it's got to be smart. It's got to have enough funding behind it for the smart suite of offices, the yacht moored down at the marina, and the private plane away at the airport.'

'You mean, it's got a string of goodies like that?'

'Oh, yes.'

Cass frowned. It was difficult to think out here. The dust, the racket of machinery . . . and some other sound he couldn't place . . . *bap-bap-bap-bap*, a fast metallic beat.

'What are you trying to say?' he asked. 'There's something wrong with this Packham company's accounts?'

'Well, put it this way,' McRae said. 'Barry's been digging around for a couple of days . . . And, all right, they're late with their tax-returns, late with every damn thing they can think of.' He paused. 'But we can't even find out how they're paying for their bloody *stamps*.'

Cass didn't understand. All he could hear was that strange hammering sound, *bap-bap-bap-bap*.

He looked on beyond the site, beyond its metal frame construction. And then he saw the pile-drivers, a row of them.

It seemed they were putting in foundations.

29

Vicky Elliott woke up around lunchtime. Woke up gradually, moving first her eyes, then her fingers, then her arm. She pulled back the sheet, saw she was still wearing the T-shirt from last night . . . FLASHMAN'S. WHERE THE . . .

She groaned.

Sitting up was a slow process. It involved not thinking about tequila, not *once* about tequila. It involved closing her eyes again before making a move. And opening them very slowly afterwards.

She made it. The room settled into place. The books, the economics books, and the paperbacks of Hardy and Böll. The seven dirty mugs, of course. And then the jumble-sale of clothes knee-deep across the floor.

Nothing else for it, she thought, she'd have to get snow-shoes. I mean, *any* decent sports-shop . . . But she got to her feet *sans* snow-shoes, *sans* any shoes at all . . . And . . . *There* you go, darlings . . . Made it to the kitchen.

She found a glass. A glass was easier to rinse out than a mug. She put it under the tap, filled it three times, and made herself drink three times. Well, that worked, darlings. Stayed down. Just a sizzle down in the tubes some-where around the Victoria line . . . So . . . It was coffee.

Which was more of a problem. It involved washing up a mug, *sans* detergent, *sans* mop. It involved boiling a kettle. Finding the Red Mountain. And finding, *of course*, there was only a thin brown crust of the stuff at the bottom of the jar . . .

She stopped the kettle before it boiled. Gripped the jar with a tea-towel, well, a tea-towel *once*. Then poured hot water into the jar and stirred.

The first, and darlings, highly experimental sip. Then the second. The third . . . Until the definite feeling began to creep over her that God could be once again in his heaven, and all could be right with . . .

Until, that was, Prewett came into the kitchen. Prewett, tall, bony in his long khaki shorts, spectacularly pale. And, where he wasn't pale, covered in engine-oil.

'The bastards have wogged it,' he said.

'Have they?'

'Bloody wogged it.'

'But,' Vicky said, 'I thought . . . I thought you were sleeping down there with it.'

'I was,' Prewett said. 'But there's a limit to how long you can go on sleeping in a basement with a Triumph motor-bike engine.'

'There is.'

Prewett brushed past her. He began to leave oilstains on a loaf of bread, a knife-handle, a pot of marmalade. Vicky left him to it.

She went, slowly it has to be admitted, into the living-room. She saw the poster of Hendrix, the posters of hardcore chic, which were Hawkins' . . . and then Haw-kins himself, lying on the sofa with a beer can. She quite liked him. He had a tuft of hair and a tuft of beard. He had muscle and intellectual muscle. And at the moment he was improving himself by watching a dog-training programme on TV.

He turned, saw her. 'You look terrible,' he said.

'Thanks.'

'I mean it.' A frown crossed his face. 'Maybe you and I should talk about your lifestyle.'

'Yes,' Vicky said. 'Well, at least I stick to drink. Not like some other people.'

Hawkins shrugged.

'And I do it out of habit and out of love.' Vicky stopped suddenly, clutched her head.

Hawkins grinned, raised his beercan. 'Well, as I always say, the important thing about drinking is to know when to pause.' He timed three seconds by his watch. 'Cheers.'

The doorbell rang.

Slowly Hawkins uncoiled himself from the sofa. He went to the window and looked down. 'Some arsehole selling double-glazing,' he said.

'Yes,' Vicky said. But then she frowned. 'What's the time?'

'Quarter past one.'

'Christ.' She joined him by the window, saw the man outside the front door, with the briefcase. 'No, it's not,' she said. 'It's my sodding probation officer.'

'Not good,' Hawkins said.

The doorbell rang again.

'Look, give me a minute,' Vicky said. 'Just a minute.'

She put the Red Mountain jar down. And Hawkins followed her down the passage and into her bedroom. She opened the window, took a deep breath.

And it wasn't as difficult as she'd thought. Hawkins helped her down on to the flat roof below. Then it was the drainpipe. And across the back garden.

Hawkins led George Adams up the stairs. The man was looking around all the time.

'Rented, is it?' he asked.

'Yes.'

'Secure lease?'

'Not really.'

They went through to the living-room. Prewett was sitting in the corner. He was still oil-streaked and half naked, looking like some mad bloody Zulu.

Adams frowned. 'Tell me about the lease,' he said.

'Well, we're fine until people dump a skip outside,' Hawkins said. 'And then start putting in stripped pine kitchens and jacuzzis.'

'And a tunnel of love,' Prewett said.

Adams looked at him strangely.

'What I'm saying is,' Hawkins went on, 'the place has been sold. Developers are coming in next year.'

'You mean, you're squatting?' Adams asked.

'No, we're paying rent, like I told you. To the Eastwood Housing Co-op.'

'And they'll re-house you, will they? Once the developers arrive?'

'That's it,' Hawkins said. 'Though we're a bit far down the list.'

'Helps if you're a black lesbian dwarf,' Prewett said.

Adams looked at him even more strangely. 'And you are?' he asked.

'Prewett. Roger Prewett.'

'And you're a student? Like Mr Hawkins here?'

'Not exactly like Mr Hawkins here,' Prewett said, 'My situation's a bit iffy.'

'Why's that?'

'I'm waiting for my second year's results.'

'Well,' Adams said, 'the best thing is to keep hoping.'

'Oh, I'm hoping, all right,' Prewett told him. 'Soon as I get that grant-cheque, I'm buying a plane ticket.'

'What?' Adams' eyebrows went up.

'And a pair of tap-shoes,' Prewett said. 'I'm going to tap-dance my way across the States.'

'Mrs Thatcher said we should all learn new skills,' Hawkins said.

30

McRae took the tray from the hotel waiter. He turned as the room-door closed behind him.

'Lunch.'

He gave Cassidy one of the plates of sandwiches. Then,

taking the other, he crossed the room to the video-recorder, and switched on.

There was the Geneva street scene he'd stared at so often. There was the Mercedes drawing up at the kerb. And the two men getting out with their suitcases.

'Who are they?' Cass asked.

'Couple of laddies with $100 000,' McRae told him. 'At least, that's what the Belgian boys say.'

The men crossed the pavement to the frosted glass door. There was the name, *AGENCE ORIENTALE*.

'Travel agent's,' McRae said. 'They've been using travel agent's recently.'

'Who have?'

But McRae didn't answer. Not until the video cut and re-started. And the two men re-appeared, coming out of the door.

'Couple of laddies *without* $100 000,' he said.

Cass frowned. Frowned harder when he saw there was a third person on the pavement, a girl with long blonde hair. 'Who's she?'

'Don't know,' McRae said. 'All we know is the blonde hair's real. She's five foot ten, and almost certainly English.'

He went over to where Cass was sitting. There was a folder on the table. And inside it, photographs.

'Blow-ups,' he said. 'I'm assured the young lady's jeans and shoes are English. And that little brooch-thing she's wearing was bought from a Devon tourist-shop last year.'

Cass looked from the photos to the TV screen. It was blank. But then the Geneva street appeared once again. And a car came down it, a different car. He saw the date in the little box was different too. A month later, May 89.

'What are we looking at?' he asked.

'Something called *hawala*.'

'What?'

'H-A-W-A-L-A . . . The W hard as in Wagner.'

'Explains everything,' Cass said.

McRae helped himself to another sandwich and sat down. 'All right. It's a banking system that comes from

India and Pakistan,' he said. 'And it's very old. Probably older than anything we've got.'

'You're joking.'

'No, I am absolutely serious,' McRae said. 'And how it works is this . . .' He pointed at the screen. 'Two men go to a *hawala* broker in Geneva. They give him $100 000, and in exchange they get a marker. A ten rupee note, say. Or a playing-card, the ten of diamonds. Or a sugar-cube with ten dots on it . . . You see what I mean?'

'Yes,' Cass said. He was beginning to.

'And what happens then,' McRae went on, 'is the Geneva broker phones a broker here in London, and tells him the deal's on.' He paused. 'And then the blonde girl, the courier, flies into Heathrow with the marker. She gives it to the London broker, and picks up the hundred thousand, minus commission.' He pointed at the TV screen. 'She's done that three times now. Watched, of course, by a minder.'

'Jesus,' Cass said softly.

'You haven't heard half of it,' McRae told him. 'The beauty of the whole thing is that no money actually *moves* between Geneva and London. There are none of your normal banking procedures or exchange controls.'

'*What*?'

'It's all done on trust.'

'With *that* amount of money?'

'Family trust,' McRae said. 'Old established Indian and Pakistani families. All these brokers being, of course, related.'

Cass shook his head.

'Don't you see it? . . . No money crosses frontiers. The transaction between these brokers isn't settled . . . Not until there's a hundred thousand dollars going back the other way. In this case, to Geneva.'

Cass sat there. It *was* beautiful, he realised, unbelievably beautiful. But then a thought occurred. '*Is* there money going back to Geneva?' he asked. 'I mean, enough money?'

'Oh, yes. Drug money, hot money going every which way.' McRae nodded, 'London–Calcutta, Calcutta–Beirut,

Beirut—Geneva . . . You remember the Johnson-Matthey fraud?'

'Yes,' Cass said.

'There's talk going around that *ten million quid* of Johnson-Matthey money disappeared like that . . . Just talk . . . It took the American SEC a year, for example, to uncover this little chain in the Far East. And the Belgians another year's surveillance to follow it up.' He spread his hands. 'The system is, as you can imagine, damn near undetectable.'

Cass turned to the TV screen. The blonde-haired girl was there again, standing by the car. 'So you never found her?' he asked.

'No.' McRae went over to the video-recorder and switched it off. Then came back to the lunch tray. There was a bottle of hock on it, with the cork half-pulled. He opened it, and filled two glasses. 'Cheers,' he said.

'Cheers.' Cass drank slowly. He was frowning again.

'What's up?' McRae asked.

'Well,' Cass said, 'what you're trying to tell me . . . what I *imagine* you're trying to tell me . . . is that there's a connection between the hot money business and this company here in dockland . . . Packham Leisure?'

'The Belgians seem to think so,' McRae said. 'That missing finance director . . . Gotto? . . . His name's come up in their enquiries at the other end.'

'But,' Cass said, 'can't you move on that?'

'Move on what, for God's sake?' McRae showed impatience. 'Anyway, at the moment we can't see what the hell Packham are up to.'

'How d'you mean?'

The man sucked in his breath. 'I told you they were a venture capital company, didn't I?'

'Yes.'

'Have you any idea how that kind of thing works?'

'Not really.'

'All right,' McRae said, 'a venture capital company finds money. And puts it into certain projects.'

'Yes?'

'And usually, *usually* the numbers go something like this . . . Out of ten projects say, one gets to be a high-earner. Six show varying degrees of profit. And maybe three go under.'

Cass nodded.

'But, here in Gotham City, things are very different,' McRae went on. 'Packham Leisure seem to be having what you might call liquidity problems . . . I mean, take that office development we both looked at. That's not going to show a profit for some years, is it?'

'No.'

'And a great many of their other projects seem to be going under . . . A theme park . . . A sailboard manufacturer . . . All the way down the card, in fact. *Except* for one bar-restaurant they own up-river. Showing a very healthy profit.'

Cass frowned. 'But,' he said, 'a bar-restaurant's not exactly going to keep nine other companies going, is it?'

'Good thinking, Batman. I see you're right up with the rest of us,' McRae said. 'Tell you what? Why don't you lend us that agile brain of yours?'

'What?'

The man grinned. 'You strike me as a pillar of Gotham City society. Have the odd dinner-party, do you? I mean, go out?'

'Well, yes,' Cass said. 'As a matter of fact my wife and I are going out tonight, with a solicitor friend and his wife.'

'A *solicitor* friend, is it? The right wines, I have no doubt. Just *edging* into the Burgundy.'

And again Cass sighed.

'So why don't you try this restaurant maybe?' McRae asked. 'It's called Flashman's.'

31

Vicky waited until two o'clock before she went back to the flat. She walked quickly up the street, reached her front door, found her keys.

And then saw Adams getting out of a Ford car, running towards her.

Her head drooped. 'I have this simple philosophy,' she told him. 'I just *hate* people who drive Fords.'

Adams took the keys from her, opened the door, and led her upstairs.

She found herself being placed gently in a chair. Then he took up position between her and the door.

'I haven't got time for this, young lady,' he said. 'Where've you been?'

'Work,' she said.

'By that, I suppose you mean the building society?'

'Of course.'

He shook his head. 'You haven't been there in a fortnight.'

'Oh yes,' she said. 'Now I remember.'

'Remember what?'

'Well, I woke up one morning and suddenly realised I was only going to have 180 weeks' holiday for the rest of my life . . . so I stayed in bed.'

'You think that's funny?'

'Not really.'

'All right,' he said. 'And have you been doing any other kind of work since?'

'No,' she lied.

And Adams saw it. He shook his head again.

'Maybe, in the circumstances, we ought to consider a job for you,' he said. 'A steady job.'

Vicky raised her eyebrows.

'I mean, you studied economics at the poly. Didn't that give you any ideas?'

'Lots of ideas,' she said.

'Well, then?'

'And,' she went on, 'they made me angry.'

'Angry?' He was surprised.

She smoothed down her jeans, looked at him coolly. 'Have you got half an hour?'

'What?'

'Okay.' She sat forward. 'Idea number one . . . every

successful European country has only been successful at the expense of its weakest citizens.'

He blinked.

'And, idea number two . . . the government of *this* country claims to be fighting inflation by controlling the money-supply.'

Again he blinked.

She got up. 'But, between 1984 and 1989 the money-supply doubled . . . Prime cause, the de-regulation of financial markets leading to a fantastic rise in borrowing, and a fall of over sixty per cent in the ratio of savings as per disposable income.' She paused for breath. 'Equals the fastest ever rise in consumption. Equals loadsamoney for some, and sod-all for the unemployed . . . It's all a sodding *con* . . . Manipulated facts. Vested interests . . . And waving the *sodding* union jack.'

She looked at him. One-nil, she saw. One-bloody-nil, darlings . . . Adams wore a red-white-and-blue jockstrap.

But later the score was edging towards one–one. And it was bad. The man was sitting close and talking earnestly. So goddamn *earnestly*.

'You see, I'm not here to poke my nose in,' he said. 'I'm here to help.'

'That's good.'

'And how I can help is tell you how the court views you.' He shrugged. 'I mean, what do they see? A girl, a nice intelligent girl, who smiles a lot, admits to everything . . . and does absolutely nothing to make amends.'

'Yes,' she said.

'There are serious criminal charges against you.' He leaned closer. 'You owe a great deal of money. Your life is at the crossroads.'

Jesus, darlings, she thought. They are going to take out my tonsils. They are going to tear up my Rupert books.

'Well, good-ness,' she said.

But he didn't get it. He just ploughed on. 'Maybe we should get to the root-cause of the problem, where it all began.'

She nodded.

'For example, at the end of your second year at the poly, you were asked to leave. Now why was that?'

'I don't know. Maybe I didn't hand in enough essays.'

'Why?'

'I don't know.'

'Of course you do.' He thought a moment. And then the clown hit home. 'Your father was very unhappy about it.'

'Ohh . . .'

'But, you know that, don't you?'

She didn't answer.

'You don't want to discuss your father?'

She still didn't answer.

'Look, what it boils down to is this, I'm asking you to do three things,' he said. 'Find a job you like. Pay back the insurance company bit by bit . . . And live at home to keep expenses down.'

'No,' she said softly.

'You mean, you won't live at home?'

'No.' It was barely audible.

Adams watched her steadily. Then he got up and went to the door. 'Mind if I take a look around?'

'Oh, help yourself,' she said wearily.

32

Cass sat at his desk. He glanced through the sun-blinds and saw that the other CPS offices were empty. He was going to be late, he thought. Late getting back home, late going out to dinner.

And the reason was Probation Officer Adams.

The man sat facing him, talking in that slow pedantic way of his, and fingering his rugby club tie.

A bit heavy, Cass remembered Sonia's description, *goes by the book*.

But at last the man got to the point.

'I found it in her flat,' he said, 'in the bathroom, of course.'

'Oh, God.'

'Hidden in a shaving-stick container. I mean, why do they always use the same place?'

Cass sighed. 'How much was there?' he asked. 'A lot?'

'Not really.'

'But, surely they're students. Students smoke a bit of dope.'

'It isn't dope, it's amphetamines. These are kids with access to hard drugs,' Adams said. 'And kids who, in my opinion, are definitely on the wild side. A bit weird.'

'What makes you say that?'

'It's all down in my report.' Adams pointed. 'Plus the fact that the leasehold of the flat is insecure. Developers are moving in.' He raised his voice. 'I mean, I *can't* recommend it as a suitable address for probation, can I?'

'I'm not sure.'

'Not *sure*?' Adams stared at him. 'Are you prosecuting this case, or aren't you?'

Cass got up. He walked to the bookcase and the photo that was there . . . Sonia and Alison.

'You're saying she won't live at home?' he asked. 'Vicky?'

'No, she won't.'

'That's quite definite?'

'No question about it.'

Cass turned. 'You know what this means, don't you? It'll have to be a probation hostel. For a girl with *her* qualifications . . . eight O levels, three A's.'

'Yes,' Adams said.

'But, she won't be able to stand it,' Cass told him. 'She'll do a runner. Then it'll be a young offender's term.'

'I'm not a fortune-teller,' the man said. 'I can't predict the future.'

'Look,' Cass bent over him, 'all I'm saying is, have one last try.'

'What?'

'With her.'

'Won't be any use,' Adams said. 'I spent a lot of time at her flat today, explained the situation and she didn't listen

99

to a word.' He shrugged helplessly. 'That young lady doesn't realise the trouble she's in.'

And *young* lady was right, Cass thought as he went out to his car. He remembered when he'd seen her in court, the freckles, the soft brown hair, the strange smile. He hoped things weren't going to happen to her too fast.

But, when he reached home, there were other problems.

Sonia came towards him in the living-room. 'Quarter to eight. We're going to be *hours* late,' she said. 'It's very rude.'

'I know. I was held up.'

'I mean, I tried ringing them, but they'd already left.'

He brushed past her and went upstairs, shrugging out of his jacket. And he was just unbuttoning his shirt when she followed him into the bedroom.

'I do hope it's not going to be another one of those evenings,' she said.

'What evenings?'

'When Marianne goes on about her new Volvo, and the private school *and* that new house they're buying.'

Cass frowned. 'Didn't hear about the new house,' he said.

'Oh, it's a biggy. Out on Ranelagh Avenue, my dear.' She paused. 'I mean, are they rich?'

'Sounds like it.' Cass left his clothes on the floor and pulled on a bathrobe.

'Funny,' she said. 'They're by no means our only friends, but they do seem to be monopolising our time nowadays. D'you think Marianne's put so many people's backs up that . . .?'

Cass held up a hand. 'Look,' he said, 'I agree with you, Marianne's an acquired taste. But Phil is nice. We've known him a long time now . . . And if you start getting all Marxist at dinner, I'll give you a kick under the table.'

She grinned. 'Okay, I'll try.' But when he went through to the bathroom, she called after him. 'This place we're going to tonight. What exactly is it?'

'Oh, just a restaurant.'

'Somebody recommend it, did they?'

'Yes, as a matter of fact,' Cass said. 'McRae.'

33

They parked in old dockland. There was a wide cobbled street leading down to the waterfront. And, on one side of it, warehouses, old brick warehouses with chain hoists and narrow windows. Two in a row were dark. But the third had lights, and a big neon sign over its doorway. FLASHMAN'S.

Inside, it was bigger than Cass had imagined, the whole ground floor of the building, in fact. The floor was bare boards, sprinkled with sawdust. There were archways and pillars of brick. And the boom of a cavern, the surf of shrieking guitars.

Sonia looked at the bar, the young execs there packed tight as a rugby scrum. 'I don't know if Marianne's going to like this,' she said.

Cass made a face, nodded.

They moved to where it was quieter and darker. There were booth-tables, every one of them crowded. And above on the walls, old school caps, school ties, canes . . .

'Oh, dear,' Cass said.

They saw Phil and Marianne at a corner table, and hurried towards them. 'Sorry,' Sonia said, 'we're *terribly* late.'

Phil got up. He reached out and kissed her. 'Doesn't matter,' he said, 'not one little bit.'

But it did, Cass saw, as he bent towards Marianne. That glow of hers, that fine summer glow, was lost in the dim wooden booth. Her lips seemed hard. And her bare shoulders were wrong, she was over-dressed.

He kissed her. 'Bet you've been here ages.'

'Oh, no,' she said. 'We're enjoying the music.'

Phil caught the edge in her voice. 'Oh, come on, lover. Heavy metal is back. A million people can't be wrong.' He picked up his glass. 'And the wine is really *rather* good.'

'What is it?' Cass asked as he sat down.

'Just the house white. Try some.'

Cass did. 'Not bad,' he said, and reached for the wine-list. 'I'll take care of this. My turn tonight.'

And the list, he saw, was surprisingly large, surprisingly well-priced. He was working his way through the clarets, when something made him look up. It was a laugh, a man's laugh, big, infectious.

Phil pointed to the next table. 'The guv'nor,' he said. 'At least we assume he's the guv'nor.'

And he was right. Because the man turned and came towards them. He was big and he seemed to have shiny points of light about him . . . his watch, the gleam of his suit.

'Are they looking after you?' he asked.

'Just about,' Phil said.

'Always the same in this place,' the man said. 'Food's good. The service is diabolical.'

They laughed, all except Marianne. And the man bowed, started to move away, when Cass called him back.

'This wine,' he said, pointing to the list.

'Which one would that be, Sir?'

'Number 43, St Emilion. Haven't heard of the name.'

The man came closer, looked over his shoulder. 'No, you wouldn't have, Sir . . . Small château . . . deceptively spacious . . . double-garage . . . split-level lounge.'

Even Marianne laughed.

'Well, it's different,' she said, as the man went away. 'I'll say that.'

And it was, Cass found to his relief. In fact the food, when it arrived, was as good as advertised . . . red mullet, *medaillons* of pork, even a rare steak that was rare.

Marianne's face began to soften. Her lipstick began to smudge as she ate. 'Why haven't we been here before?' she asked.

Neill walked to the end of the bar. He watched a customer neck back a glass of champagne in quick greedy gulps. Fifty pence, he thought, a quid, one pound-fifty . . .

Then he checked on the spiked Access forms by the till. And, leafing through them, suddenly stopped.

'Jesus.'

He looked round. Vicky was closest behind the bar. 'Oi.'
He called her over.

'What is it?' She came up, and he saw she was stumbling
a little.

'Here,' he asked, 'you been at the tequila?'

'Not so's you'd notice.'

'So's *I'd* bloody notice.' He held out the Access form.
'All right, who took this?'

She frowned at it. 'That's Simon's writing.'

'So where is he?'

For a moment she looked out at the tables. 'I don't
know. Away in the kitchen, most likely.'

'Well, you tell him.' He tapped the form. 'We won't get
half of this.'

'Won't? Why?'

'See who signed it? Mr Henderson, right? . . . The guy's
an *animal*. Drinks cognac by the bucket . . . And Access
won't meet the bill. It's way above floor-limit.'

'You're joking.'

'I am *not* joking,' Neill said. 'So what you tell Simon is
this . . . Next time Henderson's in here with a party, and
shouting for cognac, Simon doesn't go up to *him*. He goes
to the small bugger at the end of the table. And in his best
bum-licking voice, he says, "Lick yours, Sir".'

'*What*?' Vicky stared.

'"Would you be wanting any liqueurs, Sir?"'

She started laughing.

'Because,' Neill went on, 'the small bugger, he'll hesitate,
but he'll *pay*. His missus'll see to that.'

Vicky laughed louder, losing her balance, clutching on to
his sleeve.

'All right, then. You tell Simon.'

'Tell him yourself.' Vicky was looking over his shoulder.
'There he is.'

And Neill turned. He cupped his hands. '*Oi*,' he shouted.

From his table Cass looked round. He saw the big man
shouting at the end of the bar. And then . . .

Vicky. Vicky Elliott.

He was startled.

That picture of her he'd had. The freckles, the smile . . . young . . .

Old now. Something very old about the way she leaned against the man. The way he whispered to her. The way she laughed, head lolling, lips drawn back.

'Anything wrong?'

He turned. Phil was talking to him.

'No, nothing,' Cass said.

'Saw you were watching the boss-man. Certainly knows how to fill this place, doesn't he?'

'Yes.'

'And how to pick them young.'

'Yes,' Cass said, 'he does.'

He turned his back on the bar and looked at the others round the table. They were finishing the second bottle of wine and talking close.

'How's work going?' he asked Phil.

'Busy. You know, always busy.'

'That's good.'

'Not when you have to stay on till ten at night, three evenings a week.'

'Know the feeling.'

'So do I, lover.' Marianne turned and made a face.

But Sonia leaned past her. 'Phil,' she said, 'something I meant to ask you.'

'What's that?'

'Any progress on that case I sent you the other day?'

Phil frowned. 'What case?'

'You remember. Young girl from our day centre. Jo-Ann her name was. Her mother got involved with drugs.'

'Oh, yes,' Phil said. 'That one. We passed it on.'

'What?'

'To Seymour and Landgrove.'

Sonia was surprised. 'Why? It was simple enough . . . Legal Aid.'

'No, we don't do Legal Aid any more,' Phil said. 'Had to give it up last year. Didn't pay.'

'Didn't *pay*?' Sonia was more than surprised, she was angry.

Phil saw it.

And Marianne saw it too. She gave that sigh of hers again. 'Sonia's upset with you, lover.'

'I don't know why,' Phil told her.

'Well, you're not a *real* lawyer, not in her book. All you deal with is wicked property.'

'I see.' Phil started to flush.

'I mean, some of us stopped going on demos when we left university,' Marianne said. 'But Sonia goes marching on.'

All this time Cass had been feeling under the table with his foot, trying to reach his wife.

But Phil was turning back to her. 'Sonia,' he said, 'I'd dearly like to run a charity, but my partners won't let me. I mean, we all work bloody hard. We've got twenty-seven staff to pay, rent, rates, bank-loan . . . And, like anybody else, we hope to take home enough to cover the mortgage.'

Sonia wasn't convinced. Not until Cass finally found her foot and kicked it. She glanced at him and backed down. 'Okay, Phil,' she said. 'Okay, I'm sorry.'

There was a moment's silence. Then suddenly music bounced out from the bar again. One of the old ones, Status Quo . . .

Marianne remembered it, anyway. And she decided to rescue the evening. 'Whatever you want,' she sang, nodding her head up and down. 'Whatever you like . . .' And then, to Sonia, 'You know, this place *really* rather hits the spot. Where did you hear about it?'

'Oh, one of Cass's friends at work,' Sonia said, tight-lipped.

'I can't imagine any of the CPS people coming down here.'

'No, it wasn't them, it was the new lot,' Sonia said. 'Serious Fraud. A man called McRae.'

And then she turned to Cass quickly. 'Sorry, I'm not supposed to say that, am I?'

'No.' He shook his head.

'What?' Marianne leaned forward.

'Supposed to be all under wraps,' Cass told her.

'But, how *exciting*.' She looked round at Phil. 'Darling, did you hear that? Serious Fraud, no less, suggested we come here to dinner.'

But Phil, Cass saw, still seemed upset by the argument. He seemed strange, withdrawn.

It didn't last long. The man was his comforting, wide-shouldered self again over coffee. Telling Crown Court jokes, good Crown Court jokes.

And later, when he and Cass were over by the till, he insisted on paying. 'Give it here, my lad,' he said. 'I need this one. Entertaining a member of the legal profession. Oy, what?'

Cass let him take the bill. Then he stiffened. Behind Phil there was shadow, and a metal staircase going up a brick wall. And Vicky was there, legless, leaning against the big man in the shiny suit. More than that, she was hanging on to him, hauling his head down, kissing him hard.

Cass turned away. But when he looked back they were going up the staircase, to a door marked PRIVATE.

34

The Bensons' big Volvo pulled smoothly away. Cass and Sonia stood by the entrance to Flashman's, waving. Then he turned to her. 'How's the foot?'

'Okay,' she said, 'thanks very much.'

'I had to do something.'

She shrugged. 'You're right. It could have got out of hand. But I was angry.'

'I know.'

'But, the thing is, they've changed. They're not the same people we knew years back.'

'We've all changed,' he said. 'We're all getting older.'

She looked down the cobbled street at the quayside, the

dark oily water there. 'Got to get it out of my system somehow,' she said. 'Feel like a walk? Just a short walk?'

He looked at his watch. It was after eleven, and he was tired. 'All right,' he said.

They found a gate in the iron railings opposite, and started out across rough ground. It seemed endless, gravel and weeds, with every now and then a pile of rubble. And everywhere that cold blue light that was dockland the world over.

Then, in the distance, different lights.

New houses, Cass saw, village-style houses, and the swaying masts of yachts . . .

Channel Village, of course. He hadn't realised how close they were from this side.

Sonia pointed at it. 'If you really want to know,' she said, '*that's* what makes me angry.'

'What?' He didn't understand. 'Why?'

'Property-developer land,' she said. 'Phil Benson land, and sod Legal Aid.'

'Oh, come on. I don't see the connection.'

'Don't you?'

'No,' he said. 'I mean, for heaven's sake, this isn't like London. It isn't one of the banking centres of the world, high pressure stuff for yuppies . . . Here, they're doing their best by the locals. There's a shopping-mall, a big new cinema, sports-complex, restaurants . . .'

'And yachts,' she said.

'What about the office buildings they're putting up? Conference centres? Bringing in businessmen?'

'And yachts.' Sonia pointed at the masts. 'Listen, a new development starts up around here, *any* new development, and what's the first thing that happens?'

'You tell me.'

'They build a marina,' she said. 'And from day *one* it's full.'

Cass thought a moment. Then he nodded. It was true.

And Sonia turned, looking from the Channel Village houses to the dark quayside where they stood.

'You can't tell me that every twenty-five feet along this

waterfront there isn't going to be a yacht moored,' she said. 'And a 200K apartment, looking down on it.'

'Maybe,' Cass said. 'I really don't know.'

She turned again, looking at the silent cranes along the docks, then at the railway lines, rusty railway lines, that led inland towards piles of scrap.

'There are ghosts around here,' she said. 'Ghosts who used to unload crates.'

'In the bad old days, yes.'

'*Bad* days, were they? You mean it was all the unions' fault?'

'I'm not going into that,' Cass told her. 'But in the end, even you have to admit, the thing that changed it all was technology . . . The new container-port down river.'

'Employing how many people?'

'Well, less, of course. Less than before. But . . .' He nodded back at Channel Village. ' . . . There's work here now. Lots of work, putting that little lot up.'

She looked at him. 'And when the work finishes? When all the offices are full of businessmen? When the shops are full of pastrami and Perrier? And the BMWs locked up for the night?' She sighed. 'More ghosts.'

35

It was white in Neill's bedroom, white-painted brick, a lot of white carpet, and the pillow close to her head.

'Oh, *sod* it.'

'What's up?' he asked.

'Nothing.' She lay with her back to him. That buzz of tequila in her head, like a thin wire.

'Something, my darling. That's for sure,' he said. 'You seemed to be necking it back tonight.'

'I've had a bad day,' she said.

'Is that right?'

'Yes. A man came to see me.'

'So what did he want, this man?'

108

She thought about Adams the probation officer. How he'd looked round the flat. How he'd found the gear for sure, though he'd never said.

And she thought how he'd suddenly gone on about the right kind of address, about living at home, or . . .

'What did he want?' Neill asked again.

She didn't answer. He turned her round towards him, and she tried to hide the tears.

'Hey, what's up?'

'Ohhh . . .' And she began to cry harder, leaning against him. 'Ohhh . . . money. Mostly money.'

'Too bad,' he said. 'I never ask about people's money-problems . . . Money, or diseases of the bowel.'

She laughed, laughed and cried at the same time.

He pulled up a corner of the sheet and wiped her eyes. Gently. He could be very gentle, Neill.

'Look,' he said, 'is the world going to come to an end? Is Sinatra going to stop singing?'

'I don't know.'

'Course you do. You've got sense.'

'*Sense*? You don't know anything about me.'

'I know you pissed on the polytechnic, pissed on your job. But plenty of people've done that.'

'Yes, I s'pose so.'

'And if it's only *money*. Christ's sake, girl, why don't you start to think straight? Make plans? Do your own little number?'

She didn't understand.

'Tons of things you could do.' He stretched out an arm. 'Catering, for example. Catering's always been good to me . . . And, God knows, there are girls who make their way up, learn a couple of things from a Frog cookbook, start their own restaurants.'

'Me?' Vicky asked.

'Why not?' he asked. 'I mean, there are people . . . *I* know people . . . who're always wanting to put money into the right place.'

'I don't believe it.'

'Come on, it's not difficult. I could look over your

109

shoulder, put you on the right path.' He shrugged. 'I mean, back of it all, girl, you're steady. You're a grafter.'

'But,' Vicky said, 'on *my* overdraft? Plus what I owe?'

He paused for a moment, looked down at her. 'Less than five grand, is it?'

'*What*?'

'That kind of money's just there. Nobody misses it.' He leaned closer. 'Tell you what, why don't you take a holiday? Kind of a working holiday? On me? I'll sort out some notes, bung 'em your way.'

36

During the next three or four days Cass spent a great deal of time in court. Kempling, one of the other prosecutors, was away, and he had to take over part of his list.

Mostly it was the mixture as before.

There were the young men who said, no, they hadn't got a drinking problem. Eight pints was normal, wasn't it? Then a couple of vodkas, all right, four or five. And a bottle to take home.

Then the young men who were neat, in a borrowed jacket and tie. Who blinked in disbelief as they heard what had happened a month ago, or even six weeks.

The student, for example, fair-haired, not bad-looking. Who sat lower and lower in the dock as the police sergeant droned on.

'The accused replied with a well-known phrase,' the sergeant said. 'I cautioned him, but he persisted with other phrases.'

He turned a page in his notebook. 'And it was at this time that he picked up the boot-scraper,' he went on. 'He hurled it against the front door of the premises, damaging paintwork and splintering the wooden panels.'

The lady magistrate leaned forward. 'Boot-scraper, Sergeant?'

'Yes, Ma'am. It's one of those cast-iron things. People have them outside their doors.'

'I see.'

The sergeant read on from his notebook. 'The accused then told me that he was very upset because his girl-friend . . . with whom he co-habited . . . had recently left him.'

'Did you later ascertain whether this was true?' the magistrate asked.

'I did, Ma'am.' The sergeant kept his place in the notebook, and looked through later pages. 'She was a Miss Seymour. A Miss Karen Dawn Seymour.'

'Go on.'

The man found his place again. 'I then disarmed the accused and told him he was damaging private property. He became abusive, used further well-known . . .'

The mixture.

As before.

On Friday morning, early, on his way up to the CPS, Cass called in at Serious Fraud.

And he was surprised. The inner office was dim, its blinds drawn. And McRae was lying back in an armchair, his face grey.

'You look as if *you* could do with a holiday,' Cass told him.

'You're right, Batman, of course.'

'Didn't you get to bed?'

'Not really.' The man yawned. 'Only managed to get satellite-time at three this morning.'

'*Satellite*-time?'

'Oh, it's the big one,' McRae said. 'The Massachusetts computer. American SEC.'

He got up stiffly and picked up a pile of print-out paper. 'What they've got is a machine set up on anti-terrorist lines. It gives them access to flight-bookings, chain hotel-bookings, and car-hire . . . Worldwide, of course.'

'Dear God.'

McRae grinned tiredly. 'You don't know the half of it. I mean, your fortnight on the Costa del Catspiss last year was *definitely* noted.'

He let slip a concertina of paper. 'Anyway what I've

been doing since three o'clock this morning, is checking flights between Switzerland and the UK . . . on or around the dates of those *hawala* deliveries we know about.'

'Passengers' names, you mean?' Cass asked. 'But there must be thousands.'

'Right again, Batman. Though relatively few of them repeat, of course, on all the dates in question. D'you see what I mean?'

'Yes, but still . . .'

'And we've only found half a dozen so far that come from around this area.'

McRae unfolded another wedge of paper. And Cass saw a cluster of names that had been ringed in felt-tip.

Mr George Sorenson.

Mr Andrew Harding.

Mr Naim Bedawa.

Miss Karen Seymour.

He looked at this last. 'Wait a minute . . .'

Cass went up to his office. He checked his court-records from two days back, and found the notes on the young man who'd hurled a boot-scraper at a front door. -

Then he rang McRae.

Three hours later, just before midday, the man came into his office. His tiredness was gone, and he had a folder under his arm.

'Karen Seymour?' he asked. 'Karen *Dawn* Seymour?'

'That's right.'

'Okay. Have a glance at this. Then think back to those Belgian videos we looked at.'

He held out a photograph.

Long blonde hair, Cass saw, and a wide forehead. But the rest of the face was unclear, in shadow.

'Could be,' he said. 'I'm not sure.'

'Okay, how about this?'

The next picture was closer, head and shoulders. And there was no doubt, none . . . that wide mouth, the high smooth cheekbones, the faun-like beauty.

'She's a student,' McRae said, 'from the university here.'

'What?'

'Ran out on her boyfriend about two months ago. And got herself involved with a rich crowd . . . yuppies.'

Cass was surprised.

'We didn't hear about any of that in court,' he said.

'No. And I don't expect you heard *where* she got involved with them.'

McRae produced another photo.

A restaurant-table, Cass saw, a small wooden booth. The blonde girl smiling, drinking champagne.

And the T-shirt, she was wearing.

FLASHMAN'S.

WHERE THE BIG BOYS HANG OUT.

'You mean, she worked there?' Cass asked.

'No,' McRae told him. 'I know the staff wear them. But they hand the things out to good-looking girls too, regular customers.'

Then he went on. 'And, don't you see? It all fits . . . The bar-restaurant that's part of the Packham Leisure group. Rich punters. And the odd girl student maybe, with no money to her name. But just maybe she'd like a nice trip to Switz . . .'

By now Cass was trying to stop him.

'Where did you get all these?' he asked.

'All what?'

'These photos? . . . I mean, it was only this morning . . .'

McRae nodded slowly. 'Karen Seymour's on file,' he said. 'Missing Persons.'

'*What*?'

'She went missing, Batman. Well over a month ago . . . Which makes *two* people now, doesn't it? A Mr Gotto? Finance Director? And now . . .?'

But Cass had gone to his desk, snatched up the phone. 'Probation Service,' he said.

'What are you doing?' McRae was surprised.

Cass turned his back. 'Mr Adams, please.'

He waited.

'Hello, George Adams? . . . Michael Cassidy here . . . Look, about Vicky Elliott, you remember I asked you to see her again? . . . You tried to? . . . What d'you mean?'

His head came up.

'She's gone away? On *holiday*?'

37

Vicky Elliot wore a dazzling white swimsuit. She lay on a white lounger under a white parasol. And out on the lake the diving-board was white against the haze.

There were waiters too, white-gloved, white-coated. And every time she raised a hand, they brought her another Campari soda.

It was just like the TV commercials, darlings.

She glanced at her watch. Two thirty-five. She had to make a move.

In her room she showered, and dried her hair. She put on the apricot silk dress, 540 Swiss Francs, and the gold shoes, 270 ditto. Quite stunning, darlings. She was all bronzey-bronzey from the sun. And she did big things with the eye-liner and the gloss.

At five to three she walked down the staircase and came to the dim marble hall. There were pillars. There were ferns. And at the big mahogany desk the clerk said, No, Madame, her visitor hadn't yet arrived.

Which of course was the man Neill had rung her about last night. The man who was going to drive out from Geneva and give her a certain book to bring home. A very important book.

But, as she walked on down the hall, she knew it wasn't going to be like that.

For example, the man wasn't going to *drive* at all. He was going to ski down avalanches, ford rapids, swing in through the hotel windows on a wire.

And he wasn't going to give her a book. He was going to leave a box of chocolates on a table. Together with a small white card.

You remember, that other TV commercial, darlings?

Happened *all* the time.

38

Hawkins came in from the kitchen with a cold can of beer. He ringed it, sucked at the foam, then looked round at the living-room. At the Hendrix poster, the battered settee . . . and Prewett sitting cross-legged on the floor.

Prewett who was like a jelly. Had been for two days now.

'Go on,' Hawkins said, 'open it.'

'No,' Prewett answered, 'not yet.'

'Not *yet*? It's been looking at you since Thursday.'

And Hawkins went to the mantelpiece, the brown envelope that was there, the letter from the poly.

He tapped it against his beercan a couple of times, then crossed the room with it. 'Go on,' he said again.

Prewett nodded slowly. He took the letter and opened it. 'Dear Mr Prewett,' he read.

'Comma,' Hawkins read over his shoulder.

'I see from the annual report that you may not proceed to the next year of your course.'

'Semi-colon.'

'Your award has . . .'

'Comma.'

' . . . therefore . . .'

'Comma.'

' . . . been suspended.'

'Full-bloody-stop,' Hawkins said.

'If you feel,' Prewett read on, 'that your inability to progress normally has resulted from circumstances beyond your control . . .'

'Overdraft of three thousand quid,' Hawkins said. '*Plus* the plastic you flashed round the Reading beer festival.'

' . . . You are free to write and explain why an exception should be justified in this instance.'

There was a long silence. Hawkins walked over to the window. Prewett followed him with his eyes. 'How come you always manage to keep your nose clean?' he asked.

'What?'

'I mean, pass your exams each time?'

'Oh,' Hawkins said, 'nothing to it, really.'

'How's that?'

'Well, it's just a matter of picking the right courses,' Hawkins said. 'I mean, at first I thought I'd do German literature. But I went to the library with a calculator, and found the books I had to read totalled over nine thousand pages . . . That's long odds.'

He looked out of the window idly, and saw a police car in the street below.

Then he saw it stop. Men getting out.

The freaking flat *doorbell* was ringing.

In all truth Hawkins was a bit bothered by the interview-room. Though not by the sergeant asking the questions, nor by the constable taking notes. It was the two men at the back . . . The Scots guy with the long hair and the strange eyes. And the guy with the pale sandy hair they called Mr Cassidy.

What the hell were they doing here?

Still, he played for time, answered questions.

'Well yes,' he said, 'Vicky would have left, what, four days ago now.'

'Tuesday,' the sergeant said. 'And about what time?'

'Early-ish.'

'Early-ish. And did she say when she'd be back?'

'Monday night.'

'Monday *night*?'

Hawkins sighed at the boring repetitions. But the sergeant leaned forward. 'Didn't you know,' he asked, 'that she was due in court on Monday morning?'

'No.'

'Well, what do you know?'

'Not a lot.'

The sergeant frowned. 'All right, when she left, was there anything unusual about her?'

'No, nothing I could see.'

'She didn't seem under duress?'

'Under *what*?' Hawkins looked over the sergeant's head

116

at the two men beyond. 'Listen, do I have to put up with this plebeian little routine? . . . Ravel's bolero with matching tank-top?'

And he could've sworn the Scots guy grinned, just briefly. But then it was gone, and now he came forward, took over the questioning.

'You say she drove to Switzerland,' he asked, 'in a hired car?'

'Yes.'

'Why was that?'

'Sort of a week's holiday,' Hawkins said.

'Just like that? Just decided to go, and went?'

Hawkins hesitated. 'No, it was her boss,' he said then. 'He wanted her to go.'

'Her boss at this bar-restaurant place? Flashman's?'

'That's right. He said she'd worked hard behind the bar. He was throwing a little jolly her way.'

'And what was the nature of this jolly?' the Scots guy asked.

'Well,' Hawkins tried a brief smile, 'what he did was, he slung a barrel of brandy round her neck. Sent her to look for this customer in the snow.'

But the Scots guy wasn't amused, not this time. He was angry. 'Mr Hawkins,' he said, 'maybe I should tell you about this man, and the . . . jollies he's arranged for young girl students.'

Half an hour later Hawkins was more than bothered, a great deal more than bothered. The Scots guy had left in a hurry. And the other guy, Cassidy, was putting papers back into his briefcase. He snapped it shut, and started to walk past on his way out.

Then he hesitated and turned back. There was concern in his eyes.

'Look, this is off the record,' he said quietly. 'But I'd like to know, if possible . . .'

'Know what?' Hawkins asked.

'Well, how it all started.'

'How did it start for any of us?' Hawkins shrugged.

'Doing a bit of this? Bit of that? Finding ourselves maybe in kind of weird situations?'

Cassidy frowned. He didn't understand.

'Look, life at poly nowadays, it's all crap,' Hawkins said. 'It's not students there any more, it's midgets. Engineering midgets. Business Studies midgets . . . They've got their little heads down, their little calculators out. They're keeping their noses clean and rushing towards middle-age.'

But Cassidy still didn't understand.

'What can I say?' Hawkins asked. 'All the decent courses have closed down. All the decent lecturers have left. I mean, nobody wants to know about Baudelaire any more. Nobody can even *spell*.'

And Cass began to see. 'You're talking about the cuts?'

'Cuts. The obscenity of student loans. The lot,' Hawkins said. 'I mean, we all went on demos. And maybe Vicky went on too many. She missed out on the work. Got the sack.'

Cass nodded.

'And the thing was, she just didn't realise what it meant,' Hawkins went on. 'There she was, sitting around at the flat, with just three A levels to her name . . . I mean, she could get a job in freaking insurance.' He raised his head tiredly. 'She could get a job with the freaking police.' He pointed at the constable. 'Even a freaking *career* at Tesco's.'

Again Cass nodded.

'And then of course her old man came larruping round to the flat,' Hawkins said. 'Shouting the odds.'

'About her doing nothing?' Cass asked.

'And the rest.'

'What d'you mean?'

Hawkins sighed. 'Okay, she's not exactly what you'd call a looker,' he said. 'But she's always sort of figured on the sexual canvas.'

'Yes.' And Cass frowned again, trying to do the impossible, bridge the gap between himself and a nineteen-year-old. 'But . . . what I don't understand . . . I mean, why this man who runs the bar? This older man?'

118

'Maybe because he *was* older,' Hawkins said.

'What?'

'Look, remember a few years back? Remember when the first AIDS commercials came out? The *silence* there was in the cinema then?'

'Yes,' Cass said.

'Not like that now,' Hawkins told him. 'All the kids, it's got so they're like Spitfire pilots, the first of the freaking few.' He paused. 'And Vicky . . . underneath it all she's scared. Scared of everything.'

39

On the Monday evening, when he'd finished work, Cass called in again at McRae's office.

The man was on the phone.

'Yes, Sir,' he was saying. 'I do see that, Sir. But, on a surveillance operation of this importance . . .'

Cass turned away. He looked round the office and noticed an old map of the harbour on the wall. Someone had defaced it, he saw. There were scrawlings in felt-tip. There were little flags. And one of them, way upstream, was labelled Flashman's.

It gave him a sudden stab of alarm.

Behind him McRae finished talking. He slammed down the phone. 'So tell me,' he said angrily, 'is there anybody in this city who's above God?'

'God?' Cass turned.

'God the Father, Commissioner of Police.'

'Nobody, really,' Cass said. 'Not unless you've got contacts, good contacts, up in London.'

'Haven't got time for that,' McRae said. 'Vicky Elliott arrives at nine tonight. *Here.*'

'Yes,' Cass said, and thought again of the Flashman's flag on the map.

McRae got up. 'For Christ's sake,' he said, 'all I've been given, in terms of surveillance, are two unmarked cars . . .

Which is about enough to police a village flower show.'

Cass nodded. 'So why don't you pick her up at the docks?'

'That's what the commissioner said too.' McRae turned away, began pacing.

'Well, why not, for heaven's sake?'

'Number one,' McRae said, 'she's got that *hawala* marker on her, and I want to know who she gives it to . . . And number two, the situation, as they say Batman, has become rather tricky.'

'Why's that?'

'*Why?*' McRae paced towards him. 'Has it ever occurred to you that's she's coming in on the *car*-ferry? That she *drove* to Switzerland? Didn't fly, like the other girl?'

'Yes,' Cass said.

'And has it occurred to you that it wasn't like the other girl's trips at *all*? She didn't go to any office in Geneva? She only left the hotel a couple of times? And had just one visitor? A businessman?'

'But, how?' Cass asked. 'How do you know all that?'

'Oh, we traced her. And the Swiss police did the rest.' McRae was impatient. 'But, what I'm saying is their game-plan has *changed*. They've kept her well away from the action . . . Which, to my mind, Batman, can only mean one thing.'

'What's that?'

'They knew we were on to them before,' McRae said. 'Knew they were being watched.'

And Cass felt that stab of alarm again. 'Well, as long as they don't know we're on to Vicky,' he said. 'Now, I mean.'

40

It was just before opening time at Flashman's. Neill was putting change into the till. And the dark punky-looking girl, Jane, was wiping down the bar.

'Going to be busy tonight again,' she said, 'and I'm going to be rushed off my feet.'

'I'll give you a hand,' Neill said. 'I'll get back here and help you as much as I can.'

'I'd be grateful. I mean, it's not all that easy without Vicky here.'

'No.' He checked the running total, and closed the till.

'Funny,' she said then.

'What is?'

'I mean, Vicky going off like that, to Switzerland.'

He looked up. 'Why?'

'Well, for a start, she didn't have any money.'

'I don't know about that.' He shrugged.

'*I* do. She was in all kinds of money-trouble. In fact she should've been in court today.'

'What?' He stared at her.

'Oh, yes.' Jane finished the bar and started putting out ashtrays. 'She was waiting to see if she'd get probation. It was today they were going to decide.'

Neill moved. He found a glass, held it under a Scotch optic, and poured a large one.

'I mean,' Jane went on, 'if you don't turn up in court all kinds of things start happening, don't they? . . . I mean, the police . . .'

'Yes.' He drank the Scotch down.

And started thinking.

If Jane knew she'd gone to Switzerland, he thought, then who the hell *else* knew?

41

Vicky Elliott drove down the ramp from the P & O ferry. She saw where the cars were dividing ahead of her. The slow queue into the entrance marked with the red disc. The fast queue into the green, Nothing to Declare.

She chose green. And was waved through, darlings.

Easy as that.

Not that she'd *really* worried. I mean, a paperback book? Whoever in the world would worry about *that*?

And whatever in the world did it mean, anyway? Some sort of diabolical master-mind stuff? Was Neill into running the old white powder, darlings? The old Charlie? Wouldn't put it past him. Wouldn't put anything past him.

By now she was out of the dock-gates, and picking her way through the roundabouts that led on to the ring-road. The sky was wide around her suddenly. The clouds had gone, and there were the winking lights of stars.

But she was wrong.

There weren't only stars.

The night air was full of voices, though she couldn't hear them.

'*Fiver-One, Sierra Charlie. Fiver-One, Sierra Charlie . . . Target now on Inner Ring, proceeding north.*'

'*Fiver-One . . . I read.*'

Vicky drove on. She switched on the radio and found Channel Sound. Golden Oldies Night, she discovered. Before her time, really, darlings.

But there was one she knew.

Manfred Mann.

'*Sierra Charlie, Fiver-Two. Sierra Charlie, Fiver Two . . . Target on Inner Ring . . . Take roundabout Inner Ring and Cable.*'

'*Sierra Charlie . . . I copy.*'

Vicky sang.

'Hello without. Hello within,' she sang. 'You ain't seen nuthin' like the mighty Quinn.'

Then, feeling the need for the weed, she reached out to the carrier-bag on the seat beside her.

No problem, darlings. A whole carton of Rothmans came out of the carrier. And she worked at its wrappings with her fingers.

'*Sierra Charlie, Fiver-One. Sierra Charlie, Fiver-One . . . Keep 200 yards distance. This is a surveillance operation.*'

'*Sierra Charlie . . . No sweat. She's doing 40 miles an hour. It's a doddle.*'

' . . . Ain't seen nuthin' like the . . .'

Vicky got the first of the Rothmans packs out. She peeled off the cellophane, put a fag in her mouth. Then she felt for matches.

Matches?

There were none in the carrier. And she remembered throwing a box away on the boat.

Shit.

She looked ahead along the ring-road. There was a turning to the left. And away to the left she saw the lights of a garage.

It closed at ten, she remembered.

And her watch said two minutes to.

Shit.

She was almost at the left-hand turn. She braked suddenly, changed down . . . and . . . made it, darlings.

'*Fiver-One, Sierra Charlie . . . She's taken off!*'

'*Fiver-One . . . I read.*'

'*Target going fast down Saville.*'

'*Don't lose her, Fiver-One . . . Go!*'

And then, the same voice . . .

'*Sierra Charlie, Fiver-Two . . . Forget roundabout Inner Ring . . . Take Eglantine, then Dawlish . . . Go!*'

Still singing, still beating time to the music, Vicky drove fast down Saville Street towards the distant lights of the garage.

Then she heard tyre-squeals behind her.

And in her mirror saw a car turning fast from the ring-road, coming after her.

Some bloody boy-racer, darlings, she thought.

And she had two choices, she thought. Slow up and let him pass her. Or put her foot down.

She put her foot down. It was a fine night.

'*Fiver-Two, Sierra Charlie . . . Problem.*'

'*Go ahead, Fiver-Two.*'

'*Am blocked for Dawlish . . . Some wanker in an artic.*'

There was radio silence.

Then.

'*Sierra Charlie to Control. Sierra Charlie to Control.*'

'*Go ahead, Sierra Charlie.*'

123

'*Can I have assistance, junction Dawlish-Saville? Have you number-tops in the vicinity?*'

The number-top slowed.

Inside it, the two uniformed men turned to each other.

'Dawlish-Saville? That's us,' the sergeant said.

'Right, Skip.'

'Go for it then. Give her some welly.'

The constable pulled away fast, 'Not like the old days, the old BMs,' he said. '0 to 60 in 13 seconds . . . with the handbrake full on.'

They screamed down Dawlish Road.

'What now?' the constable asked.

'Turn into that garage there. See what happens.'

On Saville Street, Vicky approached the garage from the other side.

The boy-racer was still behind her. Still coming up fast.

And, shit, the forecourt was close now.

She panicked, hit the brakes hard, changed down, swung the wheel . . .

And you . . . *could* say . . . made it, darlings.

Missed the line of pumps.

But then suddenly, the police car swinging out from the far end. Out and round . . .

Paralysed, she smacked into it. Broadside.

The seat-belt grabbed her shoulders. The windscreen went white. This huge, *huge* sound of metal.

Then just her engine, screaming on.

She waited.

The door opened. A police sergeant, white as she was, leaned in and switched off the ignition.

'Are you all right, Madam?'

He felt her legs and arms to make sure.

'Why . . .?' she asked him.

'Why what, Madam?'

'Why do I always . . . hit police cars?'

42

Cass had a phonecall late that night. He got into his car and drove to a street not far from the docks.

McRae stood there alone in the darkness.

They talked. And finally Cass was angry.

'But, I can't,' he said. 'Of course I can't.'

'Why not?' McRae insisted. 'Is there anything in law to say you can't be at the interview of a person you're prosecuting?'

'Not in law. No.'

'Well, then.'

'It's just not ethical,' Cass said. 'The CPS is meant to be an independent body.'

'Batman, there *is* a certain air of urgency about this,' McRae said. 'I told you the game-plan had changed. I told you these people were on to us. I'm not going to fart around.'

He came close. And Cass saw the lines of strain on his face.

'Look, don't you see?' he said. 'For the first time in our lives we can get hold of a *hawala* marker. I want it in my hands. I want to get it checked out. I want that girl in court tomorrow morning. And I want *you* to tell me we've enough to go on.'

Cass hesitated. Then he pointed to the small hotel at the end of the street. 'But, you say you're holding her in there,' he said. 'For heaven's sake, why not back at the station?'

'Because, as I see it,' McRae sad, 'it's been one hell of a bad night for policemen.'

Inside the hotel room a woman police constable sat on a chair. Vicky sat on the bed. And she was quite calm, Cass saw, just as he'd seen her that first day in court.

She didn't turn as McRae bent to her luggage, as he pulled on a pair of plastic gloves, opened her suitcase, emptied it and slit away the linings.

Then he turned his attention to her clothes. He got the

policewoman to examine the smaller items, while he slit linings from dresses and coats, and pulled apart shoulder paddings. He broke the heels from her shoes, turned out her sponge-bag . . . and finally came to a paperback book.

'What's this?' he asked.

Vicky looked round, 'Dürrenmatt,' she said. 'He's a Swiss writer.'

McRae got up and went towards her, holding out the book.

'As a matter of fact, they're detective stories,' Vicky said calmly. 'Very unusual, almost expressionist. It isn't a question of whodunnit, you see. More of an intellectual . . .'

But McRae had the book upside-down, was riffling through the pages. A piece of paper fell out.

'Bookmark,' Vicky said. 'It shows you where you finished reading, in case you forget.'

McRae stooped and picked it up. 'Bill from the *Kärntner* department store in Geneva,' he said.

'Yes,' Vicky said. 'It was in their beauty salon. I had a facial done, wax treatment, the lot.'

'250 Swiss francs for that? Rather a large amount, isn't it?'

Vicky didn't answer.

'Fine,' McRae said. 'Last Thursday, was it?'

'That's right.'

McRae looked at the slip of paper. '9.30 in the morning?' he asked.

Vicky nodded,

McRae slipped the bill back into the paperback. Then he got a notebook from his pocket, found a page.

'Last Thursday at the Adler Hotel, Les Chaumes,' he said, 'you had breakfast in bed at midday . . . Which, it seems, was quite early for you.'

There was a crack suddenly, a crack in Vicky's face.

Back in the hotel corridor, McRae held out the book in a plastic bag. 'We're going to get her,' he said.

'Not sure if I agree,' Cass shrugged.

'A receipt for 250 francs? Equals a marker for $250 000. Right?'

'She hasn't admitted that.'

'Hasn't admitted to anything yet,' McRae said.

'And I'm not sure if she knows anything,' Cass told him. 'I mean, anything, from start to finish.'

'She'll start remembering, Batman. I mean, at half-past six tomorrow morning when the world looks *really* bad . . . And I hit her again.'

Cass sighed. He felt empty.

'What's the matter?' McRae frowned at him. 'Aren't you meant to be on my side? Prosecuting?'

And where had he heard that before? Somewhere . . . Yes, that was it, George Adams, the probation officer.

'Look, I'm in a hurry,' McRae said then. 'Got to get talking to our Belgian friends.' He started away down the corridor with the book. 'You coming?'

'No,' Cass said, 'not yet.'

'What?'

'I think I left my pen back in there,' Cass lied, 'when I was taking notes.'

And for the second time McRae frowned at him.

'Suit yourself,' he said, and marched away.

Cass went into the room again. Vicky was alone now. And she was trying to hide her face. She'd been crying.

He sat down. 'I'd like to try and give you some advice,' he said.

She didn't answer.

'I mean, it'd go better for you in court if you had someone vouching for you.'

She still didn't answer.

'What I'm talking about is some kind of reconciliation with your parents.'

'No,' she said.

There was silence.

'I've got a young daughter,' he said then. 'And I worry about her.'

'That's good.'

'And if I were your father, I'd . . .' He knew how lame he

127

was sounding, and he tried again, 'Look . . . It was pure accident, but I had dinner last week with some friends. We went to Flashman's.'

She was surprised.

'And, I mean, the difference between you there . . . and, well, how you looked in court was . . . rather . . . alarming.'

She looked straight at him. 'I've had rather a lot of advice about that, as it happens. From my parents.'

He nodded.

But suddenly she was on her feet, brave, childishly brave.

'AIDS, right?' she shouted. 'Bugger me, suddenly my father's got it made . . . God's in his heaven. The mortgage is paid. And with *one word* my old man can hate all gays, blacks, druggies, and anyone who fucks.'

'Yes,' Cass said.

There was a longer silence.

'Funny,' Vicky said then.

'What is?'

'I don't know. About sex . . . I mean, when I was a little girl, quite little, my parents were always going on about strange men.'

Cass shifted uneasily, wondering what was coming.

'And, you see, there *was* a strange man. A strange old man with shaking hands. Walked with a stick.'

Again Cass shifted.

'I would've been about nine, singing in the school choir,' she went on. 'It was Christmas time, and we were in this old folks' home . . . And this old boy came up to me, sort of from behind. He sort of put his hand out and touched me here.'

She made the shaking hand, touching her hip.

'And I knocked him away. And . . . and all these 10p pieces went spinning away over the floor.' She shrugged. 'He'd been trying to put them in my pocket.'

Cass felt the tension drain out of him, felt ashamed.

'There just aren't any nice stories like that any more,' she said, 'are there?'

'No.'

Vicky got up. She pointed at her belongings scattered all over the carpet.

'This,' she said, 'is it serious? Is it . . . prison?'

He didn't answer.

'Ohhh . . .' She made a small fluttering sound.

43

At two in the morning she felt braver, much braver. In fact she even felt, darlings, there were things she could do.

Like, get the hell out.

Two reasons for this, darlings . . .

Numero uno, the fact that the dykey policewoman was asleep outside the door. She could hear her dykey snores.

And *numero due*, the fact that outside her window was a drainpipe, about three metres of drainpipe, that went down *awfully* close to a fire-escape below.

And *if*, darlings, she could close her eyes and imagine she was only six metres from the ground, just as she was on the old drainpipe at the flat . . .

If . . .

She went over to the window-sill.

Closed her eyes.

Felt foot-holds and hand-holds,

Felt the wind tearing at her clothes.

And.

Cracked it.

The metal rail of the fire-escape.

All lean together, darlings.

And she was there, panting.

Then she was down on the street, moving fast, for the nearest phone-box.

Because Neill was the answer, the *only* answer. Had to be.

Twenty minutes later the big Jaguar pulled up by the phone-box. And Vicky ran out of the shadows, pulled open the passenger door.

'Thank God, you're here,' she said.

Neill turned from the wheel, bear-like, comforting. He put an arm round her.

'What's up then?'

'What's up?' She shivered. 'Everything. I couldn't phone you from the flat. I never *got* to the flat.'

'Why was that?'

She shivered on. 'Everything went wrong. They searched through all my stuff.'

'What?' There was a second when he was startled. But then he stroked her hair, tried to calm her down. 'Look,' his voice was gentle, 'you're too nice for this kind of racket. I never should've sent you.'

'But, you don't understand. They took everything, the lot . . . even that *book*.'

He kissed her. 'Don't worry about it,' he said. 'We'll talk later.'

He turned back to the wheel, started the engine.

And she sank back into the deep leather seat, the smell of it, the richness of the car.

There.

Wasn't the end of the world.

Was it, darlings?

44

'*General assistance call . . . Any vehicle in vicinity Bramley Point.*'

'That's us, Skip, isn't it?'

'Again,' the sergeant said.

'How far then?'

'Left when you hit the coast road. Then maybe a mile.'

They put the siren on, and weaved in and out of the morning traffic, the trippers' cars and the cars with wind-surf boards.

And, by the time they'd reached Bramley Point, they were caught in a coastal shower.

The sergeant looked down at the grey beach. At the

people gathering up their kids and deck-chairs, and running for shelter.

Then, away to the left, and much further out, he saw the one person who hadn't moved.

The girl who was sunbathing.

In the rain.

They went down to her, saw her face.

The blueness of it, the swollen cheeks . . . The fear.

45

Four days went by before all the police reports came in. Cass took the file from Roderick and began reading. Then he looked up.

'The first holiday-makers got down on that beach at half-past nine . . . and Vicky was there *then*?'

'Yes, Sir,' Roderick said.

'Were they blind or something?'

'They said they thought she was asleep.'

Cass was angry. And even more angry as he read on . . .

An hour later he got himself an appointment to see Area Chief Prosecutor Royston.

The office was on the top floor. Its windows were wide, overlooking the city. And Royston himself was tall, grey-tied, grey-suited. All of a piece.

An impressive man, Cass thought. The dark eyes, the clear way he had of thinking. Always the straight line.

Cass sat down. 'I'm not very happy, Sir, with the way this Vicky Elliott business is progressing. I'd like the inquest delayed.'

'I think we all would,' Royston said.

'I mean, as far as I can see, the likely verdict is going to be misadventure.'

'Looks that way.'

'Which would mean that Vicky escaped from custody at one in the morning, walked the fifteen miles to Bramley Point, and drowned herself by three.'

Royston nodded.

'I mean, she had no taxi-fare. The police had taken her money. All bar some loose change.'

Royston pressed long fingers against the bridge of his nose. 'The conclusion the coroner is going to come to is that she hitched a lift,' he said. 'And the motorist hasn't come forward.'

'I can't go for that.'

'Nor can I, really. But what's the alternative?'

'She had loose change,' Cass repeated. 'She made a phonecall.'

'Who to?'

Cass leaned forward and gripped the desk. 'The man Neill,' he said. 'Neill Harper, who runs Flashman's.'

But Royston shook his head. 'Harper has been questioned three times in all. His staff have been questioned twice. He left Flashman's at eight that evening. Went to a restaurant with friends. Then on to a night-club . . . He was there till four in the morning.'

Cass gripped the desk harder. 'I want,' he said. 'I want that story broken down.'

A change came over Royston. He got to his feet suddenly. '*You* want?' he asked. 'Or is it your colleague McRae?'

'What?' Cass was surprised.

Royston walked to the window, looked out at the city. 'Cassidy, you're one of my best prosecutors,' he said. 'As you know, we work very happily here . . . But every now and then our department is invaded by what I can only call . . . cowboys.'

He turned. 'We've suffered with the Anti-Terrorist Squad. And now it's Serious Fraud,' he said. 'They think they can do exactly what they like. And when they can't, they wave a hand, and priority orders come down from London.'

He stood thin and tall against the sunlight. His voice was still quiet. But Cassidy knew what was coming.

'This girl, Vicky Elliott, was removed from the police station,' Royston said. 'She was then taken to a hotel. An unsecure hotel.'

'There was a police presence there, Sir.'

'And *your* presence too, Cassidy.' For the first time Royston raised his voice. 'I can't begin to understand that.'

Cass let the silence hang. 'There were unusual circumstances, Sir, very unusual. A certain document that Vicky Elliott brought back from Switzerland . . .'

Royston came back to his desk. 'Oh yes, this document,' he said. 'So where is it? I haven't seen it. Is McRae withholding evidence? *Again*?'

'No, Sir,' Cass said quickly. 'As a matter of fact, Mr McRae's taken it with him to Brussels. The Belgian fraud people think it's very important.'

'I don't understand,' Royston said. 'They think it's important. You say your entire case hinges on it.' He showed disbelief. 'A receipt from a Swiss department store?'

'Yes. Sir.'

'I mean, think what the coroner will make of it . . . Presumably this receipt was in a foreign language. Did Miss Elliott *understand* this language? Did she even pick up the right bill?'

And again Cass hesitated. 'I'm only asking, Sir, for the inquest to be delayed until the matter is cleared up.'

'I don't see why,' Royston said. 'Unless you can prove that this piece of paper substantially affected Miss Elliott's death.'

Cass could feel the ground slipping away, 'Well, no, Sir, not exactly. But, you see, there was a previous occasion. Another girl who went to Switzerland for similar purposes. There's evidence . . .'

'I've seen it.' Royston cut across. 'But, what I didn't see was anything connecting this *other* girl with Neill Harper.'

'She used his restaurant, Sir. And she too was a student with very little money. Don't you see there's a pattern to . . . ?'

He tailed away. Royston was leaning forward, watching him over long slim fingers.

'I have read the entire file,' he said. 'And you have *no direct evidence* against Harper.'

'So you won't let me question him again?'

'Quite the reverse,' Royston said. 'In fact, the man is talking about undue police attention. He's only the manager of Flashman's. His employers are claiming that business is suffering. They're transferring him to another establishment.'

Cass went back to his office. He went through it all, step by step. And concluded, as always, that with the evidence presented to him, Royston had been fair.

But there was an alternative. Something the man hadn't mentioned.

Something he obviously refused to believe.

If Vicky Elliott had been drowned, by person or persons unknown . . . without a mark on her body . . . then it had to be a professional killing.

Here in this city.

At one o'clock, lunchtime, Cass left his desk. He got into his car and drove down to dockland. Then parked in a wide cobbled street, opposite Flashman's.

He thought back to the night he'd been here with Sonia and the Bensons. Thought about a man in a silk suit. That big laugh of his. The jokes.

A man who knew professional killers.

And was now going free.

Once again anger rose up in Cass. It surged through his veins. He needed space. And, swinging round in his seat, he saw the area of cleared ground he'd walked over with Sonia.

He drove out there, the car bouncing and lurching on the rough track. And he drove fast, not thinking where he was going, until finally he was stopped by a gate in a long wire fence.

He switched off. He closed his eyes, and gradually saw a small hotel room, a young girl standing there by a bed. 'Ohhh . . .,' she said.

A small fluttering sound.

But then there were other sounds, real sounds, making him open his eyes again.

He looked at the gate that was facing him, the wire fence. And the big sign there. BRI-RAND PARTNERS BUILDING FOR PACKHAM LEISURE.

And, through the fence, the big building site. The square steel frames and the row of tall black pile-drivers.

Bap-bap-bap-bap-bap.

CHAIN

It grew longer in the mist. Jerked down another metre . . . two . . .

To show the third body. The last.

He was a man in a good checkered suit, old-fashioned. And he was an old-fashioned man, white-haired. Hanging sack-like, plump.

And if there was horror on his face, it was of a different kind. The waiting for horror to be over, resignation, an inward look back at those he loved.

Dignity, yes.

Until, with more length to the chain, it spun.

Spun faster.

And, like the two below, the girl and the man, he swung out.

Jitterbugged, danced.

MISS
BRINKWELL

46

The multi-storey car-park was dim. It was filled with the sound of jets from the distant runways. And there was the squeal of baggage-trolleys as Barry led the way towards his car.

He opened the boot, put McRae's suitcase inside, then reached back for the duty-free carrier.

'That's for you,' McRae told him. 'You said Teacher's, didn't you?'

Barry saw the two bottles of scotch. 'Yes,' he said. 'Thanks. Thanks very much . . . But, what about you?'

McRae held out his briefcase. He clicked it open and showed the collection of malt whisky he had inside. The Macallan. Four bottles.

'I gave them a big smile in customs,' he said. 'Always knew a warrant card was good for something.'

Barry shook his head as he climbed behind the wheel. He joined the queue at the exit, and some five minutes later was driving through the shadows of the airport tunnel. But it wasn't until they emerged into sunlight at the far end, that he turned and saw how tired McRae was looking, how he was slumped back in his seat.

And he hardly dared ask it. 'So how was Brussels?'

'Cock-up,' McRae said. 'Total bloody cock-up.'

'But, I thought your friend Tuveri . . .'

'Oh, Tuveri's a good laddie,' McRae said. 'His Belgian team are *bon*. The Swiss *superbe*. But . . .'

Barry waited.

'You want a blow-by-blow?' McRae asked then. 'Okay, they traced the paperback book to a shop in Geneva. Got no further.'

'Yes?'

'And they traced the *Kärntner* store receipt an awful lot further, seeing as how it was a sizeable bill for beauty treatment.' McRae paused. 'Seems a certain Swiss lady sat in the chair and had her toenails done. Charming woman, apparently, very kind to her mother . . . Only she left home a fortnight ago.'

Barry frowned. 'But, what about the travel agent's, the *Agence Orientale*?'

'They provide a marvellous service, Barry. Not only do they find block air-bookings at a moment's notice. Concessionary rates, of course . . . They also have a nice little line in passports.'

'No arrests then?'

'Two,' McRae said. 'The window-cleaner, and the guy who sharpens the pencils . . . Nobody charged, of course.'

Barry drove on, squinting against the sun. 'So what's it all about?' he asked.

'They knew we were coming,' McRae said.

'But how? I mean, we held back at this end. We didn't go near Flashman's, or Neill Harper, until you . . .'

McRae sighed. 'I can only tell you what Tuveri said . . . He said the news came from here. At least two weeks ago.'

47

Samantha made herself small on the prosecution bench. She knew Cass was short-tempered. Knew he'd been short-tempered since the inquest on that Elliott girl. But this afternoon in court . . .

He was on his feet now, scowling at his notes. A burglary, she knew. And a bad one. A couple had been tied to a chair, knocked about.

'Ma'am, it is further alleged,' Cass looked up at the bench, 'that for the purposes of this crime, the defendant used a Citroen car without insurance. He was also disqualified from driving under a twenty-one-month ban.'

There was movement on the defence bench. A solicitor got up. He was young, and nervous.

'I'm afraid, Ma'am,' he said, 'that I have not yet received a print-out of my client's driving record.'

Cass bent to his desk, turned pages quickly. And Samantha saw his face. There was trouble coming.

'Ma'am,' he looked up again, 'a letter was sent from my office eight weeks ago, on 9 June.'

'I see.' The defence solicitor also flipped through pages. 'We . . . we . . . don't seem to have any record of that.'

Cass glared at him. 'In *addition*,' he said, 'the defence was notified fully one month ago that a print-out would be needed in this case.'

The defence solicitor was even more nervous. 'Yes,' he said, 'I now see that the matter was noted . . . But, Ma'am, it must be understood that this would only be of his current driving-licence. It could be that my client was . . . as it were . . .'

Suddenly Cass raised his voice. 'Ma'am, this case has been adjourned once before. And since valuable time is being wasted . . .'

He turned, snapped his fingers at Sam. She found the prosecution copy of the print-out, and he banged it down on the court-clerk's desk.

The man was surprised. It was a moment before he turned to the magistrates with the form.

Cass sat down.

'What the hell's the matter with that young lad over there?' he whispered.

'Only just out of college,' Sam said.

'But, for God's sake, it's nearly three o'clock. There are *real* solicitors waiting, and they cost money.'

48

Barry drove down the M3, dead against the sun. For some time now he'd thought McRae was asleep. But he wasn't.

'One good thing,' the man said.

'What's that, Bob?'

'There's been a spin-off from this little *hawala* racket. And would you believe? It works in our favour?'

'I don't get you.'

'Okay, what's been happening? A hot money pipeline's been flowing from Switzerland to a certain venture capital company called Packham Leisure . . . Now, suddenly, it's stopped.'

'And that's good?'

'It's irrelevant. It's the *amount* of money concerned that's important,' McRae said. 'The Belgians reckon it runs into tens of millions of dollars. There's high-level concern.'

Barry turned to him. 'The Belgians are worried about an *English* company?'

'No.' McRae shook his head. 'They're worried about a great many companies in a great many different countries. Legal take-over moves, and illegal.'

'It's about time.'

'Oh, yes,' McRae said. 'And there's been a sym-po-si-um, no less. A gathering of Fraud Squads across Europe. A meeting, need I say, of brilliant minds.'

'Need you say.'

'And, by the same token,' McRae went on, 'a pooling of data. Company data.'

Barry thought about that. Then he sighed. 'Something tells me,' he said, 'I've got a lot of work coming my way.'

'Quite a lot,' McRae said.

'How much?'

'Three streamer tapes, arriving at the end of the week.'

'*Three*?'

'Correct,' McRae told him. 'Three hundred and sixty megabytes of information.'

Barry drove on, his shoulders sagging. 'Round the clock work, I take it? Extra people brought in?'

'Sanctioned by head office.' McRae nodded. 'You see, Barry, it's the scale of the thing. Some very big people are beginning to deal in Europe . . . for example, a certain Eyetalian company director wakes up one morning and announces he's got an *eighteen per cent* holding in GLA. Which is one of the biggest conglomerates in Belgium.'

'Jesus.'

'And as for the Dutch, if they see one of their companies threatened, they start selling shares to the family goldfish.'

'Not quite,' Barry said. 'But I know what you mean.'

'Well, they operate by different rules over there.' McRae spread his hands. '1992 is getting nearer. Take-over's the name of the game. The big Euro-firms are getting bigger and bigger.'

'And we stay out.'

'Oh, yes,' McRae said. 'Thirty years after they built the first decent lavatory in Europe, they're buying up our country.'

Barry grinned, and pulled out to overtake a slower car ahead.

'Of course, the European Parliament's well *aware* of the situation,' McRae went on. 'Our ministers keep getting up on their hind legs . . . But it's the public-school language that offends, isn't it? I mean, we say we want the playing-field levelled. We rush up in our baggy shorts and say it's not fair, we're not going to play in your game.'

Again Barry grinned. But then he realised the other man was serious.

'I was having a little think on the flight over,' McRae said. 'And I've come to the conclusion there's some man, an Englishman, living not a million miles away, who sees all this take-over business very clearly.'

McRae sat forward, stretched his shoulders. 'I mean, he's not whingeing on about rules, about a dastardly Dago invasion . . . He's letting them *in*, Barry. He's unlocking the front door, laying out the family silver, and switching on the lights.'

49

It was already dusk, but the clouds above Fernden Head made it appear darker. There was a black curving line to the hill, and near the top a building, a large building, The Old Vine Hotel.

A new Volvo drove into the car-park. Phil Benson got out. He waited for Cass to join him, and then the two of them walked away to look out at the view.

'Amazing sight, isn't it?' Phil said.

Cass nodded.

And it was, he thought. The city far away to their right, a bright orange glow reflected by clouds. Then, below them, the huge yellow gash of the motorway, stretching from horizon to horizon. And on its far side, a vast carpet of lights, winking, stretching all the way out to the sea.

'You just don't realise how big it's become, do you?' Phil said. 'You think it's still little seaside towns . . . East Durling, West Durling, Graywell, Shanksbury . . .'

Cass didn't answer. He was looking at a place that Phil hadn't mentioned. A tiny collection of lights out on a distant point.

Bramley Point. Where Vicky had been found.

'Course it's all these people who come down here to retire,' Phil went on. 'Bloody industry that, nowadays.'

'Yes,' Cass said.

Then there were voices behind them. Marianne and Sonia were leaving the car too.

'No, I have to *drag* Phil out,' Marianne was saying. 'Make him come out . . . But the thing is, we've always needed other people around us, ever since we were married. We both realise that.'

She led Sonia away across the gravel. 'I mean, even on holiday last week,' her voice came back, 'we were always with a crowd. Mind you, it was a big place, Torre Ros. *Vast* hotel. Swimming pool and a kiddies' pool. Just perfect for Abigail. And large grounds, with hoopoes strolling around. Hoopoes, would you believe . . .?'

Phil turned to Cass and grinned. 'Bloody hoopoes.' He locked the car, and they followed the others into the hotel.

The bar of the Old Vine was strangely empty. It had stained oak panelling and flecked mirrors. And it was dim. What brightness there was came from the tables, glass-topped, and reflecting the light from overhanging lamps.

They got drinks from the bar and sat down. They talked in whispers about the changing south coast. But then Marianne pulled her bright wrap around her shoulders. 'Cold, isn't it?' she said. 'Doesn't anyone else feel the cold? I mean, after Spain . . .'

And started on the holiday again.

Phil winked at Cass. 'How're things?' he asked.

'Oh, so-so.'

'Overworking you, are they? You seem a bit quiet.'

'Do I? Sorry. It's just been a bad day in court.'

'Happens.'

'Not like today. Dragged on till well after four,' Cass said. 'There was this young junior defending. Cocked up three cases in a row.'

'Where's he from?' Phil asked. 'Which firm?'

'Napier, Selborne and Grateley.'

'Oh,' Phil said. He looked away.

'What's up?'

Cass leaned closer. 'What's wrong with N, S and G?'

'Nothing.'

'Come on. You know all the gossip.'

'Do I?' Phil asked. 'Well, it's just that I hear they're a bit short-handed.'

'And what else did you hear?'

But the man spread his shoulders, smiled. 'Why should I pass it on?' he asked. 'You never tell *me* anything nowadays, not about that secret service mob you're working for.'

'But, I can't, can I?'

'So you say.'

'Come on Phil. Tell.'

And Phil thought about it. 'All right. I s'pose you're going to hear sooner or later.' He lowered his voice.

'Trooble a 't'mill at Napier, Selborne and Grateley. Trooble among t' partners.'

'What kind of trouble?' Cass asked.

'Napier, he's walked out.'

'What?'

'Walked out on the firm, his missus, everything.'

'*Ben* Napier? The father?' Cass was amazed. 'Nice old boy? White hair? Twinkle in his eye for the ladies?'

'The very same,' Phil said. 'though maybe that eye has twinkled once too . . .'

He stopped then, as a waiter approached.

'Your table is ready for you now, Sir.'

'Be right with you.' Phil finished his drink, stood up.

They followed the waiter across the hall towards the dining-room. As they drew nearer, it seemed to be empty, quiet. But once through the door they were amazed to find it full.

The room was dim, like the bar they'd just left. And again there were those glass-topped tables and overhanging lamps. They were like pools, these areas of light. And seemingly trapped inside them were people, old people. Their faces were harsh, downlit. Slow moving carp in a dim aquarium.

The waiter sat them down and asked if they'd like some wine.

'Better make it embalming fluid,' Marianne said softly.

'Not funny, lover,' Phil told her. Then turned back to the waiter and asked for the list.

The man nodded, moved away.

Marianne looked round at the other tables, at the clicking jaws, the clacking bracelets. They seemed to upset her. She seemed to feel the need to fight them off. And, standing up suddenly, she shrugged out of her evening wrap, like a stripper.

'Da-*daah*,' she said. 'Seen my tan?'

And it was something. The colour of dark toffee, liquid toffee as she moved. And she moved dangerously, threatening to ease down the front of her dress.

'The same *all* over, my loves,' she said. 'I kid you not.'

145

'Sit down,' Phil told her.

She did so, still smiling. 'Perfect holiday,' she said. 'Sun-filled paradise. Bring the kids. Just like the ad . . . In fact we nearly didn't come back.'

'Didn't come back?' Sonia frowned. 'But, what about Phil's work?'

'Oh, that.'

'And what about you? All the things you've got going on here?'

'Like what?'

'Well, house-hunting for one,' Sonia said. 'You told me you were looking.'

There was a pause. Marianne held on to it, preening. 'Not looking, lover,' she said. 'We found. Clinched.'

'My God, that was quick.'

'Wasn't it?'

'But you managed to *sell*? I mean, in the present climate?'

'Oh, yes.' Marianne blew a kiss at Phil. 'Smart, isn't he? My husband? . . . especially when it's to do with the old dosh.'

'Must be nice.' There was an edge to Sonia's voice.

But luckily the waiter came back. He got out a pad, and started taking orders.

And Cass had the chance he'd been waiting for. He turned to Phil again. 'Look,' he said quietly, 'what you were saying just now . . . about old Ben Napier.'

Phil nodded.

'Did I get it right? Were you saying he went off with some . . . woman?'

'*I'm* not saying it. People are.'

'Well, I know he's had his share. But, what's he up to? Flinging himself about in his old age? . . . I mean, is she young?'

'Nobody seems to know,' Phil said. 'He just put his hat on one morning and walked out. Left no forwarding address.'

'When did all this happen?'

'About a month ago. Maybe more.'

'I don't get it.' Cass sat back, looked round at the restaurant. 'I mean, I thought Ben Napier's speciality was *old* ladies. Sorting out their affairs. Holding their hands. And sending them fat bills.'

50

The street was in the old residential part of the city, Georgian, with large sash windows and white porticos. Though, as happened nowadays, the houses were no longer lived in. Every one of the front doors had brass solicitors' plates.

A woman came walking slowly along the pavement, looking carefully for loose flagstones and cracks. She was old, over seventy. But she moved with the assurance of someone who had once been a great beauty. The Squadron Lawn at Cowes had known her, the racetrack at Goodwood, the polo grounds at Cowdray Park. And she still dressed with style, the wide hat, the chiffon scarf, the pinks and greys of her dress. Good clothes, bought new.

She came to a window that said NAPIER, SELBORNE & GRATELEY, and she went up the steps.

Inside there was a glass-panelled door. And beyond it an office with a long mahogany counter, and a girl hidden by a switchboard.

The woman sat down. She took off her hat and fanned herself. And only then was it possible to see the indignities of old age. The hair that was flattened at the back by her pillow. The dark stockings that couldn't hide the veins. And the skin of her face that was like paper, Christmas paper, bright, dabbed at with colour.

The girl behind the switchboard finished talking. She put down the phone, looked round. 'Oh, Miss Brinkwell. I'm sorry.'

'Doesn't matter.' The voice was well-accented, on show.

'Oh, but it does. You waiting there, in this heat.'

'No, I didn't make an appointment. I was just passing,'

Miss Brinkwell said. 'I wondered if I could have a word with Mr Napier. Mr Napier senior.'

The girl frowned. 'He's not in, as it happens.'

'He wasn't in last time I called either.' There was no reproof.

'No,' the girl said. 'He's been away . . . well . . . rather a lot recently.'

'The Test Match, I suppose.' Miss Brinkwell nodded. 'He never misses that.'

'Could be,' the girl said. 'But, would Mr Napier junior do? I think he's free.'

Miss Brinkwell shook her head. 'No,' she said, 'thank you. It was just something small. A little change to my trust-fund.'

'I see.' The girl was at a loss. 'Well, would you like to sit down for a minute? Can I get you a cup of tea?'

'No, really.' Miss Brinkwell levered herself up. 'But perhaps you could call for a taxi . . .'

The driveway was long, and the lawns around it were wide for the suburbs. The taxi drew up in front of a large Victorian house. It was well-kept, the gutterings and windows newly-painted, and the front steps scrubbed.

The driver helped Miss Brinkwell out of the car.

'Thank you,' she said. 'How much is that, please?'

'Two pounds, Madam.' The man looked at the meter. 'Two pounds exactly.'

Miss Brinkwell took her purse from her handbag. With precise fingers she counted out a pound coin, a fifty pence piece, and five tens.

Then she added another coin.

'Here's five pence,' she said, 'for your trouble.'

She turned away and walked carefully up the stone steps. The front door was open. And the inner-door, with stained-glass panels, moved easily to her touch.

Then, standing in the hall, with the colours of the glass around her, she drew in her breath. She looked at the coat-rack with its dozen or so coats. And, with a jut to her chin, a sharpness to her elbows, she moved on to the drawing-room.

It was bright. Wide windows looked out on the lawns. Armchairs, good deep armchairs, were gathered in groups. And the largest group, Miss Brinkwell saw, was clustered around the TV set. Five elderly people sat there, nodding their heads at a programme on farming.

Miss Brinkwell tightened her mouth. She went over to her armchair, removed the *Daily Telegraph* from its cushion, and sat down.

Next to her, an old lady looked round.

'Been out, dear, have you?' she asked slowly. 'Out to the shops?'

'No, I went to see my solicitor,' Miss Brinkwell said briskly.

'Oh, I see.'

'They found a taxi for me, thankfully. I mean, the roads nowadays . . . Happiest day of my life was when I gave up driving.'

'Yes, dear.'

Miss Brinkwell sat back. 'I remember I failed eight tests in a row,' she said. 'Passed at the ninth attempt . . . The man was a simpleton.'

'What?' The old lady looked up.

'Though, even then, I never could get the hang of reversing,' Miss Brinkwell went on. 'I mean, years later, *years* later, when I was working for Mrs Rubafiore . . .' She turned. 'You remember Mrs Rubafiore, don't you?'

'Yes, dear, of course.'

'Well, even then, when we went shopping, I used to make her get out. Used to make her look for a man with a nice face to park the car.'

51

A good day at last, Cass thought. Court had finished by lunchtime. In the afternoon there'd been a chance to catch up on the files. And now he was driving back home at a reasonable hour.

He parked his Peugeot in the drive, walked round the side of the house, and found Sonia in the kitchen.

She was reading the *New Statesman*. There was a big bowl of salad on the side, pasta on the stove, and an opened bottle of wine.

He topped up her glass. Then filled one for himself.

'Cheers,' he said. 'That's what I call a welcome.'

She looked up. 'You don't know the half of it.'

'Don't I?'

'No.' She put down the magazine, came towards him.

'Oh,' he said.

'Is that all you can say? . . . Oh?'

'Well, a chap doesn't like to be hurried.'

'Or grabbed?' she asked. And suddenly she crouched down. Suddenly held one hand out in front of her, and with the other guarded her crotch. 'Ball-grabbing, wasn't it?'

'*What*?' He took a pace back.

'You remember.' She moved closer. 'That little game you told me about once. That nasty little boy's game you used to play in the playground at school.'

'For Christ's . . .' Cass backed. Laughed and backed away while she circled him.

She lunged. He lunged back. She pushed him away.

Then got him.

'It's not fair.' His voice rose. 'I'm the only one with . . .'

'With what?' she asked.

And, still holding on, led him upstairs.

They lay back on the bed. The shadows on the ceiling were slow. Calm.

Then Sonia sat up, looked at him. 'You know what would be good right now?'

'Not again,' he said. 'It's excessive demands.'

'No.' She shook her head. 'A holiday. That holiday you said had been put off.'

'Yes,' he said.

'I mean, when?'

'I don't know.' He shrugged. 'McRae's got something on

at the moment. He's waiting for some computer stuff to come over from Brussels.'

'I see,' Sonia said. 'So we go on as we are?'

'Seems like it.'

'It's not as if I'm asking for much. I mean, not some sodding great hotel in Spain called Torre Ros. With sodding hoopoes in the grounds . . .'

'Please,' Cass said. 'Not that again.'

'Okay. I'm sorry.' She smiled.

He kissed her. He stroked the back of her neck where she liked it. But then she stirred. 'There is one thing, though.'

'What's that?'

'Something you could do for Alison.'

'I don't get you.'

'Alison, your daughter,' she said. 'Haven't you noticed she's out this evening?'

'Well, yes,' Cass said. 'I have.'

'She's playing with Jackie down the road. And she played with Jackie last evening, and the evening before.'

'I didn't realise.' Cass frowned.

'Look, normally at this time of year we're on holiday, all together,' Sonia told him. 'So be kind to her. Give her a little more of your time.'

After supper, Cass sat on at the table, reading *The Times*. He looked up once or twice, hearing noises from upstairs.

Then noises coming down the stairs.

Sonia came in awkwardly through the door, carrying a large doll's house. She was followed by Alison, in pyjamas, holding a tray. And on the tray, Cass saw, were balsa wood, a balsa-knife, glue, and paint.

'Daddy?' Alison said.

'Yes?'

'You were helping me make furniture. Dolly's furniture.'

'I was, wasn't I?' Cass said. 'But, I don't know, isn't it rather late?'

'No,' Sonia said gently.

She put the doll's house on the table and opened it up. And in one of the upstairs bedrooms, Cass saw, there was a

151

chair propped up on a matchbox. It had only three legs, and was unpainted.

He took it out. 'Was this where we'd got to?' he asked.

'Course.'

'All right, we'll finish it. But you've got to help me.'

And at first she did. At first she found the right bit of balsa and the knife, gave him the glue. But then she turned away and trotted a small man-dolly up the stairs.

'Who's he?' Cass asked. 'Is he the man of the house?'

'Yes.'

'What does he do?'

The dolly was half-way up the stairs, and she changed hands, reaching down from the top.

'Policeman,' she said then.

He was surprised.

'Like Sergeant Roderick,' she said, 'who comes here sometimes.'

'Golly Gee,' Cass said. 'The girl's in love.'

'Dad*dy*.'

He opened the glue, and stuck the leg he'd made on to the tiny chair.

Alison walked Sergeant Roderick into his bedroom, sat him down. 'Daddy,' she said, 'what do policemen do at home?'

'Oh, they spin drums,' Cass said idly, his fingers tight around the chair.

'What?'

'They have these drums, and they spin them.'

Alison frowned. 'What else?'

'They feel collars.'

She still frowned, lost. 'But,' she said, 'what do they like doing most of all?'

'Overtime,' Cass said.

52

There was that buzz of striplights that seemed to come only late at night. There were the creaking chairs, the yawns, of waiting men. And then, from outside, the sound of a van.

Barry looked up. 'Could be,' he said.

Then, as they all turned towards the TV surveillance screens, they saw the Securicor vehicle parking in the street.

Barry opened one door, and then the outer-door of the building. He brought the driver in with him.

'Serious Fraud?' the man asked. 'Got to be serious at this hour of night.'

McRae ignored the joke. He'd heard it too many times. He signed the paperwork. He watched the driver unfasten the security chain from his wrist. Then watched him unlock the small aluminium case.

It was about the size of a lunch-basket.

And inside were the three tape-streamers. Each as big as, and looking like, ordinary video-tapes.

And each containing a hundred and twenty megabytes of information.

Barry let the driver out again. He locked up. And then the shift gathered around McRae. The first shift, three operators including Barry, three clerks, and a secretary.

'Okay,' McRae said. 'How they brought the good news from Ghent . . . Ghent, as you may remember, being in Belgium.'

Nobody laughed.

He picked up the first tape-streamer. 'Fine. Now what we have here, thanks to the combined efforts of Euro-Fraud . . . is a complete list of EC-registered companies.'

They nodded, and he picked up the second tape. 'And here, EC company tax-returns, as of last year.'

He put it down and picked up the third. 'And this last . . . EC court-records, with particular reference to property.'

He looked at them, expecting some reaction, *something*. But they were computer men. They accepted.

'All right.' He put the tapes down. 'So now, Barry, with your well-known acumen and expertise, what have you got to tell us?'

Barry thought a moment. 'We take the names and companies that our investigations have thrown up so far,' he said, 'and put them against EC companies.'

'Yes.'

'We run those against tax-returns.'

'Yes.'

'And then court-records.'

'Correct. And what are all those three hundred and sixty megabytes of data going to give us?'

'Mega man-hours.'

There was laughter.

'I'm serious,' McRae said.

And Barry shrugged. 'All right,' he said. 'Property dealings. Purchases and sales.'

'*Company* property dealings.' McRae corrected him. 'And, as your finely-tuned nose will tell you . . . company development plans . . . take-overs.'

The operators nodded. They picked up the three small tape-streamers and went away to the machines.

McRae watched them. He still couldn't get over it. Never would.

But Barry was right when he'd said mega man-hours. Shifts came on at six am, midday, six pm, and midnight. And it went on for three days.

McRae slept little. He walked along the row of screens, saw the figures that flitted across them, the millions of dollars and deutschmarks and francs. He saw the company names, Spanish, Italian and Dutch. And he saw the chase. How patterns began to form, then suddenly fell apart.

The print-out paper piled up. The air became thick with fagsmoke and men. And by the third day McRae had retired to his office. Jesus, he thought, when *was* the damn thing going to crack?

He swung his chair around behind his desk. And then he saw the map on the wall, the old shipping map of the port.

154

He saw how it had been added to, how there were more of those bloody white flags spread across the city. Damn near every bloody property they'd looked at so far.

And under the map, Jesus, wait for it, two photos stuck on the wall. Photos of the missing, believed dead. . . . Gotto, Karen Dawn Seymour . . .

Barry, he thought. He'd get the bastard transferred to CID.

But then, right on cue, the man walked in. He had a bundle of print-out in his hand, and he was holding out sections he'd ringed.

'Got anything?' McRae asked.

'Not really.' Barry's face was lined with fatigue. 'Nothing that really gets anywhere.'

'Okay,' McRae said, 'your starter for ten.'

'Well, see here?' Barry pointed. '23 March this year? See this transfer from Packham Leisure to a company in Lyons?'

'Yes,' McRae said.

'Now, it's a paper company. We know that . . . And, on 27 March, the money moves on to another company called Viallonga.'

'Got it,' McRae nodded.

'Doesn't that mean anything to you?' Tiredness made Barry angry.

'No,' McRae said. 'Tell me.'

'Well, Viallonga Offshore was a name that cropped up back in the Lennox days.'

'Lennox Freezers?'

'Of *course*, Bob.'

'Easy,' McRae said. 'Easy.'

And Barry calmed, shuffled paper, showed another section he'd ringed. 'All right,' he said. 'But, look here. The money's now in dollars. And it's down in the books as development funding . . . for something called Rubafiore.'

'Rubafiore?' McRae asked. 'Have you tried Italian records?'

'Yes.'

'Italian-Swiss?'

'Still no go,' Barry said.

155

53

For some time Cassidy looked at the man in the dock. He was thinnish, about thirty, with short fair hair. And there was something warm about him, gentle, a smile that women would like.

Cass got to his feet and turned to the bench. 'Your Worships,' he said, 'as regards this case, I'm afraid that police enquiries are taking longer than expected. In fact they ask that today's hearing be regarded only as a holding-date. And that a further date be set for four weeks' time.'

The Chief Magistrate frowned. '*Another* holding-date, Mr Cassidy?'

'I'm afraid so, Sir.'

'But, this is the third that has been applied for.'

'Yes, Sir.'

'Well, perhaps you will be good enough to outline the . . . difficulties the police are having.'

'By all means.'

Cass put down the single sheet of paper he was holding. He turned to Sam, who handed him a thick file. And, glancing at it, he saw a note in Roderick's handwriting. It seemed that there was evidence missing. The latest police interviews hadn't yet been typed up.

Cass sighed. He thought for a moment, and then began. 'Your Worships, before you is a man called Jobelin, Charles Peary Jobelin . . . The charges against him divide into two clear areas. The first of these is rather technical, and concerns the recent property boom.'

The magistrates stirred uneasily.

'I'll keep it as simple as I can,' Cass told them. 'But the important thing to remember is, that, during the boom the big insurance companies moved into the housing-market. Competition between them was extreme, and reached a point where certain companies were granting mortgages not in months, or weeks . . . but in a matter of hours.'

A whistle of surprise from the bench.

'They managed this by taking up a minimum of credit references,' Cass went on. 'Indeed, they didn't even approach the applicant's bank in case he or she obtained a cheaper mortgage from that quarter.'

He turned to look at Jobelin. No surprise there. Just a nod. A polite nod.

Case turned a page in his file. 'It was in just such a climate,' he said, 'that Mr Jobelin managed to obtain ten different mortgages over a period of two years. He used forged references. He made not a single mortgage repayment. And when, after a period of months, the building societies forced sales of the properties, a buyer miraculously appeared . . . He was Mr Jobelin's partner, of course. He used forged references too. And the process began again.'

The magistrates looked from Cass to Jobelin.

'In a time of rapidly spiralling property-prices, the two of them managed to build up a sizeable fortune,' Cass continued. 'But then came the end of the boom. Mr Jobelin split up from his partner, and moved on to pastures new.'

He turned towards the end of the file.

'What now happened,' he said, 'was that Jobelin took on a number of cheap leasehold properties. They were all of multiple occupancy. Flats and bed-sits, occupied mainly by old people. He specialised in the elderly.'

In the dock, Jobelin unbuttoned his dark suit. He took out a ballpoint and began to make notes.

Cass flicked through pages quickly.

'Police statements will show that the defendant visited tenants shortly after obtaining the leasehold. They will show that he talked to them in a friendly manner. He told them that they were not to worry about any repair work that might be necessary. They were not to worry about increased rents or service charges. They had certain rights, he told them. The law was quite clear about that.'

And, looking up from his note-taking, Jobelin smiled.

'But,' Cass went on, 'there are also statements from local GPs. They will tell of old ladies who were prescribed tranquillisers and anti-depressants. Old ladies who complained of their flats being broken into, of windows being smashed, of water-taps left running . . .' He paused. 'Old ladies who broke down under the strain and moved out.'

After court, Sam asked him if he'd join her for a pizza. But he shook his head.

'Just a sandwich,' he said, 'back at the office.' He was going to get the typescripts of those final police interviews. That man Jobelin was going to be nailed. There were going to be no more holding-dates in court.

Shortly before two o'clock, the typescripts arrived.

Cass bent over them. He could read between the lines, see Jobelin's gentle smile, see how easily he handled Sergeant Roderick.

Except that there was a surprising crack in Jobelin's armour towards the end.

Q: Don't you realise we're making real progress now? Real progress, with those forged mortgage applications?

A: Is that right?

Q: It'll only be a matter of weeks.

A: So you say.

Q: Yes, I do.

A: Listen, I don't know why you're wasting your time with me.

Q: Why's that?

A: Why don't you go after the big boys?

Q: Like who?

A: Well, obvious, isn't it? The figures of trust in the property racket.

Q: Meaning solicitors?

A: Yes.

Q: Have you got anything you want to tell me there?

A: No, course I haven't. Well, I can't, can I?

Q: All right, then. Is there anything else that comes to mind?

A: What?

Q: Anything that might help.

A: Me, you mean? Help me?

Q: Yes. I can't promise anything. But there could be a possibility.

A: Well, I don't know.

Q: You sure?

A: Quite sure. Except, maybe, I don't know. There was one little whisper I heard.

Q: What was that?

A: Well, not so little, really. It was outrageous.

Q: In what way?

A: I'm not saying any more. Except why don't you get your street-directory out? Look for this building? Big old office building?

Q: How do I find that?

A: Not difficult. It's got an unusual name. Italian name.

54

McRae looked round. He saw sunlight coming through the blinds, and he was surprised. He'd thought it was night.

But it was all one long night to him now.

He turned back to the desk-top computer. The extra one he'd indented for and had set up in his office. He was splitting Barry's work with him now, trying to chase that Viallonga funding down the line.

Trying to.

He tapped at the keyboard. The screen filled with company land-exchanges. He slimmed them down, put each one in turn against Packham Leisure subsidiaries.

And each time got RE-SUBMIT.

Finally he left the word there on the screen. He straightened wearily, got up, and went to the door.

'Barry?' he called.

The man turned. There were dark flags of exhaustion under his eyes.

'What is it?'

'Spare a moment?'

Barry came over, and McRae pointed back through the door-way at the computer screen. 'Barry, I don't ever want to see that word again.'

'Re-submit?' the man sighed. 'Know what you mean.'

'Well, fix it, will you?'

'What?'

'Programme something else in. I mean, you can do that, can't you?'

'Yes . . . Well, yes if you like.'

'I do like.' McRae walked slowly over to the coffee-machine in the corner. 'And, Barry?'

'Yes, Bob.'

'I want it to be something that reflects a sophisticated overview of life, okay? Touch of humour. Touch of irony.'

Barry was still standing by the machine when he got back. McRae sat at the console again, and tried another way into Packham Leisure.

And got, PILLOCK.

He looked up. 'Not what I meant, Barry.'

'No?'

'Not really.'

'Sorry about that.'

'Listen . . . Among your colleagues you have university men. You have first-rate intelligences. People who have a wealth of literary allusion at their fingertips.'

'You mean, you want me to see what they can come up with?'

'Oh, I do, Barry.'

Later that afternoon, as McRae worked on, he came to another dead end.

And on-screen came the words, I GROW WEARY, EARTHLING.

He smiled.

55

Cass left his office at seven-fifteen that evening. He walked down the stairs and saw one of the Serious Fraud clerks coming out through the security doors. The man nodded at him. And on an impulse, Cass caught the door before it closed, and went in.

And he was amazed. It was like a bunker at the end of a war. The blinds were drawn, and it was dim. Print-out paper spilled from baskets across the floor. The air was thick with smoke and exhaustion. And men were like ghosts as they crouched over machines.

'Where's McRae?' Cass asked.

Nobody answered, and he went through to the inner office.

From the doorway he saw McRae, slumped over his console, asleep. And, weirdly, on the screen above his head, was . . .

I DEMAND A HUMAN SACRIFICE.

Cass got the man back to his hotel room. He helped him on to the bed, pulled the curtains against the evening sunlight, and looked round.

And all hotel rooms were impersonal, he thought. But, for God's sake, McRae had been living in this one for weeks, and about the only belongings he had, apart from suits and shirts, were four bottles of whisky in the bottom of the wardrobe.

Two full, two empty.

'You'll have a drink?' McRae asked from the bed.

'Not really,' Cass said. 'I'm expected at home.'

'You can't refuse. It's the Macallan. And it's duty-free.'

The man got up slowly, painfully. He went to the bathroom. There was the sound of water as he washed out glasses. And Cass looked on round the hotel room, saw other personal touches.

Just two.

There were the silver-backed brushes on the dressing-table. And, by the bed, a silver-framed photo. It showed a small boy on a lawn, with a child-sized cricket bat and a tennis ball.

And there was a sadness about the picture, Cass thought. Not that it was intended. The photographer had only tried to include the large house in the background, and the large garden. But the boy was small and frowning. And the lawn huge.

But there was something familiar about the scene . . . Cass turned away . . *Familiar?* How could that be? None of them knew anything about McRae. Anything at all.

The man came back with the glasses. He got Cass to hand him a bottle of the Macallan, and he poured.

'Whoa,' Cass said. 'Whoa.'

McRae handed him a tumbler that was a quarter full, poured three-quarters for himself. And lay back on the bed again.

'Cheers,' he said.

'Cheers.'

Then there was silence. Just the shifting of curtains. And Cass looked at the man, the paleness of his face, the fatigue.

'You know, you ought to get out more.'

McRae nodded.

'I mean, I keep asking you back to our place. Supper or something. You never come.'

McRae nodded again.

'It'd only be family.'

'That's nice.'

Cass moved to a chair. He found he was close to the silver-framed photo. And once again he wondered what was familiar about it.

Until suddenly he remembered.

It was something Sergeant Roderick had said.

Or rather showed him.

The transcript of an interview. An early interview, weeks back in the investigation.

The man Denton, Assistant Finance Director at Lennox Freezers plc.

The moment Denton had broken under questioning.

And the words that had seemed strange on the typewritten page. '*You see, afterwards,*' McRae had said, '*afterwards it's just a sort of a house. And of course there are memories of that other house, the nice house. Summer, kids on a lawn, cricket with a soft ball . . . all poisoned.*

162

The way a house can be poisoned for a woman.'

Again Cass sipped at the malt whisky. He pointed to the photo. 'Your son?' he asked.

'Alexander, yes,' McRae said. 'Five years old now.'

'Where is he? Back home in Scotland?'

But McRae looked at him strangely. And it was a moment before he spoke. 'The Scots move away from their homeland, Batman,' he said then. 'And, obeying sound financial advice, they invest in English pubs . . . Or stand at road-crossings, holding on to the railings. They feel it is their duty, in case these railings fly up into the sky.'

'Yes,' Cass said.

'You see, we are a civic-minded people. We are articulate, careful of pronunciation and analysis . . . But our big talent lies in severing family relations.'

Silence. And it was a sudden movement as the man sat up and reached out for the Macallan. He refilled his glass, waved the bottle at Cass.

'No, thanks. I'm okay.'

'Oh, you're okay, Batman.' McRae put the bottle down by the silver-framed photo. 'And in answer to your awfully middle-class silence . . . Yes, I do see Alexander nowadays. On a regular basis. Sundays . . . I take him to the zoo. I take him to the museums. I take him out to tea.'

There was a long pause. McRae's breathing was slow, and Cass wondered if he should leave.

But then the man's voice came again from the shadows. 'Have you ever been on the proverbial dawn-raid, Batman?'

'The what?'

Cass was confused by the change of subject.

'The raid on the rich man's house in the dawn,' McRae said. 'Which is something the bastards who employ me consider necessary.'

'No,' Cass said, 'can't say I have.'

'Tell you how it goes,' The man's voice was soft. 'We get there at seven in the morning with our squads and our warrants and our information . . . And the husband's always at the breakfast-table in his pyjamas. The wife, she's crying. And she turns to the kids and she says. "Go out and play, darlings. Go out and play in the garden . . ." And the darlings, they do. They go out and play.'

Cass sat quite still. There was a voice a long way away, he knew, crying in the darkness.

But then the voice was louder. And the man's mind moved on suddenly in that strange way of his. 'Have you never thought?' he asked. 'I mean, when you walk around this prosperous city? When you go down to dockland and see the shiny new buildings, the shiny new yachts? The shiny people getting into their shiny cars? . . . Have you *never* thought? . . . The bastards are happy. They're well-off. They don't know what the hell's going on behind it all . . . So let it be.'

'No,' Cass said.

'Why?'

'Not after the things I see in court every day.'

And McRae crabbed to the edge of the bed, came close. 'I've said it before, Batman, and I'll say it again. You're a boring old fart.'

Alone, McRae drank more of the Macallan's and stared at the photo. The big house he'd had then. The big garden. Straight after university, that had been. When he'd been head-hunted by Rinalt International.

The cars, the plane tickets.

All the caper.

He looked at his son, at Alex. The face that seemed to be shorn off, bruised. Injured by big houses.

I do see Alexander on a regular basis, he'd told Cassidy. *Sundays I take him to the zoo.*

Except that recently those Sundays had stopped.

The boy's choice.

He stared more closely at the photo. And saw just the shadow of the woman. The fine, fine woman. Sensitive too. *No doubt* sensitive too.

While he had poured money and bile and more money at her from his mouth, his eyes.

Every available orifice.

And.

When it was all over, when even Rinalt was over, and Dergal Multinational, and Basel and Tokyo and where the *fuck*?

When he'd turned gamekeeper and taken the offer from Serious Fraud. Something entirely new, they'd said, where he could write his own programme, march to his own drum . . .

When it was all over.

She'd found, that fine woman, someone with sense.

An hour later he picked up the phone and dialled.

Cassidy's wife answered.

'Is Michael Cassidy there?' he asked.

'Who wants him, please?'

'Robert McRae.'

He heard the phone being put down on a table. Heard Cassidy's voice. Then a child's.

'No, daddy,' it said. 'That's her chair for the *sitting-room*. That's where the lady-dolly sits.'

Lady-dolly. The whisky rose in McRae's throat. He didn't know if he could handle stuff like this.

But then Cassidy came on the phone.

'Batman,' McRae said, 'I think an apology is in order.'

'What? Oh, that doesn't matter.'

'It does,' McRae said. 'You brought me home. I gave you crap.'

'You were tired,' Cass said.

'Yes, that's it.'

'And I didn't really want to leave you like that.'

Jesus, McRae thought. This had been one hell of a bad idea.

'Oh, yes, maybe a little tired,' he said. 'I've been too long at the numbers-machine.'

'Yes,' Cass said.

'Thing is, I've been chasing this ghost, this phantom company that doesn't exist.'

'Oh?'

'Goes under the name of Rubafiore,' McRae said.

And then the voice at the other end said something unbelievable.

'Anything to do with Rubafiore House?'

56

It was an old warehouse building that had once been converted into offices. Once. Now the windows were boarded up. The wide double-doors were barred. And the white paint that covered the brickwork was peeling away.

But still they could just make out the lettering across the front.

RUBAFIORE HOUSE.

McRae got out of the car. He turned to Cass. 'This came from *Roderick*?' he asked.

'Yes, in an interview with somebody called Jobelin.' Cass nodded. 'Small-time property crook we're investigating.'

'And how did *he* get to hear about it?'

'He wouldn't say.'

McRae looked at the building, the size of it. The five floors and the cellar, the nine large windows on each floor.

'Nothing small-time about this,' he said.

'No,' Cass agreed. 'But where does it get us?'

'Well, according to Barry, this place was bought by some mob called Viallonga Offshore.' McRae shrugged. 'And *they* seem to have a connection with the two companies we've looked at so far . . . Lennox Freezers plc and Packham Leisure.'

'But,' Cass turned quickly, 'isn't that the big one? The breakthrough?'

'Oh, it would be,' McRae said. 'Definitely would be, if we knew where to look next.'

'What?'

'Viallonga Offshore. They've ceased trading. Vanished completely.'

'Just like that?' Cass asked. 'Can't you trace them on down the line?'

'Not in the Cayman Islands.'

McRae turned away. He kicked at the kerb.

'But that's not the half of it,' he said savagely. 'I mean, a building like that . . . What, thirty-thousand square feet of office space?'

'About that.' Cass nodded.

'And situated, where are we? On the edge of dockland?'

'Yes?'

'Sold on 12 July last year,' McRae said, 'for a hundred and thirty-five grand.'

'I don't *believe* it. I mean, who'd sell at that price?'

'Who?' McRae nodded.

57

Miss Brinkwell wore a pale blue-and-white dress. It was almost like one she'd seen at Ascot, well, Ascot on television. And the way the chiffon scarf trailed from her hat, she'd borrowed that from Ascot too.

In fact, when she'd started out for the shops this morning, she'd felt on top of the world.

But somehow . . . somehow she seemed to have strayed from the main thoroughfare. She'd seen a rose in a garden she was sure was *Zephirine Drouhin*. And then found another garden, in another street, with the most heavenly scent of *Philadelphus*.

And now.

Now she was just beginning to panic.

She was in a street she'd never been in before. It had pollarded trees on one side, with Victorian villas behind them. And on the other, a long wire fence, with what she took to be the railway beyond.

It was hot. The sun seemed to make things black and spidery. The shadows of the trees struck her as rather sinister. And when she reached the end of the street, she found a bench and sat down.

Then she turned. There was a foot-bridge over the

railway, she saw. And a movement there caught her eye.

An old man was standing on the bridge. He wore the jacket and trousers of different suits, both of them old. And he had a black dog with him. A dog that sat quietly, waiting.

There was the sound of a train.

The old man became still, looking back down the line. And the dog pricked up its ears.

The train, a three-carriage local, clattered past Miss Brinkwell. And as it reached the bridge, the dog began barking and leaping around.

And the old man, stiff as a pike, shouted something strange.

'Fetch,' he shouted, pointing at the train. '*Fetch*!'

The train passed. Miss Brinkwell was a little uneasy as both man and dog came down from the bridge. Came by. But then, when they were almost past her, she called out.

'Oh, excuse me?'

The man stopped, turned.

And he *was* strange, Miss Brinkwell saw. The madness of lonely ones. The face he'd cut shaving, the hair he'd cut badly at home. The gauntness, and the eyes.

She fought down her feeling of panic. 'I'm sorry,' she said. 'I just wondered . . .'

'Madam?' The old man came back.

Miss Brinkwell moistened her lips. 'You'll think I'm rather foolish,' she said. 'But I've walked rather a long way today. And, well, the thing is, I appear to be lost.'

'Yes.' The old man beckoned to his dog. It came over. He bent down slowly and lifted the flap of one of its ears.

'This is the captain speaking,' he said. 'Dive, dive, dive.'

The dog lay down. And the old man straightened again, gave a little bow. 'Madam,' he said, 'allow the senior service to assist.'

She didn't know whether to laugh or cry. But she followed him, along a street at right-angles to the railway, along another to the left. Then they reached the sound of traffic, and stopped by a zebra crossing.

'There you are, Madam,' the old man said. 'Taxi-rank just to your right.'

'Thank you,' Miss Brinkwell said. 'Thank you very much indeed.'

'Steady as you go,' the man said. And, as Miss Brinkwell walked out over the crossing, he put his fingers to his mouth, and imitated a bosun's whistle.

But when she returned to the rest-home, the panic came back. She was standing in the gravelled drive. The taxi was waiting. She had her purse open in her hand.

And she'd *thought* . . .

She went up the whitewashed steps as quickly as possible, and through the stained-glass door. She stood in the hallway, her pulse beating.

But Marie was dusting the banisters. Marie, the new girl.

'My dear?' Miss Brinkwell called her over.

'Yes, Miss Brinkwell?'

'My dear, it's extremely tiresome,' Miss Brinkwell said. 'But I didn't manage to get to the bank.'

'What?'

'And the thing is, there's a taxi waiting outside.'

The girl turned, heard the car-engine through the open door.

'D'you think?' Miss Brinkwell asked. 'D'you think you could possibly find me two pounds out of the coffee-tin?'

'Well, I don't know,' Marie said. 'I mean, I . . .'

Miss Brinkwell clutched her arm. 'Don't worry,' she said. 'Just put in a little note.'

The girl nodded and went away to the kitchen.

58

Cass was lunching alone in the pizza house when McRae came in. There was still exhaustion on the man's face, but he'd forced himself past it. He paced up and down before sitting at the table. Then reached out absent-mindedly and took a slice of garlic bread.

'Look, d'you want the menu?' Cass asked.

'What?'

'D'you want to order? Food?'

'No, I've eaten.' McRae munched on.

Then, wiping his hands, he took some photocopies from his pocket and opened them out. 'Mrs Rubafiore,' he read. 'Mrs Marjorie Rubafiore.'

Cass waited.

'She sold that office building we were looking at. Apparently it was where her husband had his business head-office, when he was still alive.'

'A widow then,' Cass said.

'Yes, her last address was a rest-home, Denbigh Road, out in the suburbs.'

'Her *last* address?'

'She's dead too.'

Cass stiffened.

'Nothing sinister this time I'm afraid, Batman. It was old age, in both cases.'

'Oh.'

'Well, nothing sinister apart from the *date* of the good lady's death,' McRae went on, 'September last year.'

Cass stared at him. 'Two months after she'd sold Rubafiore House?'

'Oh, yes,' McRae said. 'Somebody got there just in time.'

He turned to another photocopied page. 'And she left just under two million quid in her will,' he said quietly.

Cass whistled.

'It was in the form of a trust-fund,' McRae went on, 'benefiting two nephews and their families. One in Ontario, the other in the States.'

'So she didn't have any children?'

'No.' McRae's eyes went on down the page. 'Oh, and there's a bequest of fifteen thousand a year . . . to a Miss Brinkwell, at the same address, in Denbigh Road . . . The rest-home.'

'Probably her companion,' Cass said.

'That's it.'

'Well, have you talked to her?'

'No-oh.'

There was a long pause.

Cass smelt danger.

'Tell me,' he said, 'why've you come here? Why couldn't all this wait?'

'Wanted to get you on your own, Batman,' McRae said, 'away from all those fart-arsing solicitors.'

'Why?'

The man didn't answer at once.

'This companion, this Miss Brinkwell,' he said then. 'She's seventy-three. Probably rambling. Probably turned to Christ . . . I mean, as far as my laddies are concerned, and the kind of questions they'll want to ask . . . Well, she's a non-starter, isn't she?'

Cass shrugged.

'But then,' McRae said, 'there's your man Jobelin.'

'What?'

'Jobelin, the man Roderick interviewed. The property crook.'

'Yes,' Cass said, 'I know.'

'I want you to offer him a deal.'

'*What?*'

'I mean, he's ready for it, isn't he? I read the transcript of the interview. He seemed to be coming on a bit at the end.'

Cass leaned back in his chair. 'Jobelin,' he said. 'Jobelin breaks into old ladies' flats. He empties dustbins all over them, smashes antiques.'

'Not proven.' McRae said.

Cass shook his head. 'I can't believe this,' he said. 'I mean, what d'you think Royston will have to say about it?'

'Oh, he'll hear,' McRae said. 'He'll hear in the end.'

59

Jobelin sat down in the interview-room. And it was as if he'd come to a business meeting. There was the ease that went with the good handstitched suit, the smooth untroubled face. And McRae knew what it meant. The man had decided to unburden himself, say so much and no more.

McRae waited. The constable waited with his shorthand pad. And Jobelin lit up, blew out smoke, put his match in the ashtray.

'What are we here to talk about?' he asked.

'Well, let's start with old ladies,' McRae said. 'Old ladies in old folks' homes.'

'I get it.' Jobelin nodded. 'The Mogadon Mansion racket.'

McRae felt cold. 'Tell me,' he said.

'Been going on for years in a quiet way.' The man shrugged, 'I mean, certain solicitors, they worry about crumblies. They worry about them dying without any kids to leave their money to.'

'In which case it goes to the Crown.'

'Oh, quite.' Jobelin smiled. 'But these solicitors aren't stupid. They get out their sealing wax. They get out their pink ribbon. They set up trust-funds for surviving relatives. *Years-worth* of legal fees, that can be . . . And have you ever tried to break a trust-fund? Actually get at the money?'

'No,' McRae said. 'No . . . But, let's get on to property, shall we? Old ladies and property?'

The man sat back in his chair. 'Well, that's the biggy,' he said. 'I mean, you can see it, can't you? Some of these crumblies, they sell up houses in London for, what, three hundred grand? They come here to the seaside and buy a flat for maybe eighty. And they sell *that* when they move into a home . . . I mean, you go up the chain, and you come down.'

And, put like that, McRae thought, it made a godawful kind of sense. 'All right,' he said, 'there's money lying around.'

Jobelin nodded again. 'And certain people have access to it. So what they do is they smile at the old dears. They tell them they'll invest it and get interest at building society rates. And they *pay* these rates . . . Only the money goes into a pool, three counties wide, buying investment properties. Where the profits are *horrible*.'

The coldness grew in McRae. He got up. He paced away and came back. 'Are we still talking about solicitors?' he asked.

'Among others.'

'Who are these others?'

And the quiet voice went on.

'What you've got to understand is that there's a ring,' Jobelin said, 'a group of people who meet up . . . Solicitors, estate agents, valuers, developers.'

McRae leaned over the table.

'They get together when any property's coming up. They fix a price. Make sure it never reaches the open market.'

'And how often do they do this?' McRae asked.

'What?'

'Meet up?'

'Once a month is normal,' Jobelin said. 'But sometimes there's hurry. If some old crumbly's about to die.'

60

The clock in the rest-home said half-past three. Marie put on her white overall and pushed the tea-trolley through to the drawing-room. She left it on one side, and then went round to the old people in their chairs, setting up their trays.

Miss Brinkwell she put off till last. Miss Brinkwell was always going on about some old loony in that family of hers.

On and on.

'*Disastrous* marriage, of course,' she said now.

'Yes,' Marie said.

'You see, he could look very attractive in summer, providing he didn't wear a Norfolk jacket. He had these very short legs.'

'Yes.'

'And of course he had a great many *affaires*.'

Marie nodded.

'While she was very different. The sort of person who never cleaned the house at all . . . Which was the start of the trouble, really.'

'Oh?' Marie asked tiredly. 'Why was that?'

'Well, one morning,' Miss Brinkwell said, 'she was looking under the bed for her shoes, and she found a plate of cucumber sandwiches.'

'I see,' Marie said. She didn't see at all.

'And then she suddenly remembered . . . Nobody in the family actually *liked* cucumber sandwiches.'

Marie still didn't see.

'I must say,' Miss Brinkwell went on, 'the amount of deceit in that family used to delight us as children.'

61

By the time he'd finished with Jobelin, McRae had names.

A firm of solicitors practising in this city. And the name of the senior partner.

Ben Napier.

He went up the stairs two at a time, and on through to Cassidy's office. He needed a quiet word.

But there was one word that lifted his head in shock.

'Disappeared?' he asked. '*Disappeared*?'

'Well, nobody's said that exactly,' Cass told him. 'All I heard was he'd run off with this woman a few weeks back, and . . .'

But McRae was already out of the door.

It took him half an hour on the phone. And then he had the file in his hand.

Another file from Missing Persons.

He opened it. The date of disappearance was the same, of course. The same as the others.

For Jesus' sake, *when* were they going to get this thing together?

He turned, looked at the wall where Barry had built up his map. And the photos underneath.

Gotto, Finance Director.

Who had to be at the centre of things. The carve-up of Lennox Freezers plc. And the dollar pipeline, the money coming in from Switzerland.

Which funded firstly the sweeteners for other Lennox directors.

And secondly the bigtime, buying up half those white flags Barry had stuck on the map.

Gotto, dead now. Had to be. His job over.

And the next photo.

Karen Seymour.

Dead too. She'd been bringing in anything up to $200 000 a trip. And maybe she'd found out about that. Got her knees under the table. Started up a little poker game of her own.

And now . . .

McRae turned the pages of the file, found Ben Napier's picture. He was like an actor in a TV commercial, he thought. One of those retirement commercials for old folk. Where you picked up goodies like cocktail-cabinets and barbecues, and those sodding small Volvos that blocked up the road.

But, all the same, a reassuring face, calm. The white hair. The soft plumpish body. The old-fashioned check suit.

Come on man, McRae told himself. This was the laddie who was siphoning thousands into a three-county wide fund.

But, thousands?

And three *counties* wide?

Maybe he wasn't up to the bigtime, the millions, and the European take-overs.

Or maybe . . .

McRae looked at the photo again.

Maybe at the end, this one had scruples.

For a long time he sat there thinking. Then he picked up the phone again.

'Batman?'

At the other end Cassidy sighed.

'Just thought I'd let you know I'm getting a warrant down from head office. And a squad.'

'But, why? Why not locally?'

'I want to move in on Napier's tonight. Seven o'clock.'

'I don't get it. What's the hurry?'

'Well, first,' McRae said, 'I want to take away a truck-load of files. And second . . . Has it struck you how somebody's always ahead of us? How they've always got the news?'

'You're tired,' Cassidy said. 'Obsessed.'

'Maybe.'

'Well, what are the charges?'

'Conspiracy to defraud.'

'All right, it's a catch-all,' Cassidy said. 'But have you got enough to go on?'

'I've got what Jobelin told me.'

There was a pause.

'And, for Christ's sake,' McRae went on, 'I've got three people who disappeared on the same *date*.'

There was a longer pause.

'Doesn't sound enough,' Cassidy said. 'Not for down here. Not for Royston.'

'You think I don't *know*?' McRae slammed down the phone.

He went to the window then, and looked out. At the people leaving their offices, crossing the triangle of grass, waiting in bus-queues.

And the old brick gates of dockland beyond.

Then he heard movement behind him. Barry had come into the room, was doing his old woman act.

McRae turned. He saw the man had a drawing-pin in his hand, was pinning up Napier's photo next to the other two.

'Barry, what the hell d'you think this is?' McRae asked. 'A pop-up bloody Christmas card?'

62

There were still lights on in reception at Napier, Selborne and Grateley. And behind the long mahogany counter, the girl at the switchboard was talking.

'No, *he* wants me to stay late, of course,' she said into the mouthpiece. '*He's* got these letters that he wants to catch the eight o'clock post.'

Then she turned. A man was coming in through the glass door, a tall man, in a dark suit.

'Put the phone down,' he said.

'What?'

He reached past her, pulled out the plug.

'That's nice.'

He showed her a warrant card. 'Don't answer any more calls. You understand that?'

She was frightened. Even more frightened as the four other men in suits came in.

'You two, the back door. You two, the fire-escape,' the tall man said.

They went away. He turned back. 'Who's still here?' he asked. 'In the building?'

It took her a moment to say it, 'Well, there's Mr Grateley . . . And the two other partners.'

The man went away to the window. He knocked on it with his knuckles, beckoned to someone outside. Then he came back to the girl.

'Take me to Grateley's office.'

She led the way, along the hall, up the creaking stairs, then along a narrow passage to a door.

'Stand back,' he said.

He burst the door open, and she saw Mr Grateley, small, grey-haired, his mouth open.

'What? . . . What's going on?'

The tall man showed him the warrant-card, then some documents.

'But,' Mr Grateley said, 'this is ridiculous. I'm going out to dinner in half an hour.'

'Dinner's gone out of the window, sunshine.'

Cass was at home. He was sitting at the dining-room table, working on Alison's doll's house.

And she was watching carefully as he drew a small oblong on a piece of card, then rounded off the corners. And then drew in shading so that the flat cardboard surface appeared convex.

He cut it out, and stuck it on to the small TV set he'd made. And, he thought, it looked just like a screen.

'It's great, daddy,' Alison said. 'Really great.'

Cass caught the tone in her voice. 'But,' he said.

'But it won't fit on the dolly's sideboard, it's too big. And it can't just be on the floor.'

Cass nodded slowly. 'So it needs legs. Is that what you mean?'

'Yes,' she said.

He glanced at his watch. By now, he thought, McRae's London mob would have hit Napier, Selborne and Grateley.

But Alison was tugging at his sleeve. 'Come on.' She held out a piece of balsa wood. 'This is the bit you use for legs, isn't it?'

'Yes,' Cass said.

He picked up the modelling knife and started cutting. Alison watched him for a moment. But then she turned away, sat her Sergeant Roderick dolly down in front of the TV.

'Daddy,' she asked, 'do policemen watch television?'

'Yes,' he said idly.

'A lot?'

'Oh, yes,' he said, 'it's essential.'

She watched him make the second cut with the knife.

'Why is it . . . essential?'

'What?'

'For policemen to watch?'

'They have to know what's in fashion,' Cass said. 'Have to know what kind of haircut to get, what kind of shirt.'

Alison frowned.

'And they have to get the acting bit right as well,' Cass

178

told her. 'I mean, on TV there's always a very rude policeman, isn't there? In a smart suit?'

She stared at him. 'You're making a funny.'

'No, I'm serious,' he said. 'Sometime somebody's going to have to write a thesis . . . on the harmful effects of television on policemen.'

63

It was nine in the morning, though in the church hall it still seemed like night. There was a haze of tobacco-smoke under the ceiling, stretching all the way to the stage at the far end. And, across the wide floor, trestle tables had been set up, three long lines of them. There were men, tired men, sorting through papers. It was like a re-count on election day.

Except that it wasn't ballot-papers or ballot-boxes. Over by the wall, policemen were wheeling in filing-cabinets. Secretaries were opening them and carrying armfuls of files to the men at the tables. And there were other men too, three of them, sitting alone at the end of the production-line. They had calculators ready, different coloured pens . . . and sections of computer print-out to refer to.

But, for the past twelve hours, they'd had nothing to do.

McRae walked past them. He came to where Barry was standing. 'Not a *single* file with old Ben Napier's name on it?'

Barry shook his head.

'And where've you got to now?'

'Back to 1987.'

'So they've been at the shredder.'

'They have,' Barry said.

McRae paced away, came back.

'We've had one phonecall already this morning,' Barry told him softly.

'Who from?'

'Area Chief Prosecutor Royston.'

'*Before* nine o'clock?'

'Yes,' Barry said.

'Plays golf with a certain firm of solicitors, does he?' McRae said. 'Or is it the rolled-up trouser leg?'

'More than likely.'

'Well, if he rings again, I'm not here.'

'I know that, Bob.'

'No, I mean it,' McRae said. 'I'm away.'

He went into Cassidy's office, head down, suit flapping.

'Batman, are you in court this morning?'

'No, not as it happens.'

'Well, are you busy?'

'*Busy*?' Cass showed the papers on his desk.

'So you won't come out? A quick blast in the Batmobile?'

'What?'

Cass looked up. He saw what he took to be bright points of sunlight on McRae's face. But then he realised they were white areas of skin, where the strain was, around the eyes and the mouth. The man looked about forty-five.

'Just half an hour,' McRae said.

They drove through the city and came to wide suburban avenues.

And parked finally outside a certain rest-home.

McRae pointed at the large Victorian house, its lawns. 'The answer has to be in there, Batman,' he said.

Cass nodded.

'And we have to get it now.'

Cass blinked. 'You mean, you want *me* to talk to Miss Brinkwell?'

'Well, I can't do it,' McRae said. 'She's an old lady. And she's *really* going to be impressed by some long-haired git from Glasgow, isn't she? Who hasn't slept in a week?'

Cass couldn't believe it.

'So what about the obvious way?' he asked. 'Calling her into the station?'

'She's seventy-three.'

'All right, why not get Roderick to interview her? With a policewoman?'

'And scare her to death?'

McRae sighed. It was a thin strange sound. And then something even stranger happened. He reached out and touched Cass' shoulder. For the first time.

'Maybe I should finish with the jokes,' he said. 'Stop all this Batman business.'

'It'd be an idea,' Cass said.

There was a long pause. An embarrassing silence.

And to his surprise Cass saw the man was searching for words. Suddenly he realised McRae was going to open up a crack in himself.

'Listen . . . how d'you think I got into this little caper?'

'I don't know,' Cass said. 'University. Business Studies degree, maybe Law.'

'Ye-es.' The man hesitated. 'But there was a little time left after that. I did Medieval History as well.'

Cass was impressed.

'I'm not boasting,' McRae said quickly. 'All I'm saying is, that afterwards, there was a queue of companies offering jobs.'

Cass nodded.

'So I did the company bit. Got screwed up, got my head wrong. But then . . .' McRae shrugged. 'There was this other guy in a suit.'

'From Serious Fraud?'

McRae turned away. 'I reckoned it was worth a try. Reckoned I could put myself right with God, and Walt Disney, and Julie Andrews.'

Cass was smiling.

But McRae wasn't. He turned back. 'About Serious Fraud,' he said, 'you've got to understand *I* joined *them*. On condition that I got my own cheque-book, wrote my own time-sheets . . .'

He moved then, pointing past Cass towards the rest-home. 'What I'm saying is, if you go in there . . . just for a chat, a preliminary chat about an *extremely* sensitive area . . .'

Cass was stunned. 'You mean, it won't go down in the books?'

McRae sat back. He waved a hand tiredly. 'Okay, you're going to give me the ethical routine again. Just like last time.'

Suddenly Cass remembered the last time, standing in the street outside the small hotel.

And the girl in the hotel bedroom. Vicky, turning towards him. 'Ohhh . . .'

And he remembered something else too. The transcript of that last interview with Jobelin.

I get it. The Mogadon Mansion racket.

He turned and looked at McRae. The pale white face, the tension. The certainty there.

And it was insane, he knew. Totally insane.

But he got out of the car.

64

Cass stood in the hallway, just inside the stained-glass door. And he liked what was around him. The good Axminster carpet, the wide stairs, the smell of furniture polish. And the smell of roast beef coming from the kitchen.

Then the girl in the white overall came back. There was an older woman with her who was obviously matron. She was in her fifties, dressed in good county clothes. But her voice was clipped. And she had that severity of someone who had to distance herself from people. Who saw them die.

'Mr Cassidy,' she said, 'I understand that you're a solicitor.'

'Yes, that's right.'

'I hope you don't mind my asking.' She lowered her voice. 'But, have you come to see Miss Brinkwell about her trust-fund?'

'Well, no.' He frowned. 'No, I'm afraid not.'

'Oh.' She was disappointed. 'It's just that we were rather expecting someone.'

Cass didn't understand. He didn't understand what he was doing here, anything. He just followed the girl across the hall, and into a large sunlit drawing-room.

The television was on softly. Three elderly residents were sitting around it, watching an old Ronald Colman movie. But Cass was led to a chair some distance away, where an old lady sat reading the local paper.

'Miss Brinkwell,' the girl said, 'you have a visitor.'

She looked up. And Cass was held by the glitter of her eyes, the sudden interest. She sat upright, unlike the others around the television. And there was a quickness about her, a certain craziness of colour, a jangle of bracelets.

He sat down and introduced himself. He didn't say anything about the Crown Prosecution Service, just that he worked for the government.

'Sounds rather boring,' Miss Brinkwell said.

'Well, it is, rather,' he admitted. 'But, you see, in our office we deal with records. Check them over when the lawyers have finished with them ... It's really a tiny matter. Nothing to worry about.'

'When anybody says that to me, Mr Cassidy, I immediately start worrying.'

For a moment he was thrown. But he managed to smooth it over, say how nice the home was, and how well-run it seemed.

'Full of old trouts,' she said. 'All they do is watch television all day.'

'Well, yes,' he said, 'I suppose so.'

'As for me, I find it very important not to weaken,' she went on. 'And my defence against it is reading.'

As he watched, she produced a small leather-spined book from her chair, and held it out. 'Most enjoyable,' she said. 'But so much more enjoyable when one is read to.'

He blinked.

'Will you read to me, Mr Cassidy?'

'What?'

He took the book from her, saw it was the Folio edition of John Donne's *Poems of Love*.

'The place is marked,' she said.

Cass looked at the words. And, for the second time, was thrown.

'Go on.'

He cleared his throat, read softly . . .

'Off with that girdle, like heavens Zone glittering
But a far fairer world incompassing.
Unpin that spangled breastplate which you wear . . .'

'Louder,' she said.

And, sweating, he read on . . .

'By this these Angels from an evil sprite,
Those set our hairs, but these our flesh upright.
Licence my roving hands, and let them go,
Before, behind, between, above, below.'

Miss Brinkwell shook her head slowly, sighed.

'You read very well, Mr Cassidy.'

'Thank you.'

'Although, as a civil servant, I don't expect you understand.'

'No.' With relief he closed the book.

But she was leaning forward suddenly. There was that glitter in her eyes again, the smell of liquorice on her breath.

'You know,' she said, 'when I was a young girl, it was considered disgraceful for a young lady to admit to any kind of satisfaction.'

His mouth dropped open.

'But I'm happy to tell you,' she smiled, 'that I disgraced myself in shrubberies and conservatories throughout the south of England.'

She hadn't lowered her voice, and Cass spun round. But none of the other residents had heard. They were still watching Ronald Colman, smoothly acting on TV.

It took a moment for him to collect himself. And even longer before he could get the conversation back on track.

'Miss Brinkwell,' he said, 'I understand that you were once the companion of a Mrs Rubafiore. A lady who lived here until she . . . passed away.'

'Marjorie, yes.' Miss Brinkwell was cooler suddenly. She folded her arms.

'And I understand too . . . I mean from my records,' Cass tried to make it light, 'that there was a certain property called Rubafiore House.'

She looked at him steadily. 'I remember it,' she said.

'Can you remember anything else?'

She frowned. 'Only that it belonged to Marjorie's husband. It was the first large business premises he bought. That's why he put his name on it.'

'Yes,' Cass said.

Her head darted to one side. 'Yes, but what?'

And he knew he had to come out with it. 'Look, I know it's difficult for your generation to appreciate the value of things nowadays . . . But, well, the selling price of Rubafiore House was extremely low. Extremely . . . A hundred and thirty-five thousand? . . . It should have sold for twice as much.'

Suddenly her eyes changed. The glitter there became hard, shrewd. 'I know who you are,' she said.

'What?' Cass was startled.

'Marjorie always warned me against talking to people like you . . . You're from the income-tax.'

And she started to get up.

'No,' Cass said, 'Miss Brinkwell, I can assure you . . .'

But she was on her feet. 'Please, not another word. I won't have anything more to do with it.'

And she walked quickly, jerkily, towards the door.

He followed her through to the hall. Matron was there, and the young girl in the overall.

Miss Brinkwell stomped past them. She went angrily up the stairs and disappeared.

Cass went across to matron. 'I'm sorry,' he said, 'I don't know what I said to upset her.'

Outside in the car, McRae let his head fall back against the head-rest.

'So it's no go,' he said. 'That's definite?'

'Yes,' Cass said, 'I'm sorry to say.'

'You're sorry?' McRae turned to him. 'While you were in there I went up to the call-box, phoned Barry.'

'At the church hall?'

McRae nodded. 'Napier, Selborne and Grateley have come out clean as a whistle,' he said quietly. 'We're in what you might call trouble.'

65

The garden of the Cassidy's house faced westwards. And in the last of the evening sun, Sonia sat talking to Phil Benson. They both had gin and tonics. And on the grass between them was a bottle-shaped parcel, tied with ribbon.

'But you shouldn't have come round just for that, Phil,' Sonia said. 'We could've picked it up next week.'

'Fine,' he said. 'Except there won't be a next week. Not our little dinner party, anyway.'

'Oh?'

'Have to be a fortnight's time.'

And then Sonia understood. 'Oh, yes, I forgot,' she said. 'It's the big move, isn't it? The new house?'

'It is.' Phil nodded. 'All going very smoothly at the moment.'

'Well, that can't last, can it? Marianne'll be tearing her hair out before long. All those tea-chests? All that dust?'

'Not really,' Phil said.

'What?'

'That woman'll break me in the end.' He sighed. 'She's getting all the packing done by professionals. And *before* that she's getting new carpets down . . . curtains . . .'

Sonia frowned. 'But, can you afford it?' she asked. 'All that?'

'I try to keep her happy,' Phil said. 'You know Marianne.'

'Oh, I do.'

Phil grinned. He shook the ice-cubes in his glass, drank.

And then they both heard it, the sound of a car parking in the drive.

'That the guv'nor?' Phil looked up.

And a moment later Cass came walking round the side of the house. He seemed hot, tired.

'Cheer up,' Sonia called out to him. 'We've got a visitor.'

'So I see.'

'You don't look very pleased about it,' Phil said.

'Oh, sorry . . . Sorry, Phil.'

'And he's brought you a present too,' Sonia said, 'from when he was on holiday in Spain.'

Phil reached out for the wrapped bottle and handed it over. 'Forgot it the other night,' he said. 'Can't think why.'

Cass removed the paper, saw the label on the wine. 'Gran Riserva '76.' He whistled. 'That's kind of you, Phil. Really kind.'

And he sat down cross-legged on the grass. 'Matter of fact, I could knock it back now. I need some good news.'

'Bad day?' Sonia asked.

'My God, yes.'

But there was a smile widening across Phil's face. 'I suppose it's got nothing to do . . . with a little whisper I heard over lunch?'

'I expect so,' Cass said.

Phil turned to Sonia. 'Serious Fraud raided Napier, Selborne and Grateley. Took every damn file out of the place . . . Everybody's talking about it.'

'No comment,' Cass said. And he looked at Sonia too, in warning.

She stood up. 'I get it, the stiff upper-lip, the Empire.' She saluted. 'How would it be if I got b'wana his evening gin?'

'Be very nice,' Cass said. 'Thanks.'

She went into the house. Then suddenly reappeared.

'Oh, I forgot,' she said. 'Somebody rang.'

'Who?' Cass sighed. 'Not Royston?'

'No,' she said, 'a lady.'

'What?' He looked up.

'An old flame.' Smiling, she came towards him. 'And she wants to see you now, as it happens. Said it was urgent.'

He was lost.

She knelt down in front of him, ruffled his hair. 'How come you never read *me* poetry?'

He stared at her. Then he got to his feet, picked up his briefcase.

'I don't get it.' Phil looked at them both.

'Sorry, Phil. Got to rush.'

And Cass was away, running round the side of the house. They heard the car start up again.

Phil turned to Sonia. He grinned. 'What *is* all this?'

66

The girl in the white overall let Cass in. He saw that Miss Brinkwell was waiting for him on the stairs. She was excited, beckoning him up.

'Such a charming woman, your wife,' she said. 'So helpful.'

'But, how did you get on to her?' Cass didn't understand.

'Well, I couldn't see your name among the *solicitors*,' Miss Brinkwell said. 'So I tried every M. Cassidy in the book. I remembered you said your name was Michael.'

'Yes,' Cass said.

He was now level with her at the turn of the stairs. She led the way upwards, panting.

'You see, the point is, after you left, I was in rather a tizzy. And I had the local paper in my room, so I read it to calm myself down . . . the advertisements. I never read them as a rule.'

They reached the landing. And she paused for breath.

'The advertisements for houses,' she went on. 'And, I mean, it was such a shock. You can't even buy a decent *bungalow* for a hundred and thirty-five thousand.'

Cass looked at her. He was beginning to understand.

'And when I thought of that big office building going for that price . . . Not to mention those other properties . . .'

'*Other* properties?'

He followed her into her room.

He sat her down, and gradually she calmed.

'Tell me,' he said.

She patted at her hair. 'Well, Mr Rubafiore . . . Marjorie's husband . . . was in the garment trade.'

'Yes, I know.'

'Very wealthy man,' she went on. 'Totally crooked, of course. Which was why he needed a crooked solicitor.'

'What?'

'A Mr Ben Napier.'

And, Cass thought, it was all beginning to fit in.

But Miss Brinkwell continued. 'And Mr Napier, of course, he remained Marjorie's solicitor after she was widowed . . . It seemed only sensible to have him on our side.'

'What d'you mean?' Cass asked. 'Your side?'

She shrugged. 'Well, you see, Marjorie was in the habit of asking my advice. I mean, each time she sold off one of those properties.'

He nodded.

'And it seemed all right to me.' She was confused again, upset. 'They all seemed such *huge* amounts.'

Cass sat back. He looked round at the small room, at the old photographs, and the few pieces of furniture Miss Brinkwell possessed . . . two chairs, a bookcase, a small Georgian writing-box on a desk.

And he sighed, knowing it was a useless question. 'There wouldn't be,' he asked, 'any documentary proof of all this?'

Miss Brinkwell got up. She put her fingers to her lips. Then she went to the writing-box and opened it. Her fingers found a small brass lug inside, just by the lock. She moved it. A section of the veneered front slid forwards. A hidden drawer.

And inside it was an old creased file, tied with ribbon.

Cass sat on the bed, surrounded by documents. He read through the last of them, then looked up.

'You haven't shown these to anyone?'

189

'No,' Miss Brinkwell said. 'Never.'

'Well, you mustn't. It's very important.'

She looked pleased.

'Except to me, of course, and certain colleagues in my department.' Cass began collecting the papers. 'Can I take them away?'

There was a strange silence.

'No,' she said then.

'What?'

Miss Brinkwell fussed at her collar, her sleeves. 'Marjorie entrusted them to me. She put them in my hands.'

'I don't understand. You went to all that trouble to phone me. And now . . .'

But Miss Brinkwell was smiling. There was that glitter in her eyes again. That excitement.

'When I spoke to your wife,' she leaned forward, 'she said you were a Crown Prosecutor . . . a Senior Crown Prosecutor.'

'Yes?' He frowned.

'Well, I suppose that must mean you have certain powers.'

'Powers?'

She nodded, and then went on in a rush. 'Mr Cassidy, if I had these documents with me, would you . . . send a *police* car? I mean, *drive* me to the police station?'

Cass was amazed.

'Yes,' he said. 'Yes, I suppose it could be arranged . . . But, when? Tomorrow?'

She shook her head. 'It's been rather an exciting day,' she said. 'I'll need to rest. Get my hair done.'

'All right,' he said, 'what about the day after tomorrow? Friday?'

'Friday would be convenient,' she said. And then, leaning closer, 'Would there be . . . lunch?'

'Oh, I think we could arrange that,' Cassidy said.

It was late, but McRae was still in his office. And the man's face was very pale as he listened.

'You're quite sure about all this?' he asked finally.

190

'Positive.'

'Well, what did you see? Company names? Was there one called Viallonga, for instance?'

'Yes, that was there.'

'Any others?'

Cass closed his eyes, thought. 'One called Trötzen Gmbh,' he said. 'Another called Polstran.'

McRae moved quickly away to his desk. He checked through some print-out paper, nodded.

'What about directors' signatures?'

Cass could remember three.

They were all there.

And in the light from the desk, McRae's eyes seemed to be bulging. He seemed to be holding his breath.

67

At ten o'clock on the Friday morning Cass got into a police car with Roderick. They drove out to the rest-home, and parked in the drive.

The girl in the white overall came to the door.

'I'm here to fetch Miss Brinkwell,' Cass said.

'Oh, no,' she said, 'that's impossible. She's moved away.'

'Moved *away*?'

He was in a daze as he sat in matron's office. But then anger took hold of him as he watched that face of hers, that thin severe face, trying to explain.

'It came yesterday morning,' she said.

'What did?'

'The letter. The letter I was telling you about.'

'Tell me again.'

And she flinched at the sharpness of his voice. 'It was . . . It was about Miss Brinkwell's trust-fund.'

Trust-fund.

He remembered what matron had said when they'd first met. *I understand that you're a solicitor . . . have you come to see Miss Brinkwell about her trust-fund?*

And that interview with Jobelin.

... these solicitors aren't stupid. They get out their pink ribbon they set up trust-funds ... have you ever tried to break one of those?

He tried to make himself calm, calm.

'All right, there was a fund, wasn't there?' he asked. 'An annuity in Miss Brinkwell's favour?'

'That's right.'

'And, as far as I can remember, there were two other people named in the will. Nephews, weren't they? Living in Canada and the States?'

'Yes,' she said, 'they were the trustees. That was the whole trouble.'

'Trouble?'

'You must realise,' her voice shook slightly, 'we've been trying to get a decision out of them for some time now. About releasing more money.'

He didn't understand. He waited. And then he saw her hands were trembling, as they moved papers around her desk. 'It's distressing when residents leave here suddenly,' she said. 'Always distressing.'

'*Always?*' His head came up at that. 'You mean, it's happened before?'

'Oh, yes.' There was a strange attempt at gentility, a ghastly shrug. 'You see, this home is in what you might call the ... upper price bracket ... And, well, inflation ...'

He began to see. 'Miss Brinkwell's annuity,' he said then, 'was, what, fifteen thousand a year?'

She nodded. 'And at the time it was adequate. More than adequate.'

'When are we talking about?'

'Well, the terms were agreed by Mrs Rubafiore about two years before her death.'

'And the fees here are what?' Cass asked. 'Now, I mean?'

She lowered her voice. 'About three hundred pounds a week. Or, as you can see, just over fifteen thousand ... But that's not the point.'

'What is?'

And again she shrugged, helplessly. 'Miss Brinkwell

spent money like water. She was always buying new clothes. Always travelling by taxi . . . and, as often as not, getting one of the staff here to charge it to her bill . . . I mean, I *told* her, again and again.'

Cass was silent a moment. 'How long has this been going on?'

'For more than a year.' She sighed. 'But, of course we've kept her on. Of course we've allowed her to pay considerably less than she should . . . Because at the same time, you see, we've been trying to contact these two trustees, these nephews.'

She leaned towards him. 'And it all seemed so hopeful. Letters have come across the Atlantic to say that extra funds would be released.' She dropped her head suddenly. 'Until yesterday, that was. This letter from her solicitor. Like a bolt from the blue . . . Other arrangements had been made for Miss Brinkwell . . . So businesslike, so brutal. I mean, I . . .'

And she was crying, Cass saw.

He got up.

'I'm sorry,' she said from her handkerchief. 'Truly sorry.'

He went over to her, made his voice as gentle as he could. 'Have you got this letter?'

She blew her nose, searched through her desk.

Cass took the envelope, opened it.

The first thing he saw was the heading, Napier, Selborne and Grateley.

And then the signature.

Benjamin Napier.

68

There were three of them in the office . . . Cass, Roderick, McRae. And McRae was angry.

'But, how the hell?' he asked. 'How the hell did they get *away* with it?'

'Well, it appears the notepaper was stolen, Sir, from the solicitors' office,' Roderick said. 'And Handwriting have confirmed that the signature wasn't Napier's.'

McRae swung round. He looked at the three photos under the wall-map. He nodded.

Then he turned back to Cass. 'All right, the letter arrived yesterday morning, saying arrangements had been made.'

'Immediate arrangements,' Cass said, 'by Miss Brink-well's own solicitor.'

'And, yesterday afternoon we're told, a married couple arrived in a taxi. Not exactly a *prepossessing* couple.'

'The matron's own words, Sir,' Roderick said.

'Yet they claim to be running a smaller rest-home, a cheaper rest-home, along the coast,' McRae went on. 'They spirit Miss Brinkwell away, leaving her furniture behind . . . And the papers *you* saw, Cassidy, are suddenly missing.'

'Yes.'

'So how did they move so *fast*?'

Cass sat down. 'I'm not sure,' he said. 'Except that the whole world seems to know we raided Napier, Selborne and Grateley.'

McRae nodded.

'And half the world knows we didn't find what we were looking for,' Cass went on, 'because we said sorry, and took everything back.'

There was silence.

Then McRae looked up. 'And then, on the same day, we called on Mrs Rubafiore's companion,' he said slowly. 'Twice.'

Cass didn't answer.

'So, what happens now?'

'I don't know.'

'Well, maybe you'd better grease up the bat-pole, Bat-man.' The sneer came back into McRae's voice. 'Because the name of this smaller rest-home, this cheaper rest-home, doesn't appear to be *listed*.'

69

A day went by. Two days . . . three . . .

Then a week.

Cass didn't know how he got through it. He was useless in court, worse than useless, and he began handing most of his cases over to Sam.

And, whenever he could, whenever he was near a phone, he rang Roderick.

But Roderick was out, with the CID. There was a three-area fill-in, men from as far as Reading and Guildford. Uniformed and plain-clothes.

It was big. McRae had swung that. They'd covered the small rest-homes right along the coast. They'd covered the larger ones. They'd started inland.

There'd been the posters with Miss Brinkwell's photo on them. The radio news-bulletins.

Nothing had turned up.

And at the end of the week, on Friday afternoon, Cass took a leaf out of McRae's book. He went walkabout.

He left the office, got into his car, and drove out of the city. He took the road that led up on to the downs, the highest of them, Fernden Head. And, in the same car-park where he'd stood with Phil that evening, the car-park of the Old Vine, he looked back down towards the sea.

It was five in the afternoon, not dark like the last time he'd been here. There were no lights . . . The motorway was a screaming grey corridor, going from east to west. And beyond it, grey again, street after street after street.

People still talked about towns, Cass knew, towns and villages along the coast. But they were all one. With a population of more than a million.

And, as for the rest-homes, Roderick had given him the numbers there. Fifteen hundred registered homes, he'd said. And at least as many unregistered.

Cass was counting on these last. Counting on the fact that a *couple*, a man and wife, had taken Miss Brinkwell away. In only very rare cases did a man and wife . . . he could hardly frame the word . . . kill.

But then there was one last item. Roderick had had a name for the unregistered homes.

He'd called them hell-holes.

70

The front room was small. There were large electric-blue whorls on the carpet, large red and gold squares on the wallpaper. Everything shrieked.

And the television, the huge television, shrieked. Shrieked a chicken-like quiz-game. Where a bantam-like man strutted, with cards in his hand.

'No, Willie Wonker,' he shouted. '*Wonker!*'

Shrieks from the audience. Shrieks.

The door of the front room opened. A woman came in. She wore a bright mauve housecoat. She was overweight, her skin like lard, her hair greased. But what was truly terrible about her was her warm homely smile.

She went up to Miss Brinkwell.

'Your pills, Evelyn . . .'

And Miss Brinkwell, gaunt, scooped-out by fatigue, trembled in her chair.

'I've asked you before,' she said. 'Please don't call me that. It's my given name.'

'Oh, we're all Evelyn here . . .' The woman pointed to the four other people in chairs. Old, rag-haired people, huddled like sacks. ' . . . And Hubert . . . And Beryl . . .'

She offered the pill-bottle, saw Miss Brinkwell refuse. 'Well, suit yourself.'

Shaking her head, the woman left the room. She walked down a narrow hard-boarded passage to the kitchen. There was the blue smoke of chip-fat. And, over the deep-fry, stood a small balding man, with a perfectly round head.

'She take them, Edie?' he asked.

'No.'

Edie leaned past him. She opened a cupboard, put the pills inside. And took out a larger bottle, of liquid.

She unscrewed its cap, poured a little into a teacup. Then she flopped a tea-bag on top. 'Only work herself up,' she said.

'She will if she sees her picture on the telly,' Albert said.

'No, they're not showing it any more.' Edie boiled a kettle.

'You sure?'

'Course.' Edie yawned.

The television quiz-game shrieked on. Miss Brinkwell sat in her chair. She was through to the bone. The veins on her face had gathered in dark spider-patches. And she knew she was doped.

But she fought back. Fought. There was a Harrods shopping-bag on her lap, and from it she took a small leather-spined book. Her hands shook as she found the page. Her voice was croaky and small.

'Yet nothing can to nothing fall,
Nor any place be empty quite . . .

The television beat her back. The mouth of that bantam-like man, beak-like, cruel as he laughed.

'And now as broken glasses show
A hundred lesser faces, so
My ragges of heart . . .'

But it was useless. The dark spider-veins took over. Her eyes closed.

71

Another week went by.

Another *week*.

It was night. Cass was running down a long dark corridor. There was a man at the end, walking away. A man in a black uniform, carrying a black peaked cap.

'Commissioner!' Cass caught up with him.

'What?' The man turned. 'Oh, you startled me, Cassidy.'

'Sorry, Sir. It's just that you're a difficult person to get hold of. And they said at the desk you might be working late.'

'Yes, well, as it happens . . .' The Commissioner smoothed back his grey hair. 'So, what are you doing so far from home?'

'Well, Sir, it's just that I heard . . .' Cass hesitated. ' . . . Heard that you were calling the search off.'

'I see.'

'I mean, the last part of the search, Sir, the house-to-house, looking for unregistered homes.'

The man nodded. 'Well, it appears your information is correct,' he said. 'And it also appears that we *can* take one decision down here that can't be countermanded by somebody's head office in London.'

'Yes, Sir.'

'But, that apart.' The Commissioner came closer. 'If you were to ask me *why* the search was being called off, I would have to tell you it was shortage of men . . . in view of the coming weekend.'

'Oh?'

'The big demo on Sunday,' the man said. 'Health Service cuts.'

72

It was day.

In the kitchen, Albert watched Edie get the bottle of liquid out of the cupboard. Watched her pour a little into a cup.

'Go on, give her another dollop. Poor old dear.'

Edie did so.

And Albert went to the door, looked along the passage. 'She needs peace of mind,' he said. 'She's going outside again.'

'Outside?' Edie was alarmed.

'Like she does,' Albert said. 'It's her track.' And he watched the old lady go out of the front door, clutching on to her Harrods bag.

Miss Brinkwell moved from darkness into light, from nightmare into dream. Because it *was* like a dream, the tiny garden she found herself in, the path she walked down, and the gate she leaned against. She felt she'd been here before.

There was the narrow road outside, the pollarded trees with the strange black shadows. And opposite, a long wire fence in front of a railway.

Then she heard someone coming. It was a man, a strange old man. He wore a different jacket from trousers. And he had a black dog.

He came closer, and it didn't seem like a dream any more. Somehow she knew him.

He stopped just outside the gate. 'Good afternoon,' he said.

She nodded. 'Good afternoon.'

Turning away, he stooped to the dog, and lifted one of its ears.

'This is the captain speaking,' he said. 'Dive, dive, dive.'

The dog lay down.

Tears came to Miss Brinkwell's eyes. She *knew* him.

The old man came towards her, concerned. 'Madam,' he said, 'can the senior service be of any assistance?'

'Yes,' she said. '*Yes*.' And, letting go of her bag with one hand, she fumbled at the catch of the gate.

He helped her. They got it open.

She was through.

Then there were footsteps behind. Albert was running down the path.

'Now then, my darling.'

'I'm *not* your darling.'

He reached her. She knew the old man was backing away.

Albert turned to him. 'I'm afraid we're having another bad day.'

'I'm not,' Miss Brinkwell said. 'I'm *not*.'

She tried to pull clear of Albert. Caught herself against the gate.

Fell.

Fell badly, on one knee.

Albert bent over her. 'Oh, my poor love.'

She looked round. The old man had backed further, was whistling his dog.

Was walking away.

It was darkness, it was light. It was the living-room end of the passage where the television blared. It was the front door end, and out into the garden. It was tap, move, tap of the walking-stick. It was pain.

She reached the living-room end again. Edie and Albert were there looking at her, concerned.

'Why d'you force yourself, love? Always going up and down, up and down like that?'

Miss Brinkwell turned, started away again. She heard them talking behind her.

'Is it safe, Albert? Letting her go out like that? After last time?'

'Course it is. I got the front gate padlocked.'

And Miss Brinkwell felt the padlock, cold, under her fingers as she leaned out over the gate. As she looked . . . looked . . . out into the sunlight.

Turn. Tap, pain, tap. Back down the passage to the living-room.

'And why?' Edie asked this time. 'Why, for Heaven's sake, d'you keep hold of that bag?'

Turn, tap.

'Don't keep on at her, Edie.' She heard Albert's voice.

'No, all right . . . She's not long for this world.'

She heard that too.

She heard it often after that. But after was no longer a word, had no meaning . . . After, before . . . Time was just a grey . . . a grey . . .

There was no more pain.

There was no more tap. Her right hand no longer held the stick. Her left hand no longer held the bag.

She had let go.

There was no more movement either, as she sat quite still in front of the television. Only the television moved, in fact, went from one thing to another.

But what were they, these things?

A swimming-pool, Miss Brinkwell saw, and a man in a bathing-costume.

Heard the announcer's voice . . .

'The *entire* British team threatened by this butterfly.'

Yes, she thought.

Edie she saw too, kneeling by the television, switching channels. Trying to please her.

A man on a diving-board, diving.

'You can see the pike underwater. But maybe just a *tiny* bit of over-rotation.'

Yes, she thought.

Edie smiled, changed channels.

A man with a golf-club.

'*Definitely* threatening the hole with an albatross.'

Edie's smile was wider.

And Miss Brinkwell smiled too.

Said it out loud.

'Yessss . . .'

73

Cass went through the curtain and stood by the hospital bed. Veins he saw, dark under the marble skin. Her sucked-in mouth.

Smiling

The drip-feed he saw too, the ECG, and the stacked-up pillows.

Heard the slow breathing, catching on itself. Then not catching. Fumbling the soft ball in her windpipe.

Missing.

He sat in his office, but the day was still moving around him. The drive from the hospital. The sunlight. The edges of the world too bright.

But the world came closer. The real world, the why's, the how's, the questions . . .

Roderick opened the door, and sat down with a file.

He didn't open it at once. There was silence.

'Sir,' he said then, 'those two . . . those two who ran the home . . . Can we get them for contributing to a person's death?'

'I'm not sure,' Cass said.

'I mean, the drugs.'

'Yes.'

'And the contents of the larder.'

'What d'you mean?' Cass asked.

And he saw the strange tension there was in Roderick. The rage.

'Well, the residents there, Sir . . . Their entire diet was dried egg, orange jelly, and emetics.'

He sat in his home, at the dining-table. Alison's doll's house was facing him. She had it open, was walking her lady-dolly, sitting her down, talking to her.

Then there was a tiny, whispered swearword.

Alison came to him, holding the toy television set he'd made. One of the legs it stood on had broken.

'All right,' he said.

She fetched him the glue.

He stuck it again, held it together, then put it on the table.

And suddenly smashed his fist down on it.

She gasped. She saw with the second pair of eyes of her life. And ran out crying.

He heard her in the garden with Sonia, crying on. And after a while he went out.

Sonia was kneeling by the little girl. 'It's all right, darling. He didn't mean to.'

'He did. He *did*.'

'Well, he can make you another one, can't he? Make it now? This morning?'

Then she looked up at Cass. He had turned away. And there was something, she thought, about the way he was standing.

She got up. She went over and put her arms around him. Held him . . .

Gradually the sounds, the Saturday sounds of a housing estate came back . . . The mowers, the distant shouts, the radios.

And the sound of a van too, pulling up at the front of the house.

The doorbell rang.

Cass went in. He opened the front door and saw the Royal Mail driver. He was holding a parcel.

It was tied up clumsily with string, Cass saw, back in the living-room. It was addressed to Michael Cassidy, The Lawyer. The writing was spidery, old. And addresses were crossed out. It had been re-directed three times.

Cass opened it.

He saw a Harrods bag.

Inside was a leather-spined book of poems.

And an old creased file, tied with ribbon.

74

The footbridge ran over the railway line. And an old man stood up there, leaning against the handrail. He had a black dog.

The dog pricked up its ears as there came the sound of a train.

It began leaping about, barking.

The train came up. It passed beneath them. Went on. The old man pointed after it. 'Fetch,' he shouted. '*Fetch*!'

CHAIN

The mist began to thin over the building site. The pile-drivers showed more clearly, and the deep shafts of the footings. And some distance away, past rough ground and stacks of scaffolding, there was movement. The door of a portakabin opened.

A man came out, a big man, shambling. He was a site-worker, twenty-seven years old, and gone to gut. His jeans hung low over a big belly. And his hands were low, the hands of a man who fell down every night.

Trevor Gummer had done the gallon by nine o'clock last evening. He'd done the gallon-and-a-half by the time he'd been thrown out. And he'd managed that, he'd always managed that, by giving a miss to landladies, by sleeping rough on any site where he worked. By getting a key, or using a thin strip of metal.

And now he'd got up to have a pump out.

He stood there, swaying, checking out the rubble and bricks in his path. He looked up.

And, across the new site, the footings, he saw the chain hanging down.

There was maybe thirty feet of it, between the ramp and the shaft of the footings below. And there was a gap of maybe four feet between each . . .

Between each . . .

Body.

A tiny sound welled up inside the big man. He clamped a fag-smelling hand over his mouth. Shit, he thought, a gallon-and-a-half. . . .

He closed his eyes. He opened them again. The bodies were still there, swinging slowly.

And the two men above. The fair-haired guy and the guy in the leather jacket, who were hauling their way up on to a truck. Because the chain came from there, from a winch on the bed of the truck. And the fair-haired man went towards it. He picked up a hammer. He lined up on the pawl of the winch. Swung.

There was a shriek of metal links, a cloud of rust, as the chain kicked out. As the bodies kicked down, snaked into the mesh-lined shaft below.

Gummer shut his eyes again. Opened them again. The chain had gone. But there was another sound as the truck drove down from the ramp.

And Gummer knew what that ramp was. In another few hours there were going to be more trucks coming up it. There were going to be hoppers hauled up from them to the chute above.

There was going to be concrete pouring down into that narrow six-by-six shaft.

Gummer turned. He left the portakabin open. And he started to run.

DAVID LYNTON

75

On the far side of the marina, Channel Village was raucous with its jazz. There was the wail of buskers from the red and blue pavilion, the rattle of juke-boxes from the bars, and the tannoy directing tourists to the Maritime Museum.

But on this side, the Yacht Club side, it was quiet.

It was the slow time of the afternoon. Yachts had motored out this morning. They would motor back this evening. But at the moment the wooden pontoons were deserted in the heat . . . Gentle sounds, the creak of fenders, and the flap of sails hung up to dry.

From the Yacht Club balcony a figure looked down. David Lynton was a tall powerful man nearing fifty. Strength came up from his neck muscles to the squarish shape of his face. And his face was burned red on red, the curse of a fair-skinned man who went from office to yacht. He wore canvas trousers and a blazer, and the tie he'd put on for the club dining-room. Though normally, when he was at play, his style was shirtsleeves and claret.

He finished his glass of wine and went in through the balcony door. The bar inside was decorated in Cunarder style, pale wood, light-blue walls, cream ceilings. It was dim after the sunlight, and there were dim prints of J Class yachts long gone.

Lynton went over to the bar and put down his glass. 'Sorry to keep you on your feet, George,' he said.

'No, there's others.' The barman nodded away to the far corner.

'Getting more beautiful with every drink they take?'

'That's it, Sir.'

'Always the way . . . See you at the weekend, George.'

Lynton's voice was quiet, Harrow and Cambridge. And he moved quietly on yachting shoes as he crossed the car-park to his car.

He was fond of the big Merc. It had the knack of reducing the city to a cinema film. A slow silent film. Buildings, vehicles and faces unreeling around him, while he touched brakes and throttle, fingertipped the wheel.

Then out in the country he lowered the windows, needing to smell the air. That dry air, that sickled air of harvest. The silver-white stubble fields and the straw-coloured sky. The year that had been gathered in.

While his harvest, he thought, his personal harvest, was almost ready too. Only his had taken five years, not one. Five years of slow and careful planning.

He turned off on to a long winding drive. Dust was thick and white in his mirror, and ahead of him the house appeared over a crest. A hazelwood copse stood above it. A paddock sloped down towards its walls. The farmhouse that had begun as Elizabethan, with a well under a stone flag in the kitchen, and ended up as Georgian.

He parked in the drive and walked past a white flint wall. A green gate led him through to the garden, where he stopped for a moment. The summer flowers were going, he thought, there were now only the roses. And the dark figs and peaches in the shadows where he stood. Grape-coloured shadows. And the sun a squashed grape in the sky.

He stood quite still, listening, until he could identify every sound between himself and the horizon. It was a trick he had, a trick that calmed his nerves.

Then he moved on. Crossing a small stream, he came to the south wall of the house. There was a wide stone patio with cane loungers. And, on one of them, a novel held open by a pair of glasses. He looked round. 'Viv?' he called out. 'Viv?'

There was an answering shout from the pool, and he climbed a slight rise through bushes. She lay in a strip of sun by the water's edge. Vivienne, his wife.

She was his age, forty-nine, and in a gesture that slightly upset him she covered her body with her wrap. But her face had a striking beauty. It had affected him deeply at times. Times of fire, he remembered, times of slow shuttered shadows. And times of hate too, of course, though for the past five years there had been a gentleness between them. She was not only beautiful, she showed him beauty. She took all the decisions between the four walls of their home. And, as for decisions outside, she never asked.

He bent and kissed her, tasted sun-oil on her lips.

'What's it like in?'

'Perfect,' she said. 'Just perfect.'

He touched her shoulder, and walked on towards the summer-house, taking off his blazer. 'Anything come in the second post?'

'Yes, a letter from Charles.'

He kicked off his shoes, felt pleasure. 'Where is he now? Back from Turkey?'

'Yes, he's seeing friends in Cambridge. Says he'll come here for the weekend.'

'Good. *Good*.' In his mind's eye Lynton saw the fair hair, the serious eyes of their son.

'And you?' Viv asked then. 'You're back early. Didn't you go up to town?'

'No, I told you. I lunched with some local government people at the yacht club.'

'Local government?' She frowned.

'Very boring.' He shrugged out of his trousers, unbuttoned his shirt.

Then, naked, he ran from the summer-house and dived flat. He covered the length of the pool in six crawl-strokes, and hauled himself half out of the water, facing her.

Water glistened on his hair, his face, but she saw past it. 'You look tired, David. Worried . . . Are you?'

'No, not really,' he said. 'It's just that certain things are coming to a head. It's a waiting time. Planning the game through. Right to the final whistle.'

He arched away from her, swam another length, and came back. Then he got out, dripping water on to the stones.

'So, how was your day?' he asked.

'I don't know. I shopped, did a couple of hours on the hospital car-run, made some chutney . . .' She shrugged. 'Oh, and your tree-man called. He looked at the disease in the walnuts.'

'What did he say?'

'Well, either we can leave them until they die off. Or we can chop them down, sell the wood . . . and plant new ones.'

'Not sure about that,' Lynton said. 'What's the point of planting new trees, if people are only going to chop them down again in three hundred years' time?'

76

Cass sat alone in his office.

On the desk in front of him was an old creased file, tied with pink ribbon. He opened it, leafed through the faded contracts and the letters. He closed his eyes for a moment, shivered.

Then he got up. People were waiting. He added two newly-typed sheets to the file, closed it, and took it down to Serious Fraud.

But McRae wasn't in his office. Only Barry was there, moving between a length of print-out and the computer-screen. He looked round, saw the file, then Cass' face.

'Barry, I want you to handle these with care,' Cass told him. 'An old lady died getting them to me.'

Barry nodded. He'd heard. All of them had.

'Now, these are the originals.' Cass showed the contracts, and letters. 'But I've also had extracts typed up. In the form of lists, as you can see.'

Barry took them from him. 'Property,' he said. 'My God, and the rest.'

'Not all of it's here,' Cass said. 'We're still waiting for the last of the transfers from Land Registry. Somebody'll have to go over there and get them.'

'Right,' Barry said. He started reading. Then, a few moments later he moved over to the map on the wall. He found little white markers from a box. And began sticking them up.

'Getting to be quite a slice of the city,' he said.

'It is.' Cass nodded. 'But, that's not all . . . The second sheet you've got there gives a detailed list of people . . . solicitors, estate agents, developers . . . '

'That ring, you mean? The property ring?'

'Exactly.'

Barry glanced at it. 'Some of it goes back a long way.'

'Five or six years, yes.'

'But, are all these characters still around?'

'Most of them,' Cass said. 'There are going to be some very frightened people in this town shortly. It could be just what we were hoping for.'

He sank down into a chair.

Then the door opened. McRae came in, fast as usual. He seemed irritated.

He shot just one quick glance at the map. 'So it's back to the pop-up bloody Christmas card, is it?'

And sat down at his desk, his back towards them.

'Ignore him,' Barry said softly.

'I heard that, Barry.'

'Yes, Bob.'

'But, what I *don't* want to hear from you, right now I mean, is some half-assed lecture on property empires.'

'Right, Bob.'

Cass got up. 'Look, it's not just property,' he said. 'As I was just telling Barry, we've got names. Men who were known associates of Ben Napier, for example. Even that Lennox director, Gotto.'

'Terrific.'

'And, if we could just prove . . . '

McRae swung round. 'Batman,' he said, 'if we could prove Napier was shagging Catwoman, and Gotto was shagging Adam the butler . . . If we could prove the Police Commissioner was on the take . . . '

Cass drew in breath, annoyed.

211

'Look, all I'm saying is, forget the bloody map,' McRae went on. 'Just concentrate on what's happening *now*.'

'And what's that?'

The man sighed. 'All right, there's word that an Italian white goods combine is making a play for Lennox Freezers.'

'There is,' Barry said.

'And, in addition, there's word of big business interest focussing on this city.'

Barry nodded.

'Fine,' Cass said. 'But, where does all that get us?'

'Where it's got us before, with other Serious Fraud investigations.'

'What d'you mean?'

'Batman,' McRae said patiently, 'there comes a time when all the shenanigins are over. All the back-door stuff, the land-grabbing, the hot money.' He paused. 'And then it goes quiet, like now.' He hissed the words. 'It goes respectable.'

77

They were still by the pool, Viv lying in the last patch of sun, and Lynton pulling on his clothes in the summer-house. He came out, hung up his towel. Then he glanced at his watch.

'My love, I don't want to hurry you.'

Viv looked up at him. 'Oh, I see,' she said. 'It's time to make myself scarce.'

''fraid so. I mean, I hate to ask you, but . . .'

'But you do,' she said. 'And I shower and change, and drive over to Elizabeth's. And she serves tennis balls at me at ninety miles an hour.'

'But, you knew what I'd planned for this evening.'

'Oh, yes, you booked.' She smiled at him gently. 'So, how long is this little party of yours going to go on?'

'I don't know. Two hours, maybe three.'

She got up, knotting her robe around her. 'And what about food? You didn't ask me . . . Have you got caterers coming?'

'No, I've brought it back with me in the car,' he said. 'And I put some bubbly in the larder fridge this morning.'

'All very mysterious,' she said.

He didn't answer. There was silence over the garden, over the whole valley. Until they both heard it, the car approaching along the drive.

'Sounds like one of them's arriving early,' Viv said.

Lynton listened. The car stopped, ticked over for a while, then moved away again.

'No, it's a taxi,' he said. 'It's Robbie.'

'Robbie?' She was pleased. 'Is he part of it?'

'Yes, as a matter of fact.'

'Oh, I am glad,' she said. 'Haven't seen him for *ages*.'

They waited, looking down towards the house. And in a moment a man appeared. A large fat man, walking on his heels. He had yards of striped City cloth around his body. And as he drew nearer, they saw the map of veins on his face. The map of the cognac area, as he called it. The very *best* of the cognac area.

Viv ran down towards him, kissed him. 'Robbie, marvellous to see you.'

'And you, my darling.' He drew back, mopped his face. 'God, I thought it'd be cooler in the country.'

'Not this year,' she said. 'But has that husband of mine dragged you all the way down here by train?'

'Seems like it.' He nodded. 'Hardly call it a train, though. More like a cattle-truck. I mean, they crammed us in everywhere. I was *driving* the bloody thing up till Basingstoke.'

Viv laughed. She pointed back to where Lynton was standing, by the pool. 'So, why don't you have a swim?' she asked. 'Cool down?'

'Can't,' he said sadly. 'My darling, I've lusted after you for fifteen years now. Just can't afford to show you my body.'

She took his arm and walked him on towards the house.

'Well, at least you're involved with this thing of David's,' she said. 'I was beginning to have my doubts. It all sounds so secretive.'

'Secretive?' He smiled at her. 'No, just a group of businessmen, a consortium. The usual swindle.'

The consortium arrived at half-past six in two large black cars. They made their way through the house and out on to the lawn. A table was there under a cedar tree, laid out with glasses and champagne.

The sun was low across the valley now. The *kok-klok* of pheasants came from the hill. In the slanting light the lawn seemed pale and wide. And the six businessmen who'd arrived stood close together.

And mostly they were quiet men, Lynton thought, men who drank little. The sort of men you would see driving out to the smart suburbs of Milan or Frankfurt or Grenoble. He spoke to them in their languages, without ever once attempting their accent.

Except for one man, that was, the tall stoop-shouldered man who spoke perfect English. Willi from Salzburg, or *Onkel Willi* as he called himself. And he looked the part, with his chins and his cigar.

'David,' he said, looking round at the lawn, the house, 'this is the way I like to do business.'

'How's that, Willi?'

'In a person's home, where I can see his taste, his character.'

'Glad about that.'

'Because usually,' Willi went on, 'usually I am taken to Wimbledon or to polo, or to the Open Golf.' The chins quivered. 'Golf is not for me. It is rather a draughty game. I would rather watch two flies crawling up a wall.'

Lynton laughed. He moved on, pouring champagne, until he met Robbie coming the other way. And then, looking at his watch, he saw it was time to begin.

He went behind the table. He tapped a fork against a glass until he had their attention. Then he nodded at Robbie to join him.

The man went to the end of the table. There was a white cloth there, and he whipped it away.

To reveal a large model, three feet by four. A model of a marina with yachts moored at pontoons. With rows of loft-houses looking down at them. And with a shopping precinct, restaurants, an office complex.

A marina of some size.

There was applause from the businessmen, the sound of soft hands clapping.

Lynton took up a knife.

Quickly he cut slices, of shops, of offices.

Slices of blue and white cake.

There was more applause as Robbie handed them round.

Willi was among the first to get a plate. He looked at the cake, tried a small mouthful, then a larger one. Then crammed the whole slice into his mouth and held out his plate for more.

There was laughter.

78

It was seven in the evening, and Cass was trying to edge his way towards the door.

But McRae was still talking. Was still standing with his back to the map, refusing to look at it.

'Barry, it's awfully pretty,' he said. 'It shows definite artistic promise, but for God's sake I only needed to clock it once.'

'Why's that?'

'Because it told me we were wrong.'

'What?'

'On the wrong track.'

'Not sure if I'm with you, Bob.'

McRae came towards him. 'All right, what's the big news here in Gotham City? Where's the smart money?'

Barry shrugged. 'Has to be dockland, doesn't it?'

'Oh, yes, dockland. And how does investment work there?'

'Well, you have to get a group of people together. Get hold of a sizeable chunk of land. I mean, it has to be sizeable to make it pay.'

'Exactly.' McRae nodded. 'And where, among your little white flags . . . your *anal* white flags . . . are there dockland properties?'

Barry flushed. 'Well, there's that office complex going up for Packham Leisure.'

'*One* office site,' McRae said. 'Some way from the water, yes.'

'And then,' Barry moved past him to the wall-map, 'there are these other two sites, way up-river.'

'Oh, yes,' McRae said. 'That pub-restaurant, Flashman's . . . And, if I'm not mistaken, a paint-shop that belonged to Lennox Freezers.' He paused a moment, winked at Cass. 'Those would be big sites, would they, Barry? Worth a bob or two?'

'No,' Barry said. 'One's an acre, the other an acre and a half.'

'And are they what you would call *contingent*? In a property parcel?'

'No, not really.'

'Not contingent,' McRae said. 'And not very close to that Packham office-site either. In fact they're more than two *miles* away.' He spread his hands. 'So, all in all, Barry, wouldn't you agree they had very little commercial value?'

'I would,' Barry said, 'yes.'

'Whereas the big dockland sites, valuable sites,' McRae went on, 'Channel Village and Westergate, down at the mouth of the estuary . . . Well, they've already been bought up by developers, haven't they? *Years* ago?'

'Yes, that's right.'

Over by the door, Cass stirred uneasily. 'I don't understand,' he said. 'What are you saying?'

'Simply this, Batman,' McRae told him. 'We know they're after dockland properties, and none are available. What's more, we know they're after *big* properties, fifty, seventy acres, like the ones we've just talked about . . .'

And again he paused, took his time. 'I mean, that's the kind of land to kill for.'

There was silence.

Then both Cass and Barry looked round at the photographs under the map.

Gotto, Karen Seymour, Ben Napier.

McRae sat down.

'Let's be honest,' he said. 'I told you we'd been in this situation before with Serious Fraud . . . Not strictly true.'

'No,' Barry said.

'We've had witnesses hustled away before, hustled halfway around the world. But, Jesus, not three of them killed in a row.'

He swung his chair back and forwards for a moment, then slowed. 'I mean, has it ever occurred to you that all this has happened in a provincial city? Where murder is rare?'

Cass nodded.

'And has it ever occurred to you that nobody's come forward? Nobody's seen anything?'

79

The sun went down over Channel Village. The yachts had come back in, but the bars were quiet, waiting for the supper trade.

While away on the far arm of the harbour, behind hoardings that announced a new site for village housing, was a small development on its own.

Cardboard City.

There was a huddle of superstore cartons, upended to make shacks. There were tents made from polythene sheeting, old bits of timber. And dirt-black men, rising up out of a mess of newspapers and plastic-bags.

A group of them.

The two Paddies, construction men, losing a summer on acid.

Ronnie, the old squat man with the pram.

Carl, still fit, still saying he was going to make it down to the Channel Tunnel.

And Gummer.

Gummer who was unrecognisable, who had lank shoulder-length hair, who had a week's worth of stubble on his round moon face. Stains down his T-shirt, a thick black shine to his jeans.

Gummer looked round at the other men. The four of them. Though yesterday, he thought, there had been five.

There'd been Derek, the small kid.

The kid with the blood, the broken bridge to his nose.

Where Gummer only had a bruise on his forehead.

And Derek's tenner in his pocket.

He got up, spat into the fire, and pulled on a torn leather jacket. Then he walked off without a word.

It was strange, that walk of his. There was something glass-thin, fragile behind his great size. And something jerky about his movements, his sudden smiles, his crazy talking to himself.

Something strung out.

He walked past the water. He ducked away from the cars of Channel Village and the bright new bars. He walked for some time, getting deeper into old dockland, the wide rutted streets, the rumble of lorries. And he couldn't work it out, which lot to try first. The John-boys or the Brethren?

He settled on the Brethren. It was going to be a smoker's pub, he knew, but there was the chance of other stuff. And as he went in through the door, he was careful . . . You were the only whitey in the place, and you watched out.

He went up to the bar. He uncrumpled the tenner and showed it around as he got a half of Stella. He pocketed the change, looked at the golden liquid, felt the chill of the glass. Shit, he thought, the thirst on him.

But he made himself hold back. He took the Stella over to a corner table and sat down. Garvin was there. Garvin was always there, with those rings of his, that Rasta hair. But Garvin, like always, was sitting with a mob of them.

Gummer made himself sip. He waited. He saw another

whitey come in, go up to Garvin, saw them talk. Then whitey went off to the can, and in a moment Garvin followed. They were away only a minute before whitey came out again, smiling.

Gummer took another sip. He watched Garvin sit down at his table again. He took another sip, another. Then he went up.

'You know me, Garv?'

'Sure I do, man.'

'You doing any trade?'

'No.'

Gummer let his arms fall. He smiled, he cringed, he took inches off his height.

'You done some trade just now,' he said.

'Dif-rent, man. Dif-rent. Old Cozzo, he make me laugh.'

'I can make you laugh too, Garv.'

'No, Gummer, not you.' Garvin turned away.

The meat stood out on Gummer's face as he thought. 'Listen . . . Listen, you seen that one on the telly?'

'What one on the telly?' Garvin didn't look round.

'Where it's this guy from *Minder*,' Gummer said. 'And he's got all these cameras. And there's this other guy with just one camera. And the guy from *Minder* says to him, "who d'you think you are? David Bailey?" And it is David Bailey. It *is*.'

Garvin looked up. 'Shit, man, that was years ago. *Years* ago.'

The Brethren turned their backs.

And Gummer knew when to get out.

He tried the John-boys. He didn't want to, they were getting too young for him nowadays, too quick. But he reached their pub and went in to the sound of Simple Minds.

The bar was full of them, their sharp mouths, their sharp high-street suits, their screw-faced Tinas, and their sodding aftershave.

There was no sense messing around. He went straight into a group, started talking.

219

'Listen,' he said, 'you seen that one on the telly?'

They looked round.

'Where it's this guy getting married, and he's standing outside this church. Only he isn't marrying some tart, he's marrying his *boss*, and . . .'

'Fuck off, Gummer,' they said. 'Just fuck off.'

He fucked off. The wires inside him were beginning to hurt now. And that *thirst* . . .

He dropped by an off-licence, got two four-packs in a carrier. He ringed back the first one in the street outside, and sucked it down.

There was only four pounds-twenty in his hand.

It had to be Steve.

80

The fact was that Cass had forgotten they were going out. Unbelievably a fortnight had gone by, and they were due to have supper with the Bensons again.

And of course they were late.

He sat behind the wheel of the Peugeot and drove fast, faster than he would have liked.

While Sonia held on to her safety-belt. 'Steady on,' she said. 'Five minutes won't make any difference.'

But there was something else he'd forgotten too.

'No, don't turn off!' she said suddenly. 'Stay on the ring-road. Keep on towards Hawkham.'

'What?'

'Love of my life,' she said, 'the Bensons have moved.'

He sighed, stopped the car, turned.

'You mean, you haven't *heard*?' she asked then. 'For God's sake, that woman's been on the phone at least twice a day.'

And she imitated Marianne's low voice. 'Oh, yes, we're out on Ranelagh Avenue now, darling. Come in from your end. Take the first on the right, and we're half-way down on the left.'

'Ranelagh Avenue?' Cass whistled. 'That's going some, isn't it?'

'Certainly is.' Sonia nodded. 'They paid three hundred and twenty-five grand.'

'You mean, she told you that too?'

'About a dozen times.'

They reached the avenue. They slowed, and found the turning. It was a private road, with laurel hedges on either side, and wrought iron gates.

'Here we are,' Sonia said. 'On the left.'

And even Cass was surprised. There was a new white gravel circle with a fountain in the centre. And beyond, a great modern barn of a house. There were darkwood framed windows. There were two separate wings with dark hanging tiles. And between them, a long brick-arched portico.

As they drew up in front of it, a light came on. Marianne appeared in one of the arches. She wore something slim-fitting. It was a light grey, and for her, subdued. Until Cass saw how it showed off her legs, her suntan, her pearls.

And she in turn showed off the house.

'*Da*-daah.'

'That woman,' Sonia said quietly, 'is becoming impossible.'

They went through the hall. There was a double stair-case, redwood, going up around a large mirror. And the kitchen, of a lighter wood, and steel, was enormous.

Luckily Phil Benson was there, filling it with his wide shoulders, his laugh, his hellos. And the seven year-old Abigail was with him, taking the glasses of wine that he poured, and handing them round.

'Thank you, Abigail,' Sonia said. 'Gosh, you're looking very smart tonight.'

'My party dress,' Abigail nodded. 'Mummy said I could wear it if I went to bed before supper.'

But Mummy was impatient to start the conducted tour. She brushed past them and walked over to a massive cooker.

'Came with the house,' she said. 'They threw it in, plus the extractor-hood, plus the microwave.'

'That's marvellous,' Sonia said.

'Then there's the twin-sink plus waste-disposal . . . *Ample* storage . . . Swedish . . . Fitted, of course.'

'Of course,' Sonia said.

'And here at the end, hot water and central heating. Wall-unit, as you can see . . . Amazing, isn't it? That something so small can heat such a large house.'

'Darling,' Phil said gently.

'What?' She looked at him.

'Are we throwing the place open to the public?'

She made a face at him. Then turned to Abigail, who was clicking the hood-light on and off. 'Darling, I've told you about that before.'

The tour went on, through the drawing-room, the dining-room, the study.

Then upstairs.

Abigail led the way into her bedroom. 'See?' she said. 'My Roger Rabbit bedspread, my Roger Rabbit poster, my Roger Rabbit light.'

Sonia bent down to her. 'And where d'you keep your toys?'

'Here.' Abigail led the way over to a large cupboard.

But Marianne was holding out the Roger Rabbit curtain. 'Lined,' she said. 'I had them lined. It does make sense.'

Cass ducked out. He found Phil out on the wide landing.

'Mortgage frighten you?' he asked quietly.

'Not half.'

'I mean, it's a bad time, isn't it? Interest rates right up? House prices falling?'

'Ye-es,' Phil said.

'You mean, they're not falling?'

Phil came closer. 'Not round here,' he said. 'Not on the avenue. There's a bit of a queue. Eighteen people looked round this place in three weeks.'

Cass shook his head. 'You amaze me.'

'Look,' Phil said. 'I am in the business, remember.'

'But, what's it all about?' Cass asked. 'I mean, the sort of tales I hear . . . '

'Simple.' Phil shrugged. 'It's big firms, moving their staff around. Taking care of the expenses, not to mention the risks.'

Cass still didn't see.

'Come on, man, the big new dockland development,' Phil said. 'Fast as they put up offices, people move in . . . National names . . . Hall Charterhouse have taken over an entire block. General Union, the same . . . The thing is, we're near enough to London, way below London prices, and it's an environment people want to be in.'

'You sound just like the brochure.'

'Don't I?' Phil grinned, and led the way on.

They passed two, three bedroom doors.

'You've certainly got enough room,' Cass said.

'Oh, we have that.'

They reached a turn in the landing, and a single door at the far end.

'What's that?' Cass asked.

'It's over the garage,' Phil said. 'The last people used it as a granny-flat. But as you can see . . .'

He took Cass down there, opened the door.

Inside there was a large bare-ish room with a fawn carpet. It was fitted out as an office, with desk, phone, filing-cabinet, safe.

Phil leaned against the doorway. 'These fine summer evenings I thought to myself, why work on downtown? So I bring stuff back here, sit by the window, hear them in the garden.'

Cass looked on round the room. 'Fax machine, too?'

'Oh, the works,' Phil said.

81

It was an old dockland street that led down to the water. The houses were two-up two-down, damp peeling brick. And Gummer stood there, the bag of tinnies in his hand, watching just the one yellow light.

Steve's front room.

He went over. There was the sound of a kid crying inside, and he knocked on the door. A few seconds later Steve stood there. The spikes of his thin red hair showed up against the light. He didn't look pleased.

'Steve,' Gummer said. 'Look, I tried everyone tonight. You're my last hope.'

'Is that right?'

'Yeh.' Gummer put his hand in his pocket, felt the four pounds-twenty. 'Look, I can manage a couple of quid. And I get my giro Thursday.'

Steve looked at him, at the crut on his T-shirt, his jeans. 'You don't pick up no giros, Gummer. You int got no address.'

'I have. I got Jackie's. They still think I'm there.'

Steve wasn't sure.

'Go on. Do us a couple. I'll pay you by Thursday.'

'No,' Steve said.

'No?' Gummer sucked in his breath.

The child inside the house cried louder. Steve pulled the door to behind him.

And Gummer began his cringing act, his smile. 'Look, Steve, in the past . . . '

'Oh, in the past it was fine,' Steve said. 'Couple of months back you had work. You had money. We did a bit of whizz.'

'Right, Steve. Right.' The smile again.

'But then you packed up work. And, okay, you brought me your giro, and we still did some trade. You took twelve grammes off me, kept back four, knocked out eight at a good mark-up.'

'Right.' Gummer tried a wild laugh.

But Steve felt crowded by his huge shape. He pushed past, stood on the pavement. 'Christ's sake, Gummer, it's just not bloody on. Look at the state of you.'

'What?'

'You're living rough now. Sniffing your own bloody giro.'

'No, Steve. No.'

Steve started away down the street.

And Gummer went after him, his carrier bag clinking. 'Look, it's not like you think.'

'Int it?' Steve pointed at the carrier. 'Got a serious thirst on you, Gummer?'

'Just a few tinnies.'

'No.' Steve shook his head. 'Listen, one thing I know about is whizz. You get heavy into that stuff and you get a *thirst*. You don't eat. You don't sleep. The chemicals get to you, and you get seriously paranoid.'

'No.'

'And what's more, you start shouting *seriously* paranoid things around pubs.'

Gummer's head jerked up. His cringing act went. 'What you on about, Steve?'

But Steve was walking fast. '*You* know,' he said over his shoulder.

'No, I don't.'

Steve swung round. 'It's about that time you quit working. *Why* you quit working? Why you went and dossed up at that cow Jackie's . . . Know what I mean? Disappeared?'

Fear broke out suddenly on Gummer's face. It was wet.

They were down near the river, under the bridge. The new concrete road-bridge that rose up high above them, and went out over the dark water.

Steve stopped for a moment, out of breath. He was angry.

'For Christ's sake, Gummer. You just don't *understand*.'

'Understand what?'

'There are these people. They keep coming up to me.'

'What?'

'And they want to know who this whizz-head is, shouting his mouth off.'

'*What*?' Gummer shook, shook violently. 'Steve, you never . . .'

'Course I didn't.' Steve told him. 'But listen, Gummer, you got to face up to it . . . Nobody around here's going to sell you stuff . . . Nobody.'

A squeal came from Gummer. He looked up at the bridge, the great arch of it. The cars up there, and the cold blue light.

But Steve was going on. 'Know how much they spent on that?' he asked.

'What?'

'On that bridge?'

'No.'

'Thirteen million,' Steve said. 'Thirteen sodding million, then they ran out of money. Never linked up with the motorway where it was meant to.'

Gummer didn't answer.

And Steve turned to him, still angry. 'Bridge to Nowhere, that's what they call it . . . And you know what, Gummer? That's what you're on.'

Gummer heard that. And over and over again he heard what Steve had said before. *Nobody around here's going to sell you stuff . . . Nobody.*

He spun round and got it just right. The bone high up on his forehead against Steve's nose.

There was that crunch. That blood.

Then Steve was down. And Gummer was pulling the man's shoes off, rolling down his socks. The small plastic bags spilled out on to the pavement. Then the roll of notes.

82

Abigail had gone to bed. The four of them were sitting round the dining-table. And it was strange, Cass thought, that pale polished table of Phil's, and the white chairs, now dwarfed by the large new room.

But one thing was still the same, Marianne's cooking. The large sea-bass she'd steamed in onions and peppercorns and wine. The smell of it, the flakes of white flesh.

Phil wiped his mouth. He leaned forward. 'How's that fraud business of yours coming along?'

'I don't know.' Cass was evasive. 'So-so.'

'You always say that.'

'You'll just have to give up asking.' Cass sipped at his wine.

'Lover,' Marianne looked up, 'Cass's glass is nearly empty. And mine *definitely* is.'

Phil frowned at her. 'You're going it a bit tonight.'

'It's good wine.'

'Only Muscadet.'

'But it's the kind *you* buy, my love.' Marianne blew him a kiss. 'Anyway, it's a sort of house-warming isn't it?'

'Fair enough.' Phil picked up the Muscadet, poured.

'We're going to need another one.' Marianne looked at the bottle. 'Loads more in the pantry.'

Phil got up. He put his napkin on the table and went out.

Sonia was giggling.

'What's so funny?' Marianne asked.

'Sorry.' Sonia waved her hands. 'But, *pantry*? We didn't hear about that.'

Marianne shrugged. 'Well, for three hundred and twenty-five . . .'

'We heard all about *that*,' Sonia said.

'Sorry.' Marianne nodded. 'Promise not to mention it again.'

She picked up her glass, drank a great gulp.

'Matter of fact,' she said then, 'price apart, we were lucky to get this place in the end. Phil had to move very fast.'

'What d'you mean?'

'Another couple were after it. There was even talk of them going up three thou.'

'Up?' Sonia stared at her. 'Gazumping? In this day and age? I thought the new thing was gazunders.'

Marianne shook her head. 'Apparently not. Not in this case anyway. And Phil knows about these things.'

'S'pose he must.'

'Anyway, these other people, their offer was sort of accepted over the phone,' Marianne went on. 'Sort of . . .'

There were soft footsteps on the carpet. Phil was back in the room. He signalled at Marianne to stop.

But she didn't.

'Anyway. Luckily Phil knew this solicitor . . .'

'You're joking,' Sonia said.

'No. And he got him on the phone and . . .'

'Bloody *joking*!' Sonia's face was white, angry.

Marianne stared at her.

Phil sat down in silence.

'It's out*rageous*,' Sonia said then.

Marianne turned to Cass. 'Lover, do tell your wife what the real world's all about.'

'*Real* world?' Sonia asked.

'Yes,' Marianne said. 'Number One.'

'That's pathetic,' Sonia said.

Marianne shrugged elegantly. She was still looking at Cass.

And maybe it was the dining-table, he thought, suddenly small in the new house. Maybe it was the lined bloody curtains in the bedroom upstairs, the Roger bloody Rabbit . . .

'I go along with that,' he said.

The silence changed. People were edging back.

'Hey, steady on.' Phil tried his laugh. 'All right, I admit it . . . Maybe I was in a position just to ease the rules.'

'*Ease* them?' Cass asked.

'My old lad, the property game is rough. Everybody knows it's rough'

'Jesus,' Sonia said.

Marianne turned to her icily. 'Lover, it's all there in my little colour supplement . . . Life today, it's success. It's money-making without guilt. A return to dear old Victorian values.'

Sonia nodded. 'Every Victorian value bar one.'

'Do tell.'

Sonia turned away angrily, looked at the room. 'All right,' she said. 'All right, they used to have these little embroidered texts, didn't they? Up on the walls? You know the kind of thing . . . God is Love . . . I Will Lift Up Mine Eyes . . . ' She turned back to Marianne. 'So what should it be now? . . . Slip'em A Couple Of K?'

228

Marianne smiled. 'Well, if you've *got* a couple of K, lover. Is that what we're talking about?'

Cass felt cold. He couldn't help himself. He started pushing back his chair.

'No, it isn't,' he said slowly. 'What we're talking about is a gazump. A gazump by a solicitor.'

He turned on Phil. 'For God's sake, when we were starting up north, if a senior partner had done that, you'd've resigned.'

Phil looked at him steadily. 'No,' he said. '*You* would.'

But then he wavered. 'Look Cassidy . . . old mate . . . Where is all this getting us?'

'To *exactly* what I've been investigating over the past few months.' Cass raised his voice. 'Only it isn't just one solicitor. And it isn't just a few K.'

'Very touching,' Marianne said.

'Oh, yes,' Sonia swung round, 'it's that too. Listen, I'll tell you something . . . ' She pointed at Cass. 'Not so long ago I saw him in *tears*.'

Marianne played an imaginary violin.

And Sonia was furious. 'It's true. There was an old lady. She sent him documentation of how many property rip-offs? And what happened? Somebody had her *killed*.'

'Try Police Five, lover,' Marianne said, 'not me.'

Cass shook his head. He knew he should have stopped Sonia but he'd been angry, very angry. And now, as he looked round the table, all he could think was, dear God, how do we pick up the pieces?

83

The morning sun yellowed the old bricks of the farmhouse. But further down the valley there was mist. A coldish mist, David Lynton thought. The summer had been dry, the leaves were falling early, and it smelt like autumn as he walked over to his car.

He got in, and moved away down the drive. But, as he neared the main road, he stopped and pulled over. The car-phone was ringing.

He picked it up. The man's voice at the other end was high and excited. Lynton heard it out. He was calm.

'Yes, I do see that,' he said. 'But old ladies are funny. They keep things hidden away. I mean, I had an aunt once who kept a small Canaletto hidden in a picnic basket. Didn't want any of her children to get it. Didn't like them very much.'

The voice at the other end was higher. It spoke faster.

'No,' Lynton said. 'Not if we see the pattern of the game clearly. See where it's going.'

'I don't know,' the voice said. 'I mean, there's another little problem. No so little, really.'

'Oh?'

'You see, what was actually said . . .'

But Lynton broke in. 'People die,' he said. 'Natural causes. It's an unfortunate fact. So, why don't you check the death certificate?'

'Yes.'

'That answer your question?'

There was hesitation. 'Yes, as far as that goes, fine. But . . .'

'But, what?'

'Well, there've been other grey areas.'

Lynton waited.

'I mean, when I've gone along to a certain building-site. Paid over money.'

'For cement,' Lynton said. 'Yards of cement.'

'Very expensive . . . cement.'

Lynton thought a moment, sucked his teeth. Then he brought the club-room into his voice, the tie. 'Dealt with your profession all my life,' he said. 'A profession, as they say, founded on distrust. But, my dear chap, I find you quite *invaluable* at a local level. And I don't see why it should end there. You could be quite . . . the coming man.'

'Yes.'

The voice at the other end changed. Lynton could almost see the man's face, taking on new ideas.

'Be in touch.'

He put down the phone and drove on.

84

Cass finished the morning's court-work and went back to his office. He dumped his brief-bag down on the desk, then turned. McRae was there by the window.

He seemed thin against the light, drawn. The man had reached a dead end, Cass knew.

'Got a message on the Bat-phone. Heard you wanted to see me.'

'Yes,' Cass said.

'So, what's it about?'

Cass hesitated. 'Probably nothing,' he said. 'Just a tiny breach of office security.'

'Oh, that kind of nothing.'

'Well,' Cass spread his hands, 'we went out to dinner last night, and the evening got a bit out of hand.'

'You mean, you took *off* the little black boots and the jump-suit?'

'I'm serious,' Cass said. 'I mean, my wife just happened to mention Miss Brinkwell, and that list of properties.'

McRae's face changed. '*What?*'

And Cass was surprised. 'Honestly, I'm sure it doesn't matter. We were with friends. And he's in the same line of business. A solicitor.'

'What's he do?' McRae asked. 'Litigation work?'

'No, conveyancing mostly. I think it's commercial property.'

'I see.' McRae nodded. 'Reasonable line of business, that, I suppose?'

'Oh, yes,' Cass said, 'he does all right. Smart holidays. New Volvo. Big house.'

'Not like the old CPS then?'

'You're right.' Cass sighed. 'But, he's a good friend. We go back a long way. And, you know, we have dinner together. Sort of a weekly affair.'

McRae came away from the window. He smiled, relaxed. 'Well, as long as he's a good friend, goes back a long way.'

85

Roderick followed the big new Volvo. He'd picked it up as it had left the office car-park. He'd kept with it through the early evening rush-hour, and turned in towards the centre of town.

Well, he thought, we're going shopping.

He waited, double-parked in the street. Which was a risk, he thought, seeing as how he wasn't using a CID pool car. For some reason McRae had said no local numbers, and he'd wangled a car from Special Branch. For some reason it was all being kept very quiet.

Roderick looked down the street. The evenings were getting colder, he thought, but the days were just as hot. People were still coming out of their offices like dishrags. There were still swarms of flies round rubbish-bags, and dried-up looking veg in the shops.

He watched Benson come out of the deli. He had a couple of small parcels tied up with ribbon. Flash, that, if you could afford it. Most likely something special for his wife. And she was a looker, judging by the photographs.

The man got into his Volvo and eased out of the parking-space. Roderick followed, dictating time and place into a tape-recorder. Which was another of McRae's little whims. No radio-contact, except when they changed over shifts. And the surveillance tapes were to be handed directly to him.

The high square back of the Volvo was ahead, two cars ahead, taking him out through the traffic to the ring-road. They went towards Hawkham, then chucked a right on Ranelagh Avenue. Top of the pile, that was.

He slowed at the entrance to a private road, knowing Benson's address, and making sure he turned in there.

But then he saw something else. Parked cars, a lot of them, just beyond Benson's house.

Roderick drove up and slotted in among them. He wound down the window. There was a crowd of people on the far side of a hedge. He heard the thwack of tennis balls, and a lot of half-cut voices saying sorry.

Tennis party then, next door.

Should've brought his racket.

86

It was six in the evening, and the pool-balls in the public had been clicking all day. Gummer had been sitting there all day, up at the corner of the bar, on the Stella.

He was crying.

He'd reckoned to get clear of the city last night. Well clear. Only he'd had these tinnies with him. And the whizz.

The buzz and flap of his head, the crash of decisions, the *moves* he had to make . . . Only he'd found a club at midnight. Got kicked out at four. Found this pub this morning.

And they'd let him alone, crying and talking, crying and laughing. Watched him go out to the can every now and then for the zag, the lightning. And come back in again for the thirst.

Around him there were puddles on the bar-counter, puddles on the floor. And his mouth was slow and wet, miles behind his brain.

'I couldn't help it,' he said. Then shouted. 'Couldn't *help* it!'

The barman swung round. 'You want to stay here?'

Gummer nodded. He drank, spilled beer around his chin, handed over his glass.

The man poured.

'Fucking chain.' He knew he was going to shout again.

'This fucking *chain*! And then, shit, it was *gone*! Wasn't nothing to do with me!'

The barman stopped pouring. 'Out,' he said.

He watched Gummer go.

And through the bar, in the saloon, somebody else was watching. A man with elastoplast on the bridge of his nose, and heavy bruising there.

Steve.

Steve gave it five minutes. Then he went out to the cinder-smell of the city. His nose was hurting, and there was crap all round him, old cans, supermarket trolleys. He kicked them savagely out of the way.

Down on the waterfront there was more crap, tourist-crap. The ugliest sodding people in the world were waiting in a queue for the Maritime Museum. And the ugliest kids in the world were crawling all over the ships they'd got on show there, the old light-ship, the steam yacht, and the schooner with the two big masts.

Steve walked on. He passed the whispers from the bars. He passed new yuppy-style houses with their sodding lace curtains and their sodding cars.

He came to sunlight, and open ground.

Some way ahead of him was a big wire fence with a gate.

There was a sign, BRI-RAND PARTNERS BUILDING FOR PACKHAM LEISURE.

Steve knew a few people on the site. He gave a name to the security man, and walked through.

He went past a building they'd nearly finished. Then another, finished up as far as the third floor, with big box-frame girders above.

And beyond, by a pile of scaffolding tubes, was a portakabin.

He walked up the steps, knocked on the door. It opened, and a man in a leather jacket stood there.

Steve talked to him. And as he talked, he felt good, he felt calm. At the end of it all, the man came close. He got a roll of notes from his leather jacket, and peeled off a fifty.

Steve walked away over the rough ground. He turned

back once and saw the man in the cabin was lifting the phone.

On the Ranelagh Avenue estate, Roderick got out of his car. He stretched his legs, moving away from the shouts of the tennis party. And, as he reached Benson's house, he heard a sound.

Did McRae want that down on his tape? he wondered.

18.30: Thursday. Target's phone ringing?

87

07.00: Friday. Detective Sergeant Roderick taking over from Harper. No lights in target house. Nothing to report.

08.45: Target leaving front door of house. Opening garage door. Am taking up position in turning-circle of close opposite.

08.55: Target now on outer ring-road, proceeding south. Three ahead. No sweat. For sure he's going to take the city turn-off.

08.56: Target taking Docks. Repeat. Docks. Am getting over to the slip-road if this prick behind will . . .

09.01: Target past Dock Entrance 3–4. Getting into left filter. Looks like he'll take Channel Village.

09.02: Target through lights to Channel Village. Proceeding towards . . . No, chucking another left. Taking . . .

09.06: Sorry about that. Bit of a scramble there. Target took service road to new office-building site. Packham Leisure site. Couldn't follow. I was too exposed. I gave him three minutes, got lucky. He was through gates, proceeding general direction new sites. I kept on outside perimeter gates. Got the car tucked down behind earthworks.

09.18: It's a bit of a fucking story. I just saw a switch. Kept target under observation with glasses. He parked by second of new building-sites, Packham sites, went into a grey portakabin. There were others inside, and target came out again with another man, medium-height, slim-build, leather jacket. They talked maybe five minutes. And at the end I saw this switch. A brown envelope. Target passed it to . . .

09.23: Missed the bugger. Target drove back fast to site-gates, took direction Channel Village. I couldn't reverse in time. And you said no radio communication. Am still up on this mound of earth, getting it all over my John Law suit. Be sending you the bill for that . . . Sir, I mean . . .

09.30: Target Two. Man in leather jacket. Hot off the press, Sir . . . Kept him under observation, and there's a new little number going on . . . From the beginning, he went back into the portakabin, picked up a hard-hat, and then went up a lift on the site. The second site, that is, the unfinished one. He went along a third-storey walkway, approached a group of men by a chute, talked to one of them. Call him Target Three. Tall, around six-two, heavy build, fair-haired when he took off his hard-hat . . . And there was another switch. This time Target Two gave Target Three the envelope, folded over now, and smaller. Definite fix on this because the two of them turned away from the other men, towards me. They talked some time. Then Target Three went back to where he was working on the chute, operated it, poured cement.

McRae switched off the tape. He took it out of the recorder, locked it away. Then he called Roderick.

The man came down from the CPS floor.

'Sir?'

'Something to say to you, Sergeant.'

'Sir, if it's about the . . . well, the informal nature of my report, well, Sir, you said the tape was only for your . . .'

'It's not about the informal nature of your report.'

'Yes, Sir. Only you see, normally, normally I'd have it transcribed, and it would all be set out, you know . . .'

'It's not going to be transcribed, Sergeant.'

'Not?'

'No. And you and your two oppos in this surveillance

operation are to hand your time-sheets in to me. And I'm going to sit on them for a while.'

'Sir?'

But McRae didn't give him any explanation. He just sat there, thinking.

'Tell me, Sergeant,' he said then. 'Benson has been under continuous observation since two o'clock yesterday afternoon?'

'That's right, Sir.'

'And at no time, I mean during banking-hours, was he seen to go to a bank?'

'No, Sir.'

'And this morning, these switches you described, the brown envelope,' McRae paused. 'Was it big?'

Roderick frowned. 'I'd say about twelve by eight, Sir. Inches.'

'And, what's the word they always use . . . Bulky?'

'Bulky, yes, Sir.'

McRae stared at his hands. 'So he's got the money at his house,' he said then.

Roderick waited. There was something he had to ask.

'Sir?' he said. 'You said there were going to be no transcriptions of evidence. And, I mean, we're using a Special Branch car . . . Am I to take it, Sir . . .?'

'Oh, you are, Sergeant.' McRae cut across him. 'There's to be no mention of this upstairs.'

'Even to Mr Cassidy, Sir? I mean, we've all been working on this a long time.'

'*Especially* to Mr Cassidy.'

And Roderick was alarmed.

Suddenly there was this wolf-like thing about McRae's mouth. This cruel thing he hadn't seen before.

88

At about half-past four that afternoon the Mercedes came up the long drive to the farmhouse. David Lynton got out.

He crossed the narrow strip of grass outside the kitchen window, and poked his head inside.

Viv was at the long scrubbed table, peeling dark figs and putting them into a bowl.

'David?' She was surprised.

He blew her a kiss.

'Back early on the fatcat's train? That's not like you.'

'No,' he said.

'Is there anything wrong?'

'Not really. Just that the phone's been ringing all morning.'

'But,' she frowned, 'wouldn't that keep you up in London?'

'No,' he said, 'ringing from down here, this end.'

'I see. Your consortium, you mean. Your swindle.'

'That's it.' He smiled.

But behind the smile, she saw, there were deep lines of worry.

He leaned further into the room, and saw the rucksack by the door. The rucksack, the bedroll, and the worn-out trainers.

'Charles?' he asked. 'Is *Charles* here?'

She nodded.

Flesh came back to his face. He breathed out slowly. 'But, that's *marvellous*. I just didn't realise . . .'

'But I told you.' She got up. 'I told you he was coming back this weekend . . . David, are you sure there's nothing wrong?'

Lynton stood in his son's bedroom. He saw the pop-posters, the *Tintin* books, the cricket bat. Then his son as he was now. Nineteen years old, deeply tanned, with great knots of muscles for shoulders. And a way of sitting cross-legged that came neither from Viv nor himself.

Which was the real pleasure of being a father, he told himself. Not to look for resemblances. But to see someone entirely new. Someone who woke with excitement each morning with the slate wiped clean. Who saw new things with new eyes.

Firm eyes they were too. They made white creases in the deep tan, saw a long way. And the hair bleached to the colour of tow.

'So, how was it?' he asked.

'Fine, dad. Just fine.'

'Did you see much of Turkey?'

'More of Greece, really.'

'My old stamping-ground,' Lynton said. 'So where did you go? Olympia? Epidavros?'

'Well, just briefly. Yes.'

'Briefly?'

'I hitched around,' Charles said. 'I sat in the sun, talked to a lot of people. Read a lot of books.'

Pleasure, Lynton felt. Pure pleasure.

They did what they always did when any of the children came home. They got into the Land Rover, all of them on the front seat, and drove up on to the hill.

The stubble was below them. There were the shadows of round straw-bales along the hedgerows. And the first ploughing had begun. The first of the chocolate-coloured strips of earth.

And maybe because his son was with him, Lynton talked of times past, of times his own father had known. Of the shearing-gangs coming in, and the big harvesting-gangs. The barrels of mild ale set up in the barn, the palliasses in the loft, and the gangers required by their contract to turn up in church.

But then he looked away, at the farmhouse below, and the wide lawn with the cedar tree. He thought of the men who had stood there earlier in the week. The new gangers. *Onkel Willi* and the rest of them.

And he frowned. He didn't like business spilling over into his private life, into his home. But there was no other way.

He waited a moment, caught Vivienne's eye.

'My love,' he said, 'there's something I should've mentioned earlier.'

'Oh? What's that?'

'Well, I know it's not exactly the right time . . . I mean, Charles being here with us, but . . .'

'But, what?'

'Well, as it happens, I did ask somebody down for the weekend.'

Viv frowned slightly.

'D'you mind?' he asked.

'Depends who it is.'

'Only Robbie.'

But she was relieved. More than relieved, pleased. 'Oh, that's all right,' she said. 'Robbie fits in.'

And Robbie did fit in, Lynton thought.

Definitely, after the news of the last two days.

The phonecalls from that local solicitor, Benson.

The one he'd taken yesterday in the car.

And the calls this morning.

About the new payment to the men on the building-site.

The new cement that was to be poured.

89

Gummer was back in Cardboard City. It was the only place he could think of to go. Not that he was thinking. The whizz had seen to that. The whizz and the Stella.

Though he had thought a couple of things out. He'd got what was left of the little white packets in one sock, what was left of the money in the other. And he had two big carriers of tinnies.

But the sodding Paddies were on to these. Watching them, never taking their eyes away. And Gummer got up, pulled the bags close to his body, and shambled away to his cardboard shack.

He stuffed the tinnies inside, turned, straightened up . . .

And fuck's sake.

Fuck's *sake*.

He saw the car, the old beaten-up Datsun parked away over the rough ground. And the two men by it.

One in a leather jacket. The other, tall and fair-haired.

Fear stoked up in Gummer, red, burning his insides. He turned and ran.

He tried keeping the cardboard huts between him and the two men. But they saw him.

He tried smashing his feet down harder on the ground, tried to get clear, *clear*.

But the Stella came at him, rose up in his throat. He was down on his knees, spewing.

He got up, ran *on*.

But in the end it was the whizz, the sodding whizz, screwing up his head.

He got it wrong.

He'd been trying to run for the water, the harbour. But he'd come the wrong end. The big wall of the Maritime Museum was to his left. And the grey hoarding that cut off the quays, straight ahead.

The two men slowed. They closed in.

Gummer screamed. He just ran, ran crazy, smashed at the hoarding when he got there. Turned, smashed with his boot.

There were cracking sounds. One of the panels gave.

He went through, tearing his hands on nails. And, fuck's sake, nearly went *in* . . .

There was maybe three inches of stone quay. And then water, a mess of water. Oil, crap, dark sucking ropes.

Gummer shook. He reached up, grabbed with his hands for the top of the hoarding, and hauled his way along. The water was below him. And behind there were those ships they'd got moored for the museum. Big ships. Big iron buggers. But they were shut for the day, their gangplanks up.

He crabbed his way on, sweating, crying. He got past the big white bugger, the steamship. Then the red lightship . . . And then, he saw suddenly . . . then, crowds, safety, the line of cafés.

Channel Village.

Gummer got there. The tall guy was maybe ten feet behind him and he ran on, past tables, past people grabbing their kids away.

He reached the pavilion, the big blue building with the red metal girders.

He found steps, red metal steps, and ran up them. There were double-doors at the top, leading inside. And he smashed his way through them.

Glenn Miller.

Glenn *Miller*?

He found he was in a crowd, a dense crowd. They were on some kind of terrace, done up like a steamer's deck. And they were looking over the rails at the floor below.

Fuck's sake, a five-piece sax-combo down there. Tuxes, Jesus, the lot. Blowing *In The Mood*.

Gummer hit the crowd. They wheeled round. Some of them made to swing back at him, but they saw his size. He smashed his way on, using shoulder, the bone of his head. Then he was on the far side where it was dim. There was empty space along the wall, and these trick fucking portholes, like you were in a steamer, looking out.

He looked back. Back the way he'd come. The crowd was closing together again. Sort of, they were angry. Maybe there was still a path through them that showed.

And beyond. Beyond, coming through the swing doors.

The tall guy.

Gummer went away in the shadows. He was looking for stairs down. But there was only one lot. Back behind him.

He came to a passage. It was dark. Maybe a fire-escape, he thought. But it went the wrong way, along the length of the building. He went down it. There were doors, all of them locked.

He kicked open the last one, tried to make it look like it was shut again behind him. But it stayed hanging crooked. He turned. He was in a small office. Desk, that kind of crap.

A phone.

He started shaking again. Shook more as he went towards it. Jesus, he thought, a *phone-lifter*?

He hesitated.

Behind him he heard *In The Mood*.

He lifted the phone, did the three nines.

'Police, Fire, Ambulance. Which service do you require, caller?'

'Police,' he said.

He was through, and the words came out in a rush.

'Listen, there's these two guys. They're trying to kill me. And they killed before. Couple of months back. A building-site down this way. Killed two guys and a tart. And . . .'

He stopped.

There was a question from the other end.

Gummer gave the phone number. Then he heard a noise. Turned.

The two guys were there. For real. They started with the boots . . . Shit . . . *Shi-i-it* . . .

90

It was about half-past six when Robbie arrived at the farmhouse. He'd come by car this time not wanting to risk that dreadful train journey again. He had a leisurely cup of tea with the Lyntons in their kitchen. And then he went upstairs to shower and change.

He came down again half an hour later. There was the sound of a motor-mower. David, he saw, was out past the cedar tree, mowing silver and green stripes against the sun.

While Charles was sitting alone on the patio. He was reading a book. And there was a drinks-tray next to him on a table.

'Ma's getting the supper,' he said. 'She said to help yourself to a drink.'

'Splendid,' Robbie said. But when he got close to the tall glass jug on the tray, he frowned.

'What's this?' he asked.

'Pimm's by the look of it.'

'Oh, dear,' Robbie said. 'Half a hedge and a golf-ball.'

Charles smiled. 'Your ma?' Robbie asked then. 'D'you think she'd mind if I helped myself to a gin?'

'Not in the least. It's through in the dining-room, on the side.'

Robbie went into the house. He came back with a fairish G & T, sat down.

'What's the book?' he asked.

Charles showed him the cover.

'Chekhov?' Robbie was surprised. 'Haven't I slept through most of his plays?'

'Probably.'

'Part of your course at Cambridge, is it?'

'No, not really. I'm reading history.'

Robbie sipped at his gin, grunted. 'And what are you going to do when you finish?'

'Don't know yet.'

'They all say that.'

'Yes,' Charles said. 'But, what I'd *like* to do is get over to Mexico. Sit around on a pavement for a year or so.'

Robbie made a face. 'Your father happy about that, is he? After all the money he's spent?'

Charles nodded. 'He says the only thing he requires of his children is to be articulate.'

Robbie glanced at the Chekhov once again. 'Thank God, Jeffrey Archer's good enough for our leader.'

He crossed himself.

David Lynton finished mowing. He went to the summer-house, and came back with an armful of croquet-hoops and a peg. He set them out on the lengthening shadows of the lawn. Then went back for the basket of coloured balls, and the mallets.

Robbie strolled up. 'Croquet, is it?'

'Yes,' Lynton said.

'Filthy, nasty, dirty game.'

Lynton nodded. 'Ever played before?'

'Not so's you'd notice,' Robbie said. But he smiled as he examined the mallets, chose one, and hefted its weight.

Lynton turned back towards the patio. 'Charles,' he called out, 'you playing with us?'

'If you like.'

'Well, bring the Pimm's, will you?'

'And the gin and the tonic?' Robbie called. 'There's a good lad.'

Charles arrived with the tray. He put it down. Lynton chose a mallet, and turned. 'House rules,' he said. 'No pooftah shots, like putting your foot on the ball. And the playing-area is the whole lawn, as you see it.'

'Fine by me,' Robbie said.

'So who goes first?'

'How about young Charles?' Robbie asked. 'See if he can get away?'

Charles could. He went through the first hoop cleanly. And then laid up, at the far end of the lawn.

'You next, Robbie.'

Robbie took his time sighting up. He went through the hoop like a rocket, and stopped some twelve feet from Charles.

'A-hah,' he said.

And he gave Charles the treatment, the full treatment . . . The croquet, the roquet, through the second hoop . . . Then the croquet, the roquet, through the third hoop . . . Until he was way ahead. On his own.

'A-*hah*,' he said. 'Pretty to watch.'

91

Gummer lay in a cubicle in Casualty. His face was dark, split, stitched, one black bruise. And there were more ring-bruises on his white body.

It was bad, Sergeant Roderick knew.

He turned as footsteps came up. McRae appeared, carrying a briefcase. He beckoned Roderick away.

'What's he like?' he asked.

'The doctors say fifty-fifty.'

'From a *beating*?'

'More of a kicking.' Roderick lowered his voice. 'They gave him a hell of a working over.'

'How long ago was that?'

'Two hours.'

'Half-past five?'

'Yes,' Roderick said. 'I picked it up at six-thirty, when I was coming off-duty. And I thought it best to check it out, you know, before I rang . . .'

McRae nodded. 'Is he talking?' he asked.

'Just.'

'Have you seen him?'

'For five minutes.'

'And what did he say?'

'The same as on the phone, Sir. These three bodies he saw, dumped on a building-site.'

'Where? The site, where?'

'The new development. Packham Leisure.'

McRae came close, grabbed his arm. 'You *sure*?'

'Yes.' Roderick was startled. 'I mean, he was working there at the time. He knows the place. Reckons he can pinpoint the spot.'

McRae's grip tightened. He was hurting. 'And the bodies?'

'Two men and a girl, Sir.'

There was a long moment, and then McRae swung away. 'Can you get another five minutes with him?'

'Not sure, Sir.'

'Get five minutes.' McRae reached down to his briefcase, opened it. 'And show him these.'

He held out the three photos.

Gotto, Karen Seymour, Napier.

Roderick didn't take them. 'But, Sir . . .'

'But, Sir, what? Isn't the man up to it?'

'They say he's fighting. They say he's strong. It's not that, it's . . .'

'Just bloody do it, man.'

McRae pushed the photos into Roderick's hand, watched him walk back towards the gap in the curtains, go through.

There was another cubicle, and it was empty. McRae went into it. He sat on the bed. There was this terrible

246

strain about him, this whiteness. It was the same as the whiteness of Gummer's body. He was willing him to live.

Then Roderick came out again with the photos. He nodded.

McRae got up. 'We're there,' he hissed. '*There.*'

92

Darkness had come to the croquet lawn. It was almost night. Though the three men, who'd been playing for over an hour, had hardly noticed.

Until, that was, Robbie walked away to the edge of the lawn. Where his ball was, where that young bastard Charles had hit him.

And the shot he had now was all of fifteen yards, nearer twenty. An important shot. He had only to hit the peg, and he'd won.

He bent over his mallet, aimed. Then he straightened up.

'David, it's dark.'

'What's that, old son?'

'Nearly night-time. Bloody *is* night-time, come to that. I mean you can't see that lovely wife of yours, can you? And she's only yards away.'

'Darling, he's right,' Viv called from the cedar tree.

'Course he's not right,' Lynton said. 'Come on, Robbie. Play the shot.'

But Robbie waved a huge arm. His voice rose. 'Look, David. That young kid of yours is waiting for me up there. If I miss, he's going to knock all *hell* out of me.'

'That's the game.'

'It *isn't* the game. The game is played in bloody *day-light.*' Robbie was angry. 'My dear man, I suggest you concede, since I'm two hoops ahead.'

'Two hoops is nothing in croquet. It all depends on the last shot.'

Robbie let his mallet fall on the grass. 'This is ridiculous.'

Then he heard Lynton moving, going away round the side of the house. In a moment a car engine started in the drive. And he saw the big Mercedes, lurching and bumping, as it climbed the grass slope of the paddock. It swung round, stopped. Headlights cut through the darkness and found the croquet lawn, blinding Robbie as he stood there.

Lynton's voice came down the hill.

'Right,' he said, 'we play on.'

93

It was just before eleven am as Cass walked down the corridor. Thick-carpet was underfoot, there were framed reproductions on the walls. And at the end, a door marked AREA CHIEF CROWN PROSECUTOR.

Cass knocked and went in. He wondered how Royston would feel about being dragged out on a Saturday morning.

The man sat in front of wide windows. And for a moment Cass didn't recognise him. He wore his gardening clothes. There were none of the usual clearcut lines of suit or dark tie. And, strangely, none of his clearcut way of handling people. He seemed subdued, hesitant.

And on his right was the Police Commissioner. Black uniform, silver buttons, short grey hair.

Warning bells, Cassidy heard.

Royston pointed at the file in front of him. He cleared his throat. 'I'm rather at a loss, Cassidy. I'm not quite sure why you feel there's such urgency about this matter. Why you feel that . . . certain take-over moves are imminent.'

'Sir?' Cass waited.

'The Commissioner and I, we've put in an hour or so on your report. Not much more than a skim-through, as you'll understand . . . But, the way seems clear enough. We'll go along with two of the investigations.'

'Two, Sir? Only two?'

Royston nodded. 'Lennox Freezers and the Rubafiore properties.'

Cass was amazed. 'But, what about Packham Leisure? I mean, surely, that underpins our whole case.'

'Exactly.' Royston glanced at the Commissioner. 'And the problem there, Cassidy, as I explained once before, is that we have no direct evidence.'

'I don't understand, Sir. You've seen the file. The unexplained fundings.'

'They claim they haven't got complete figures yet. They're late with their tax-returns.'

'But, what about the surveillance videos?'

'Not *direct* evidence, I'm afraid.'

The Commissioner looked round. 'And they're Belgian.'

He made it sound like Martian.

Cass was more than amazed, he was stunned. 'For God's sake,' he said, 'what about last night's news? The news that links everything together? The three bodies on the Packham Leisure site?'

Royston hesitated.

And the Commissioner got up. 'All right, I'll take it, Alan.' He walked to the window, turned.

'Mr Cassidy,' he said then, '*I'm* here because you have made a request. You want a certain company's assets frozen, and an investigation made into the foundations of one of their sites.'

'Yes, Sir,'

'Have you been down there recently?'

'What?'

'It isn't foundations any more. That site is three storeys *high*.'

And Cass shouldn't have said it, he knew he shouldn't. 'If you'll excuse me, Sir, is this really a police matter?'

The Commissioner's head came up. His face was red under his grey hair. 'All right,' he said, 'we'll forget that Packham are one of the biggest investors in this city. We'll forget that you have no documentary evidence against them . . . Let's just talk about the source of your latest information, shall we? A man called Trevor Gummer.'

He walked fast to the desk, leaned across Royston, flipped through the file.

Warning bells, Cassidy heard.

'Gummer, unemployed bricklayer,' the Commissioner read. 'His personal effects in carrier-bags. And inside one of them, an empty tape-cassette box and the tube of a ballpoint pen . . . D'you follow my meaning?'

'Yes, Sir. He sniffs amphetamines.'

'More than that, he's known to us. He has *dealt* in amphetamines . . And you want me to halt a multi-million pound construction site on *his* say-so?'

Royston was looking away, Cass saw. And he didn't understand why he was in this on his own.

'Sir,' he turned to the Commissioner again, 'as I understand it, last night in Casualty there was a photo-identification.'

'There most certainly was *not*.'

'Come again?'

'Mr Cassidy, as you well know, photo-identification involves twelve photographs of like appearance on a board. Only one of them being of the subject.' The man raised his voice. 'In this case, Mr McRae instructed a Detective Sergeant of mine to show Gummer just three pictures. One of each subject.'

Cass looked down. His shoulders sagged. He hadn't checked it out with Roderick. It had been two this morning when he'd finished his summary.

The Commissioner came round the desk. He turned briefly back to Royston. 'I'm sorry, Alan. This is your office, and your man.'

'Yes.' Royston waved a hand tiredly. 'But go ahead.'

The man came close.

'I am writing a report about Mr McRae. A rather *long* report. It will be sent to his head-office towards the end of next week . . . But in the meantime, just as the Chief Prosecutor here has to look after his own men, I have to look after mine.'

Cass nodded.

The Commissioner drew himself up. 'This fraud

investigation has been one long *circus* of corner-cutting,' he said. 'My policemen have had their time-sheets removed. They have been excluded from interviews. I've even heard that you, Cassidy, a *Senior* Prosecutor, questioned a certain old lady alone . . . I mean, who the hell d'you think you *are*? Some American-style *DA*?'

94

Cass went to McRae's office. He told him about the Commissioner's report. He told him that his own attachment to Serious Fraud was to be reviewed on Monday.

McRae was silent, his back turned.

Suddenly he smashed his fist down on the table. 'You know, I said it once before, and I was *joking*.'

'What?'

'About the Commissioner being on the take.'

Cass was shocked. 'Oh, come on.'

McRae whirled round. 'No?' he asked. 'So, Batman? What's your opinion?'

'Well,' Cass thought for a moment, 'if I were in Royston's shoes, for example, and one of my Prosecutors came in with this kind of evidence . . .'

'Christ.' McRae started out of his chair.

But as he got to the door, it opened. Barry was there with an armful of papers. They were knocked to the floor as McRae brushed past him.

'Charming.' Barry looked down the corridor after him. Then he turned to Cass. 'What's up?'

'Oh,' Cass said, 'it's a long story.'

Barry frowned. He bent to pick up the papers. 'Well, so is this,' he said. 'A very long story.'

'What?' Cass asked absently.

'The last of the Rubafiore land-transfers, you remember, from Land Registry?'

'Yes,' Cass said.

'D'you know those buggers aren't even on the computer?'

'Yes, I do.'

'Took me bloody days.' Barry went over to the big wall-map. He referred to the papers, then started sticking up new white flags.

'That's funny,' he said then.

'What is?' Cass didn't look up.

'Well, you remember those two properties? Way up-river on their own? . . . Flashman's? And that paint-shop of Lennox's?'

'Yes.' Cass frowned.

'Well, we seem to have got another couple here, linking the two of them up.'

Cass straightened. He went over to the map. And it was just as Barry had said, a thin strip of property, running along the river.

He thought a moment.

'Barry,' he said then, 'refresh my memory, will you? I mean, in the past we decided there wasn't room for anything like a marina, didn't we? Here up-river?'

Barry nodded.

'Why was that?'

'The sites weren't big enough for serious investment.'

'And are they now?'

'No,' Barry said. 'Take a look. Can't be, what, more than five acres in all?' He pointed a finger. 'And it can't spread inland, can it? That's an industrial estate. Newish industrial estate.'

'But, it must mean something.'

'Well, what?' Barry asked. 'There's no sense looking further up-river. That road-bridge gets in the way, doesn't it? . . . Can't get a sailing-boat under that. The mast sticks up too high.'

'You're right.' Cass sighed.

But then he looked at the land-transfers Barry was holding. The nearest one.

The back of it.

He went out to his car. He felt quite cold as he drove towards the ring-road. And when he reached it, he turned left, the way he never went as a rule. Because of the traffic-jams.

He came to the tail-back, the long line of cars snarling in the sun and the dust. They inched forward, and the sign came up ... REGRET INCONVENIENCE UNTIL SPRING 1990 ... URBAN MOTORWAY IMPROVEMENT SCHEME ... NEW DOCKLAND SPUR ...

Shadows passed him. Big earth-moving machinery, and then the great dirt banks they were piling up for the overpass. He parked the car. He got out. He fought his way up a bank. But before he reached the top, he knew what he would find.

The new spur, levelled earth, graded, went away in a long gentle curve. But in the distance he saw it. The great concrete span. The new bridge, as it was still called, that went out over the estuary.

The locals had another name for it, he remembered.

The Bridge to Nowhere.

Bridge to somewhere now, he thought.

He went back to the car, drove until he found a call-box, and made two phonecalls.

Then, driving more leisurely because he had time, he threaded his way up-river to that other bridge. The road-bridge Barry had pointed to on the map.

And he waited, glancing at his watch.

McRae was the first to arrive, in a taxi. And shortly afterwards a car drew up, a small family-car, polished, looked-after, eight years old.

A man got out. He was in his fifties, but looked older. There was an old-fashioned quiff to his hair. He wore a thick tweed sports-jacket in the heat. And had a row of pen-clips in his top pocket.

Cass introduced the two men. 'Robert McRae,' he said. 'Frank Nichols ... Highways Department.'

The three of them walked out to the middle of the bridge. Traffic blasted past them, occasional traffic, in gusts. Then they leaned against the stone parapet and looked downstream, towards the south-west bank.

The sun was in their eyes, but they could see the lit sign, FLASHMAN'S. They could see the old Lennox paint-shop, and the properties in between.

Cass pointed. 'Frank,' he said, 'suppose I knew people were buying that strip of land over there. Five acres in all.'

'I'd say they were very wise.'

'Why?'

Frank hesitated. 'Access,' he said then.

'What?'

And Frank spoke softly. They could hardly hear him above the sound of the traffic.

'Grade 1 Access,' he said. 'Four lanes, central reservation, roundabout.'

'For *this*?' Cass pointed at the two lanes of traffic on the bridge.

Frank didn't answer. He led the way on. They reached the eastern bank, and he showed them a section of stone parapet that had been repaired.

'About a year ago,' he said, 'there was a driver with a ten-and-a-half ton artic. He had a fit of coughing coming on to the bridge . . . We made good, reckoned it was perfectly safe . . . But, in the opinion of the Head of the Steering Committee, Highways . . .'

'A new bridge,' Cass said.

'No,' Frank said, 'Lock-gates.'

They crossed over then, to the upstream side. The sun was behind them, and they saw a quiet backwater, shabby, smalltime, a world on its own.

Frank pointed at the river. The tide was low, and there was just a silver curl of water between mudflats.

'With the lock-gates,' he said. 'And good piling, good foundations . . . you could get a marina in there.'

Cass breathed out slowly. 'How big?' he asked.

'Well, just talking about the quays and the pontoons alone would give you eight to ten acres.'

Cass looked down to the bank below them. There were

ramshackle boatyards, and jetties where old houseboats and cabin-cruisers were moored.

'And that?' he asked.

'Every one of those yard-owners would get out for real money,' Frank said. 'Say, another ten acres . . . That's before you even look at the far bank.'

And the far bank, they saw, was a wide area of green common. There were groups of people strolling across it. A dog rolling on its back.

'But,' Cass said, 'I mean, for God's sake, that's common land.'

'Oh, yes,' Frank nodded. 'But you could get a quid pro quo . . . Reclaim a bit of the river up under the next bridge . . . Only a short walk.'

'How many acres are we talking about there?'

'Fifteen, maybe more.'

Cass shook his head. 'I don't understand. Won't people complain?'

'They won't know anything, not yet. Right now it's just a road being moved, which is local council.'

Then the man pointed on. 'And we haven't come to the real dilly,' he said, 'not yet.'

It was an overgrown section of the bank. A big site, with low concrete buildings, and fat peeling pipes.

'Water Authority land,' Frank said.

There was a long silence.

'Jesus,' Cass said then.

Frank nodded. 'And you know what they'll call it? Bloody uplift, they'll call it, in terms of the environment.'

Suddenly Cass heard it, the hiss of breath from McRae. McRae who'd said nothing so far.

And he saw where McRae was looking. Not at the Water Authority site, but back at the grassland.

At the wicket that had been chalked on a tree. At the small boy standing in front of it with a large cricket bat. Missing the ball his father bowled at him.

And McRae's face was strange. It was animal. Vicious.

Frank drove away in his car. And McRae got into the

255

Peugeot with Cass. He seemed calmer.

'Old Frank,' he said. 'He's a pal of yours, is he?'

'That's right.'

'Must be. To come out with all that.'

Cass started the car. He drove off. 'It's quite simple,' he said. 'He's worked for Highways all his life. He's saved, voted Tory . . . But he says, and I quote, the powerblocks lining up all around us are beginning to get bloody frightening.'

'Bloody frightening is right,' McRae said.

He didn't say anything else for quite a while. And when he spoke again, his voice was quiet.

'There's going to be a report out on me by the end of the week. Could rather link in with this powerblock idea.'

'Yes,' Cass said.

'What I mean is, if I'm to finish what I started, I've got to make my move. Now.'

'Yes.'

'You don't seem surprised.' McRae turned. 'You don't say, "Oh, what move would that be? What's it all about?"'

'No.'

Sweat was glistening on McRae's upper lip. 'Batman, I'm trying to tell you I've got just one line of enquiry. Turns out . . . Turns out it's a local man . . .'

'Local solicitor,' Cass said.

'You mean, you *know*?'

Cass slowed the car. He stopped at the roadside. His head bowed forward over the wheel.

'I knew this afternoon.' He only just managed to say it.

'How?'

'Well, you see, land-transfers, they have the acting solicitor's name on the back.'

'Yes. But so far they've all been Napier's haven't they?'

'Not today's.' Cass' voice was calmer. 'Today's were more important, as we both know. They had a different name.'

He was still calm when he got back home. Calm when he heard from Sonia that Alison had gone out.

But not calm when he heard where.

'Phil picked her up,' she said.

'*What*?'

She looked at him in surprise. 'But it was all arranged weeks ago,' she said. 'It's Saturday, they're having a kids' party, in the new house.'

'Jesus,' Cass said. He sat down.

'I don't see why you're like that about it. I mean, Phil rang. He was very nice. He said just because all four of *us* were behaving like children, he didn't see why it should spoil Alison's fun.'

Cass thought a moment. 'Are we fetching her?' he asked.

'No. Phil's bringing her over. He's doing a delivery run.'

'When?'

'I don't know. Seven-ish.'

Cass looked at his watch. Twenty-five minutes. 'I'm going out,' he said.

'Out *again*? . . . Look, what *is* all this?'

'Nothing. Just something I've forgotten.' He got up.

She came after him. 'You're not still worrying about that dinner-party? The row?'

'What?' Cass asked. 'Yes, of course I am.'

But she gripped his shoulders, stared at him hard. 'No, it's not that,' she said. 'You're scared. *Scared* of meeting him.'

'That's crazy.'

'And you've been working till late, on a Saturday . . . No court on a Saturday . . . It has to be Serious Fr . . .'

She stopped suddenly, went white. 'That new house of Phil's,' she said. 'The new car, the . . . For Christ's sake, nobody's making *that* kind of money conveyancing. Not nowadays.'

'Course they are.'

But her eyes saw straight through him. 'You can't lie to me.'

Suddenly she broke away. Stood with her back to him, by the fireplace. 'How deep is he in?' she asked.

And just as suddenly he gave up. 'Deep,' he said.

He looked at his watch again. It was twenty to seven.

Sonia turned round. 'Well, I can't face him,' she said. 'I just *can't*.'

They tried to think it out. They couldn't both leave the house, not if he was bringing Alison back. They couldn't hide.

It was a quarter to.

And then there was a sound from outside.

A car hooter.

Phil was early.

They saw him getting out of the Volvo, honking the horn. They saw the two children getting out behind him. They had balloons. They had party-hats. They were covered in streamers.

Sonia ran upstairs, crying.

95

The shadow of the cedar tree was lengthening once again. David Lynton looked out at it from his study. He could hear Viv and Charles talking together on the patio. And he closed the window, turned.

'How's your glass, Robbie?'

'Fine, old son, thank you.'

'Let's sit down then, shall we?'

'Why not?'

Lynton took the small armchair. Behind him the long-case clock ticked slowly. It had ticked through his father's time, ticked through his grandfather's.

'Robbie,' he leaned forward, 'obviously I didn't invite you down just to beat you at croquet.'

'*Beat* me?' The man's face quivered. 'Dear God, you and your car headlights both. Shining in my eyes.'

'Quite.' Lynton shrugged. 'But, that apart . . .'

He heard the clock again. It had never been moved. There were five different layers of wallpaper cut around its shape. Because it had been the only accurate timepiece in the valley.

He smiled at Robbie.

'I need to have a little talk with you,' he said, 'about our European chums.'

The man nodded.

'It seems that Willi . . . *Onkel Willi* from Salzburg . . . is throwing a bit of a wobbly. Seems there's a chance he could back down.'

'What?' Robbie was surprised.

'We're after a steadying hand, d'you see? And, as it happens, I did a bit of phoning last night, got hold of most of the consortium . . . Thing is, we'd rather like you to sit above the salt on this one.'

Robbie was more than surprised. But, as Lynton watched, the idea took root in him, grew.

They sipped their drinks.

'Mind if I say something?' Lynton asked then.

'By all means.'

'Well, no names, no pack-drill, but I did hear you'd paid a lot of money to duck out from . . . the Guinness affair.'

Robbie's face went blank suddenly. He held Lynton's eyes, stared back.

'Not that I'm probing, d'you see? Only trying to help.'

'Yes.'

'And what I've done,' Lynton went on, 'is I've had a word with my local solicitor here. We're going to swing you seventy a year, plus twenty for expenses . . . And, as a little drinky-poos, we thought we could back-date the payments over, say, twelve months.'

Robbie breathed out slowly. He smiled. There had been real tension in the man.

'Very white of you, old son.' He raised his glass.

96

There were still streamers and balloons tied to the Bensons' twin staircase. Abigail came slowly down in her nightdress. With one hand she held on to the banisters. With the other she clutched a new and gleaming present, a small transistor radio.

'And now,' it said, 'to take us up to the eight o'clock news, here's a little offering from Andrew Lloyd Webber . . .'

Music echoed through the hall. There was a shout from upstairs. 'Darling, can't you let anybody sleep on a Sunday morning?'

And in a moment Marianne came down, a robe tied around her. She took Abigail's hand, led her through to the kitchen.

'I s'pose you'd like some milk,' she said. 'And I s'pose daddy would like his cup of tea.'

They went to the fridge. Marianne poured milk into a glass. She yawned and put the kettle on.

'Be a pet, darling. Go and see if the papers have come.'

Abigail nodded. She put down her radio and went out to the hall. She slid the bolt back on the front door, and turned the Yale.

The papers were outside on the porch. She moved towards them, but then looked up.

At the far end of the lawn, men were moving along the hedge. Men in suits.

'*Mummy*!'

'What is it, pet?'

Marianne came out of the kitchen. To hear strange sounds. Feet running across the lawn. Cars racing up on the gravel.

Then people pouring into the house.

She screamed, ran towards her daughter.

But a strange woman got there first, in a light fawn costume.

Marianne stopped. It wasn't *happening*.

Then another woman appeared, came on towards her. Took her arm.

And the men. How many men? All in the same dark suits. Pounding up the stairs. Going straight past her along the hall. Standing by the kitchen door, the back door.

Then, dreamlike, the woman in the fawn costume picked Abigail up, brought her over.

There were shouts. A thundering down the stairs. Phil was there in his pyjamas. 'What are you *doing* to them?'

He moved towards his wife and daughter. But men appeared silently. Four of them. Phil swung round, hit out.

McRae got out of the car. He crossed the gravel and went in through the front door. He saw the balloons and the streamers. He felt pain.

He walked on, towards the sound of shouting in the kitchen. The man Benson shouting. The squeak of bare feet on vinyl, gasping breath.

He pushed at the door as he came to it, walked straight up to Benson. Showed his warrant card.

The colour of the man's face deepened. He closed his eyes for a moment. Then he nodded.

'Let him go, Sergeant,' McRae said.

He walked away, leaned against a table.

The man in pyjamas, he thought. The wife crying. And the child . . .

Pain.

Benson bent to the little girl. He tried to calm her. Wiped her eyes.

And McRae knew what the man was going to say.

'Darling, would you go out and play in the garden a moment? With mummy?'

'No,' the little girl said.

Benson signalled an urgent yes at his wife. She moved. And the two plain-clothes women moved too. They all went out through the glass door.

They stayed there, a strange little group, on the paving stones. One of the plain-clothes women brought a bike from the lawn. But the little girl shook her head, looked straight back through the glass door, crying.

Pain, McRae felt.

Pain.

97

There was a flush about Benson that was like the flush of an athlete, McRae thought. The man was pumped up, confident. He wasn't afraid.

Not of the interview-room. Nor of the files that they'd brought from his home, the office there above the garage.

And why, McRae thought, wasn't he afraid of the files?

He spread them out on the table. He stepped back from Benson's chair, gave him room. As he always did at first.

'Well,' he said, 'it's all here, isn't it? . . . You're the local man. Handling Lennox property, Rubafiore property. Negotiating with our Euro-friends *well* before the For Sale signs hit the streets.'

Benson shrugged.

'Though, of course, the actual contracts always went through other solicitors.'

'What's wrong with that?' Benson asked. 'It's happened before. It'll happen again . . . With big take-overs.'

'Yes,' McRae said. 'Yes. But then we come to the contracts you handled *personally* . . . Concerning a marina, no less.'

'Marina?' Benson laughed. 'For God's sake, what is this? . . . Marina where? . . . All the dockland here has been leased out by the British Port Authority. The same as in every other major city.'

'Marina up-river,' McRae said. 'I make it just short of sixty acres. Including the access, of course. Grade 1 Access, dual carriageway.'

A flicker. The first flicker in Benson's eyes.

'Oh, yes,' McRae said, 'we've found certain communications between you and the Highways Committee.'

He kept it there for the next half an hour or so. Didn't take it any further. Just went back over details, dissecting them clause by clause. Boring details, quite safe.

But every now and then that flicker in the man's eyes.

Wondering how the hell they'd got on to the Highways stuff.

McRae moved closer. He reached into his briefcase, got out a sheaf of faxes.

'Didn't find these in your office,' he said. 'Found them on a bookshelf downstairs, among your collection of *Autosports*. A couple of faxes inside each magazine.' He kept talking. 'And we wondered about that for a bit. Then we thought, well, it's a new house. He hasn't had time to get his carpentry set out yet, make little cuts in the floorboards . . . And, of course, a safe's *bugger*-all use.'

All the time he was watching Benson's face, giving the man time to settle, time to narrow down the exits, choose the right one.

'Faxes.' McRae fanned them out in front of him. 'Sent and received by you over a period of eighteen months. Quite a few different organisations involved. The Highways Department, for one, as I said . . .'

'How d'you know that?' Benson asked suddenly.

'Quite right,' McRae said. 'How do I know?'

He let the silence hang.

'Well, to be quite honest,' he said then, 'Highways was easy. We knew the acreages, the sites, the suggested plans for the new road. But as far as the other faxes are concerned, I know what you mean.'

Benson was wary.

'I mean, look at them.' McRae dropped fax after fax onto the table. 'No names, no company names, no fax numbers . . . Rather unusual.'

There was a pause.

'I asked for my solicitor,' Benson said then. 'Where is he?'

'It's a Sunday,' McRae said. 'We think he's playing golf.'

Half an hour later he brought Roderick in, and gave him some reading practice.

'O9.18,' the man read. '*It's a bit of a . . .*'

'Go on,' McRae said.

'O9.18: *It's a bit of a fucking story. I just saw a switch. Kept target under observation with glasses. He parked by second of new building-sites, Packham sites, went into a grey portakabin. There were others inside, and target came out again with another man, medium-height, slim build, leather jacket. They talked maybe five minutes. And at the end I saw this switch. A brown envelope.'*

Benson sat forward in his chair. A network of lines began to appear on his face.

'What is a switch?' he asked.

'The passing of an object,' McRae said, 'from one person to another.'

'In this case, an envelope?'

'Brown,' McRae said.

'Who says so?'

McRae pointed at Roderick.

'Was he close?'

'Not exactly,' Roderick said, 'outside the perimeter fence. But I had glas . . .'

'A couple of hundred yards.' Benson cut in. 'Maybe more.'

Roderick nodded.

'And correct me if I'm wrong,' the man said, 'but this sounds like somebody talking, sounds like a tape-recording. Not a written statement. Witnessed.'

'We work in pairs,' McRae said, 'on surveillance.'

But Benson turned, caught Roderick's face.

Young Roderick's face.

'Show me a signed statement,' he said, 'with a witness's signature.'

Not bad, McRae thought. Not bad at all.

Benson seemed to perk up after that, as they talked about the Packham Leisure site.

'You said it was a couple of hundred yards,' McRae told him, 'from the fence to the site.'

'Yes.'

'You know it then?'

'Oh, yes, I go there from time to time.'

'Why?'

'Why?' The man even smiled. 'I'm a solicitor. I handle commercial properties. We have clients interested in units

264

on that site. I check the work as it progresses. Do it in other places too.'

'Don't you have people under you who do that sort of thing?'

Benson smiled again. 'I'm thirty-seven, getting a bit fat,' he said. 'Maybe I want to put on the yellow hard-hat and prove to myself I can still walk about on scaffolding.'

'Quite,' McRae said.

And then, quickly, 'Talking about scaffolding . . .'

'What?'

'The man you saw on the site that morning . . .'

'The man I didn't see.'

'The man in the leather jacket,' McRae insisted. 'He went up on the scaffolding after you'd gone, talked to another guy, tall, fair-haired. He passed money to him.'

'Witnessed, of course.'

McRae had had enough.

'*Plenty* of witnesses that evening.' He raised his voice. 'More than a *hundred* bloody witnesses over in Channel Village, when these same two men kicked the *shit* out of a site-worker.'

That flicker again.

'I don't know anything about that,' Benson said. 'I don't know about site-workers when they're tanked . . .'

'Kicked him damn near to *death*,' McRae went on. 'A man called Trevor Gummer. We thought there was a chance he'd pull through, but suddenly there's clotting on the brain. He won't last the night.'

And the flicker.

It was more than that.

The panic button.

And McRae knew when to start shouting. Shouting loud. 'I'm going to have you, Benson. Accessory to *murder*!'

'What?'

'Oh, *yes*!' He kept the volume up. 'Because this Gummer, he was going to pull through, remember? And we were there with him, in Casualty, weren't we? We heard about the footings of that Packham site, the main structural footings, the exact *place*! . . . Three *bodies* down in that cement, Benson! Three people *killed*!'

McRae moved then, in front of Sergeant Roderick, hiding his face this time.

'You want more, Benson? You want to hear about a photo-iden in that Casualty ward? A *full* photo-identification? Twelve pictures of like appearance on a board?'

He grabbed Benson's head, hauled it round.

'You want names, I'll give you *names*!' he shouted. 'A girl, Karen Seymour. And two men . . . Gotto . . . And a solicitor of your acquaintance . . . Ben Napier.'

It was the last two names that did it. Had wires crossing inside Benson. Panic leaking from his eyes.

McRae let him go.

'You're in this. You're in this over your head,' he said quietly. 'But, let's get to where it's at . . . A consortium we hear about, waiting to carve up dockland . . . I want the name of the man at the *top*.'

And there was always that edge, he thought.

Which way it would go.

Until Benson nodded.

98

David Lynton was at the wheel of his yacht. It was an old mahogany wheel, brass-bound. And there was gleaming brass around him. The cleats on the deck, and the rows of fat barrel-shaped winches.

A yacht of great beauty, of age, he thought. He'd had her restored to her original condition. The hull, Scots-built in 1932. The long pale holystoned deck. And the tall gaff-rigged main rising slowly above him, as the two crewmen hauled it up.

The jib was already set, and he called for a staysail. They filled. He winched slowly in on the mainsheet, and the boat heeled over. There was that slow deep burble, and the hiss of the waves.

Later, when they left the lee of the land, and the wind was stronger, he called Robbie up from below. The man was like a large crumpled cushion, hanging on to everything in sight.

'I told you, there's no motion, not when we take the wind,' Lynton said. 'Not in a boat of this age.'

'No, old son.'

'And you're better off up here than below.'

'Is that right?'

The water was wide. There was dark cloud over the island. But closer at hand, waves were folding in on themselves like silver.

Robbie saw none of it. His eyes were inward-looking, nervous. But Lynton knew the answer. He handed the boat over to the professionals, and led the man carefully for'ard along the deck, wedging him between the skylights. He fetched champagne and opened it, the wine lipping up with the spray.

Then he looked round. Towards the south, the dark cloud, he saw a fleet of ocean-racers. Their hulls were bright race-car colours. Their sails were a strange mixture of gleaming plastic and dull brown. They cut through the water, and yet there was a stillness about them. The crews still. And each helmsman taut, concentrating, flicking the steel spokes of his wheel.

Lynton turned to Robbie. 'Fine sight, aren't they?'

'Yes,' Robbie said. The champagne bringing life to his face.

'Come from New Zealand, the States, Germany, France, just to race here,' Lynton went on. 'Finest stretch of sailing-water in the world.'

'If you say so.'

'I do,' Lynton said. 'And until recently there was a seven-year wait for a berth along this coast. Till recently it was ghastly food in worse pubs ... Queues ... The English way.'

He sat up, and looked back at the shore. 'And, d'you know what? For years there's been an airport just a couple of miles away. Thirty minutes flying-time from London, fifty minutes from Brussels, fifty-five from Paris . . . I tell you, Robbie, this isn't just going to be a leisure-centre. It's going to be *the* leisure-centre . . . *Mammoth* . . . Hotels, restaurants, night-spots, sports-complexes . . .'

He smiled suddenly. 'Oh, and I left out the shops, didn't I? Shops selling French designer-clothes and Italian freezers . . . With factories, of course, just around the corner.'

'Gotcha,' Robbie said. He held up his glass for a refill.

The sails of the racing fleet were distant now, like pointed white shark's teeth against the cloud . . . Until they rounded an invisible buoy. And small sails burst out into huge round spinnakers. They were balloon-like, the shine of onion-skin about them, and the dazzle of luminous designs.

Lynton turned back. 'I give you a toast,' he said. 'To . . . Inner . . . City . . . Development.'

They raised their glasses, drank.

'Coupled with the name of our leader.'

Robbie crossed himself, grinned. 'Praise her and magnify her for ever.'

'Who in her wisdom has given us the inner cities,' Lynton said. 'Fought over and lost. Put to the bloody torch . . . Thirty years of loony schools, twenty years of drugs, ten years of tabloids and quiz-games.'

'Quite right.'

'I tell you, there is a brave new world coming, Robbie. Ill-spelling, ill-informed . . . and, need I say it, fully-employed.'

'Hyah-hyah,' Robbie brayed, House of Commons. And laughed.

'No, I mean it,' Lynton told him. 'A great many economic indicators point that way . . . Ironic, really.'

'What is?'

'That this country invented the steam engine *and* the jet engine. And yet, in five years' time, d'you know what our biggest industry will be?'

Robbie nodded. 'Catering.'

'That's it,' Lynton said. 'The British are going to be waiters to the world. They are going to stand on the quayside and tie up the world's yachts.'

99

In the marina a section of the mooring-pontoons had been cleared of bystanders. Fifteen men in suits stood there. And at their centre was McRae.

Cass saw them from some way off as he approached. Approached slowly until he stood by McRae's shoulder.

'Got a call from your office,' he said.

'You did, Batman.'

'But, should I really be here?'

'What's that?'

'My attachment to Serious Fraud, I mean. D'you remember?'

'That's Monday. Today's Sunday. You're still with us.'

McRae was speaking quickly. And he was nervous, Cass realised, as nervous as he'd ever seen him.

Then the man pointed. 'Look, there isn't much time. Park yourself up there on the walkway. Get yourself a deck-chair and a raspberry ripple.'

Cass nodded. He went back the way he'd come. He found a ramp up to the walkway, and moved out along it.

By which time, he saw, there was a tall mast coming in through the marina entrance. Lynton's yacht.

They'd reached the end of the whole business, he thought. But he shared none of McRae's tension. He just wanted it to be over.

The men in suits had left the pontoon. And, one by one, Cass was able to pick them out on different yachts, crouching down in cockpits, behind wheelhouses.

Around the gap at the quayside that was Lynton's mooring.

The yacht moved slowly in the centre of the marina. Its long white hull edging round in bursts of throttle.

The air was still. There were sails, racing sails, hanging up to dry. Hanging limply in coloured folds.

The white stern came back towards the quay. There was that sharp spat of diesel on water.

Then silence. A crewman leapt ashore with a rope, tied up, took a second line.

And in the cockpit of the yacht Cass saw two dark figures. One tall, distinguished looking. The other awkward on a boat, a fat man.

The crewmen helped them over the stern.

The men in suits moved.

There was a sudden flurry of wind. The dazzling colours of the sails swung out, hid the end of the quay.

And when the squall had passed, the sails fallen back, Cass saw the men in suits again, bringing the fat man in.

100

David Lynton picked up his gin and tonic from the yacht club bar. 'Thank you, George,' he said.

He went out on to the terrace and looked down at the car-park. Where, half an hour ago, he'd seen them take Robbie away. The man looking back through the car window, shouting.

Well, Lynton thought, they'd find the contract in a day or two, those Fraud boys. The back-dated contract, covering the past year.

And the back-dated faxes too, twelve of them, showing Robbie's salary as head of the consortium.

Robbie would do a lot more shouting, of course. But nobody would believe him. People didn't really *tend* to believe him. That slight sweatiness of his. That panic under pressure he could never *quite* conceal.

And, of course, the real bonus . . . He knew nothing.

The same with Benson, really.

He might have guessed about the cement business. Probably *had* guessed. But he wouldn't do anything. Not after his misdirection of justice earlier today.

All in all, even if Benson started his new career in Ford prison, he was definitely the coming man.

Lynton swirled the gin round in his glass. He glanced down at the car-park again. And saw the man. The pale man with the shoulder-length hair and the designer suit. The rage in him as he looked up.

270

McRae got into the front seat of the Peugeot. Cass started the motor, and they drove away from the marina, away from the blue and red pavilion, and reached the queue of cars by the traffic lights.

Cass looked away to his right. He saw the service road and the wire fence beyond. Then the two building sites, both of them completed now, roofed, glazed.

'Well, we didn't get it all. We didn't find those bodies,' he said. 'But we got the people who mattered.'

McRae swung round. 'Batman, we didn't get *anybody*.'

'What?'

'A fat man and a solicitor.'

Cass didn't understand.

'Oh, you were blinded,' McRae said. 'Blinded by that great chum of yours with his hand in the till ... I mean, don't you *see*?'

'No. No, I don't.'

'Think back to that yacht. Think who *owned* the bloody thing, a boat like that.' McRae's voice rose. 'I ran a check with Barry before we came down here. The guy's a broker. Nothing on him, *nothing*. He picks up the phone, never signs his name. Plays what they call the long game.'

Cass shook his head.

'For Christ's *sake*, he's going to collect in the end,' the man went on. 'A year or two's time, and another Euro-mob will come along. That marina will get passed. That bridge will go. That bastard, *bastard* playing-field will go.'

And Cass saw it then, saw it again. That vicious animal in McRae. That look he'd had on his face when he'd stared out at the playing-field. And seen the small boy with the large cricket-bat.

Cass turned away.

'I'm sorry,' the man said then, his voice quieter. 'I'm tired.'

'Yes.'

'Don't you listen to me. You just stick to prosecuting. Put on the cape and the little black boots. Go through the whole damn comic-book in court.'

He reached out, touched Cass gently with his fist.

'Ker-Pow.'

101

It was late when Cass got home. And Sonia saw his face.
'What's up?' she asked.

'Oh, nothing.'

'Have they taken you off the investigation?'

'For the moment.'

'After those *arrests*?' she asked. 'All that excitement I saw on TV?'

He nodded and walked past her, to where Alison was sitting, her legs out stiffly in front of her, wearing a pair of new shoes.

'I like those,' he said. 'Very smart.'

'No, they're not.' She shook her head. 'They're school shoes. We go back to school tomorrow.'

'Oh.' Cass sat down beside her. 'So I s'pose, tomorrow you won't be wanting to sleep on the bunk bed.'

'What bunk bed?'

'The bunk bed next to the porthole.'

'What?'

'The bunk bed next to the porthole on the ship.'

'*What*?'

'I'm taking you off school for a fortnight,' Cass said. 'We're going on holiday, to France.'

He flopped P&O tickets down on the table.

'A *holiday*?' Sonia spun round.

'Yes,' Cass said. 'And then it's back to prosecuting for McRae. Official.'

Upstairs there were suitcases open on the bed. Alison came into the room with sun-tops, pairs of shorts, two dolls.

She saw Cass getting shirts out from a drawer. Then an old floppy sailing-hat. He put it on.

'You're not wearing *that*?' She was horrified.

'Oh, yes,' he said.

He put it on, did a little dance, grinned.

'Dad*dy*!'